17 ⁹⁵

D0349988

OTHER BOOKS BY SANDRA DALLAS

Colorado Homes

Colorado Ghost Towns and Mining Camps

Sacred Paint

BUSTER MIDNIGHT'S CAFE

BUSTER MIDNIGHT'S CAFE

SANDRA DALLAS

RANDOM HOUSE  NEW YORK

Copyright © 1990 by Sandra Dallas Atchison
All rights reserved under International and Pan-American Copyright
Conventions.
Published in the United States by Random House, Inc., New York and
simultaneously in Canada by Random House of Canada Limited,
Toronto.

Library of Congress Cataloging-in-Publication Data
Dallas, Sandra.
Buster Midnight's Cafe / by Sandra Dallas.
          p.   cm.
     ISBN 0-394-57651-9
          I. Title.
     PS3554.A434B87   1990
     813'.54—dc20   89-77811

Manufactured in the United States of America
24689753
First Edition

FOR KENDAL,
"JOY OF MY LIFE"

THANKS TO JANE JORDAN BROWNE AND SUSAN KAMIL,
THE UNHOLY THREE'S BEST FRIENDS,
WHO MADE THIS A BOOK.

BUSTER MIDNIGHT'S CAFE

CHAPTER 1

You want to know about Butte, you go over to the twenty-four-hour Jim Hill Cafe & Cigar Store on Silver Street and ask for me and Whippy Bird. The lunch counter, not the bar since Whippy Bird doesn't drink anymore, not after she got half of her stomach taken out.

Whippy Bird can't eat very well unless she lies down. When I get invited to her house for dinner, she serves it in the bedroom, where she can stretch out. With real company, she lies down on the couch, but me and Whippy Bird have been family all our lives, so we eat in the bedroom. "Whippy Bird," I say to her, "you have more fun in that bed with a pork chop than you ever had with your husbands." And she laughs and says, "You're right. You are surely right, Effa Commander." Though I surely am not.

Everybody knows the Jim Hill on Silver Street. That's because there's a big sign in front that says JIM HILL CAFE in pink neon. Even without the sign, you'd know it was special. The front is covered in stainless steel just like an old North Coast Limited streamliner, and in the window is a blue neon champagne glass with pink bubbles coming out of it as flashy as May Anna's diamond earrings, which she left me in her will.

Classy. That's what I told Whippy Bird the first time we saw the Jim Hill all spruced up like that. "Whippy Bird, that's classy. Just like May Anna's house," I said. Of course, that was forty years ago when people knew who Jim Hill was. Now people think Jim Hill is Joe Mapes. Sometimes Joe Mapes even gets confused. Whenever a customer calls, "Jim!" he answers, "Yo!" I doubt Joe even knows who Jim Hill was. That was the name of the restaurant when he bought it in 1964. He didn't have the money for a new sign. Then or now.

I don't know how the word got out to the tourists about the Jim Hill being the place to learn about Butte. Maybe it's the newspaper people from back east. Every time some paper wants a story on Butte, their boys come whipping into the Jim Hill and say hi, I'm a reporter from *The New York Times,* like we're supposed to swing around and fall over backward off the stool. Then they ask a couple of fool questions like will the price of copper go up. Or down. How the hell should we know? Then they go back and write us up like we're cuter than a bug in lace pants. Local color, it's called.

You've seen those stories. They quote me and Whippy Bird, then they tell you Montana's so quaint the governor has his home phone number listed in the telephone book. I asked Whippy Bird once if that was true, and she said she didn't know; she didn't have any reason to call up the governor.

Maybe all those tourists read about the Jim Hill in the newspaper stories or maybe they read about it in Hunter Harper's book, which you might have seen. Its title is *That Hellhole Called Butte,* which I think is a stinking name. Nobody but Hunter Harper ever called Butte a hellhole. I never liked Hunter Harper much, and I hated him after that book came out. He hangs around the Jim Hill counter, sitting on the corner stool with his legs crossed, smoking one of those little cigars, the kind that look like you can't make up your mind if you want a cigarette or a real stogie. Hunter Harper wears Levi's and boots and a hat that's too big and a yellow kerchief around his neck. He thinks somebody might mistake him for a cowboy. But anybody who knows cowboys knows yellow scarves are bad luck.

I started reading Hunter Harper's book, but I never got to the end. It's just made up of stories he picked up around the Jim Hill that he never got right. He tries to sound like he's one of us, but he isn't. Nobody who grew up in Butte uses words like *heretofore* and *built environment*. You have to have a dictionary just to get through the first page. Of course, Hunter's not a Butte native. He's just a summer person, who teaches history in Iowa the rest of the year. Folk history, he calls it, us being the folks, I guess.

I asked Whippy Bird if he was a queer, but she didn't think so. Not that we care. Butte had "sissies," as we called them when we were growing up, but not very many. It isn't a good idea to be a fairy with all those miners and tough cowboys in Montana.

It's a funny thing about tourists. They come here to see us, but they really don't want to get to know us. They want to find somebody who's like them. You see tourists walking down the street in their baseball caps saying SIOUX FALLS ELKS and wearing orange jumpsuits with the Expand-O waistbands. They nod a little to everybody, but when they see another tourist in a baseball cap and an Expand-O jumpsuit, they get real friendly, like they just found they were war allies in enemy territory. Even though Hunter doesn't wear a jumpsuit, the tourists spot him for one of them just the same.

Your better class of tourists, however, look for me and Whippy Bird.

Mostly they say the same things, like how far they drove that day or is it always cold up here. Then real friendly like, they ask about the history. Whippy Bird likes to go into detail about the copper kings who got rich here and had big mansions and race horses. Or she tells them about Columbia Gardens because it was the best amusement park in the state of Montana. Also, it's the place where Buster got his start.

If she's feeling sassy and has the time, she draws it out so those people are sorry they asked. If she's busy, she lets them get to the big question right away. Sometimes she even brings it up herself. But mostly, she makes the tourists get around to it on their own with a lot of heming and hawing. Sooner or later, they always do, like it was something that occurred to them just then over their bacon and eggs.

Take yesterday. Whippy Bird was behind the counter as she sometimes is when the Jim Hill is shorthanded or Alta, who's the regular waitress, has trouble with her bunions. Me, I help, too, if they need me, but I've cooked about a million meals in my time back when we had our own restaurant, and enough's enough, so I was just sitting on a stool in front, enjoying my morning coffee.

Whippy Bird was half paying attention to what this particular tourist was saying, a real windbag, I thought. First, he had to talk about everything on the menu, asking were the eggs fresh and was it link or patty sausage? And did the Jim Hill serve skim milk, and could he have blueberry pancakes instead of regular? Then he said to his wife did she remember when he got fresh-picked blueberries in his hot cakes in the year of 1979 in the state of Vermont? Your fatties surely like to talk about their food. Then after he ordered the short stack of pancakes, even though they didn't have blueberries, he cleared his throat. "You from around here?" he asked in kind of a casual way.

"I been a native all my life," Whippy Bird said.

"You know, I read Marion Street was from Butte."

"Marion Street?" Whippy Bird asked.

"Yeah. You know Marion Street?"

"Is that a person or an address?" She pronounces it *"ay-*dress." I've heard Whippy Bird ask that about a thousand times, but I always have to put down my coffee and laugh.

The tourists think that address business is funny, too, but not for the same reason. You see, me and Whippy Bird know that Marion Street took her name from an *ay*-dress. Hunter's book tells you that her real name was May Anna Kovak, which it was not. It was Kovaks—but it doesn't explain that when she turned out, she wanted a fancy name, and me and Whippy Bird came up with it. We just looked up at the street sign and got the same idea at the same time. May Anna thought it was the funniest thing she ever heard. When I told Pink about May Anna's new name, he said she was lucky she wasn't standing on Porphyry Street when we got the idea.

Then that tourist at the Jim Hill leaned over the counter on one elbow, with his Expand-O waist riding up halfway to his armpit, and said in a low voice, "I heard Marion Street used to be a hooker here."

He sat back down, and his wife punched him in the arm and said, "Now, Harold."

Whippy Bird was flipping a pancake just then. She turned around and let the pancake land on the floor. "Marion Street was a hooker?

You mean a whore?" She said it so loud you could hear her outside, only nobody from Butte who was walking by ever paid her any mind because she'd said it so many times before.

The tourist turned red as Heinz 57 ketchup—which isn't really Heinz 57 at the Jim Hill because Joe Mapes fills the Heinz 57 bottles with the cheap kind you buy by the gallon. Then Whippy Bird slammed down his short stack, which was even shorter since one of the pancakes was on the floor, turned back to the grill, and pretended to cook, but I knew she was laughing.

That pancake on the floor was a good touch. The timing doesn't always work out like that. Even Hunter, who was sitting with his legs wrapped around each other puffing on one of those smelly smokes of his, making you wish the Jim Hill was no smoking, started laughing.

Whippy Bird cleaned off the grill with the edge of the pancake flipper and turned back to the tourist, who had his head in his hot cakes. "Where'd you get an idea like that?" she asked him.

He shrugged, keeping his eyes on his breakfast.

"I guess when you get to be as beautiful and as famous as Marion Street, people just naturally say nasty things about you." Whippy Bird clucked her tongue. "And her being dead like she is! She was just as famous as Marilyn Monroe. And just as sad. You know, she was older'n me?" That's true, though not such a big deal as you might think because Whippy Bird was talking only three weeks' difference in age.

I thought old Harold would gag at that. People remember pictures of Marion Street with her platinum hair and her mouth a red slash of Max Factor at the Bob Hope USO shows or at the Cocoanut Grove with Cary Grant, and you forget they were taken during World War

II, more than forty years ago. Once she became a star, there wasn't
a picture of her that wasn't glamorous. She'd even get dressed up just
to take out the garbage. Your actresses had class back then.

I could see Harold there compare that image of the glamorous
Marion Street with Whippy Bird in her road-stripe orange corkscrew
curls and rhinestone earrings, looking like she was going to a canasta
party. That's not to say Whippy Bird isn't pretty. She always was
prettier than May Anna. In fact, even with the sickness she's had,
Whippy Bird doesn't look as old as she is. Still, she looks plenty older
than May Anna did in those pictures Harold remembered.

The rest of us, we got old, but not Marion Street. She's frozen as
a Hollywood Legend Sex Goddess now, and people remember her the
way she looked when she died in 1951. Just like they do Marilyn
Monroe. You don't think, why she'd be in her seventies now. You
just remember her being about thirty or thirty-five. Or at least me and
Whippy Bird do. The rest of the world thought she was younger,
since May Anna always lied about her age.

"Did you know her?" Harold was back in the saddle.

"Did I know her? I guess me and Effa Commander knew her
better than anybody." Whippy Bird is always willing to share the
credit.

"Do you know about the Love Triangle Murder?" Nothing could
stop that boy now.

"That was a long time ago," Whippy Bird said. Me and Whippy
Bird don't like it when the tourists ask about the murder. We talk
about May Anna, her being a famous tourist attraction in Butte now,
but the murder is none of their business. I expect old Harold read
Hunter Harper's book or those articles that came out after the book

was published. Hunter picked up on all that old Hollywood gossip and thought he figured it out about the murder, but he was dead wrong. With May Anna and Buster gone, me and Whippy Bird are the only ones still around who know what really happened, and we never talked. Especially to that damn fool Hunter.

Whippy Bird turned to scrape off the grill, and Harold there slurped down his pancakes and grabbed his wife and beat it out of the Jim Hill. Funny thing. You'd think tourists would be mad at Whippy Bird for embarrassing them—take the wind out of her "sales," as Whippy Bird says—but they never are. Good old Harold left Whippy Bird a two-dollar tip.

After they left, Whippy Bird wiped off the grill again, looked me straight in the eye, put down her pancake flipper, and said, "Effa Commander, it's time somebody told the truth about the May Anna Kovaks–Buster McKnight murder or else the world will keep believing what that damn fool Hunter Harper said in his book. And you are that person," she said. "I am going to the Ben Franklin as soon as Alta comes in and buy you some steno pads, and I'll even get you Flair pens instead of ballpoint. You write it down, and I'll type it up for you. You made a promise to Buster once that you would do the right thing."

"I thought I did the right thing," I told her. "At least I did what Buster wanted."

"That was then. Now the right thing is to tell the true facts," she said. "You owe it to Buster and May Anna and the world." Then she added softly, "Mostly to Buster. Don't you think he deserves the truth being known?" I thought it over for a long time while Whippy

Bird poured me more coffee, then I said thanks to you, Whippy Bird, for the coffee, and maybe you are right like you always are.

"It's for you to do, Effa Commander, because I may not last that long. Besides, I'll look over your shoulder and tell you if you go wrong."

She surely did that, all right. Whippy Bird surely did that.

CHAPTER 2

Me and Whippy Bird met May Anna Kovaks the day we saved her life.

We were always getting May Anna out of scrapes. One time, when we were standing on the sidewalk in Centerville, Chick O'Reilly dared her to put her tongue on an icy sled runner, and she did, and it stuck. Me and Whippy Bird dashed into the closest house, grabbed a pan of soup that was cooking on the stove, and poured it over May Anna's head. That got her tongue loose, all right. I always wondered what those people thought when they came home to find an empty pot and no supper.

Whippy Bird remembered about that sled runner after May Anna became famous and said wouldn't it be funny if we hadn't been there that day and May Anna would have to be a movie star with a sled hanging out of her mouth.

The first time we saw May Anna, she was standing right at the edge of the Little Annie glory hole. The glory hole was fenced off because it was just a big open pit, but the fence never kept anybody out, especially kids. May Anna stood at the edge real quiet, just looking down into the hole.

When we spotted her, me and Whippy Bird were playing on a mine dump. We thought the whole world was made up of mine dumps. We must have been ten years old before we found out other places didn't have dumps the way Butte did. Butte was just lucky, Whippy Bird said.

On bad days in old-time Butte the smoke from the smelters turned the sky dark, even at noon. Sometimes the town left the street lights on twenty-four hours a day. You'd see the miners coming down off the hill in the middle of the day with their carbide lights like a chain of moving stars. That's what it was like when we spotted May Anna.

At first, we just stood on the mine dump, watching her in the smoky air. Later when I saw *Wuthering Heights* it made me remember May Anna up there at the edge of the Little Annie glory hole with the wind blowing, and the mist swirling. Only with the sulfur fumes from the smelters that day, it was like *Wuthering Heights* in Smell-O-Vision, Whippy Bird says. It's too bad May Anna didn't play in that movie. She surely looked the part that day.

The sulfur made you sick to your stomach and kind of woozy if you weren't used to it. Of course, it didn't bother me and Whippy Bird, but as I say, May Anna was new. All of a sudden the sulfur fumes must have gotten to her, and she started to weave like her legs were giving out. If May Anna had fallen into that hole—which goes down about a million feet—you never would have seen Marion Street win an Academy Award for *The Sin of Rachel Babcock*.

We were ready for her. We had just ducked under the fence, when Whippy Bird yelled, "Look-it there, Effa Commander. That little kid's in trouble!" So we scrambled up those rocks as fast as we could, just in time. As she started down that hole on her way to kingdom come, Whippy Bird grabbed one side of May Anna's dress and I took hold of the other. Together we pulled her out.

"You're a damn fool," Whippy Bird told May Anna. We were five and had just learned "damn fool" and liked the way it sounded.

"I was trying to see to China," May Anna retorted once she collected herself. She wouldn't admit the fumes got to her.

"Then you're dumber than damn fool because the Chinamen live over on West Mercury Street, not at the bottom of the Little Annie glory hole. Ain't you never been down to the Chinese laundry or the noodle parlors?" Whippy Bird asked.

May Anna drew herself up like she did later in *Moon Blood* when she told her husband she was leaving him for another man and said, "China is straight through the earth from Butte, and if you dig far enough you will reach it. How do you expect the Chinese got here— walking across the ocean?"

Whippy Bird started to reply, but she stopped and thought it over. "Do you think she's right, Effa Commander?" she asked me.

It sounded like it made sense to me, I told her.

"I never saw no Chinamen around this hole." Whippy Bird took some convincing.

"I didn't say they came out of this hole. I said they came out of a hole, and I was wondering if it was this one. Any damn fool knows most of these holes are from mining."

Me and Whippy Bird liked that. May Anna was real quick in picking up our style.

Whippy Bird stuck out her hand and said, "Hi, my name's Whippy Bird, and this is Effa Commander."

"May Anna Kovaks."

"That's a funny name," Whippy Bird said after she thought it over. "How come it's not Anna May?"

"What kind of a bird is a Whippy Bird?"

People were always asking her that, even when she was five years old. I expect Whippy Bird's been asked that five thousand times. She told me once, the reason we were good friends from the first day we met was I never asked her about her name.

All the Birds had odd names. For instance, Whippy Bird's brothers were Stinky Bird and Bummer Bird. But the worst of the lot was Myron Bird. Who'd name a kid Myron and expect him to amount to anything? Which is what happened. He left the union, voted for Ronald Reagan twice, and used to pay money to get his shoes shined.

Another thing about names while I'm on the subject, we always called each other by our full names, Whippy Bird and Effa Commander. I don't know why. Nobody ever called Whippy Bird "Whippy" unless they didn't know her, like Hunter Harper and the tourists. So when May Anna became our friend, it just sounded right: Whippy Bird, Effa Commander, and May Anna. Only most people called us the Unholy Three.

May Anna said, "OK, I won't ask you about your name if you don't ask me about my dad." So right away we did, but she wouldn't say anything except he died in a mine accident in Arizona, so they moved to Butte where her mother came from. We knew May Anna a long time before we found out there never was a Mr. Kovaks. Some people said that was one of the reasons May Anna turned out, but there were better reasons than that.

May Anna wasn't a looker back then. She had skinny legs and hair the color of mine runoff. Later, of course, she changed it to platinum blond, and she claimed it was natural. Funny thing, people around here got to believing that. Not me and Whippy Bird, though.

Sometimes when people remember May Anna, they say what beautiful blond hair she had when she was a little girl. Me and Whippy Bird laugh at that since we know for sure she wasn't a blonde. That's because we were the ones who helped her peroxide her hair the first time, and we put on so much bleach, it almost fell out. That sure would have ruined her career. Who ever heard of a hooker with no hair?

Still, May Anna had a pretty face when she was a girl, with that Greek goddess nose everybody wrote about and eyes that looked like two glory holes. They were that dark and that deep. Some writer in *Photoplay* said they were like "twin pools of moonlit water." Maybe so, but I never saw May Anna's eyes except that they reminded me of two mine pits.

May Anna's teeth weren't much either. She'd already gotten her second teeth when we met her, and they were slantways and black, which is why she smiled with her lips closed and put her hand over her mouth when she laughed.

She did that even after she went to Hollywood and got china caps on her teeth. Everybody thought May Anna putting her hand over her mouth was sweet, but me and Whippy Bird knew the real facts. After she got the caps, May Anna had to be careful about what she ate or her teeth would break off.

Of course, in the beginning, when we were all five years old, she was just like anybody else. You could look at a picture of the whole grade school, and you never would have picked May Anna as the one to become famous. Or Buster McKnight, either.

Maybe you'd of picked Whippy Bird because she was as cute as a button with her red curls. Those curls she has now when you see her at the Jim Hill aren't a perm. They're natural. What's more, unlike May Anna Kovaks, Whippy Bird always had nice straight teeth.

Whippy Bird was little. Me, I've always been tall and skinny. People we didn't know called us Mutt and Jeff. Being little didn't mean Whippy Bird wasn't tough, though. When we got older and Buster got famous, we laughed about how Whippy Bird used to beat him up. Buster laughed about it, too, claiming he could have won their fights only he didn't want to hit a girl. But he couldn't fool us. We knew that wasn't true.

"Whippy Bird was too fast for you," I kidded him once.

"Only with her mouth," Buster replied.

Whippy Bird claimed she was the one who turned Buster McKnight into a fighter, that he was so embarrassed at being beat up by a girl that he learned to fight to save face. I think she was wrong, though I don't often go against Whippy Bird. Growing up in Butte, you just naturally learned how to protect yourself, so he had something going for him to start out with.

The real reason Buster became a fighter, though, was to impress May Anna. He fell in love with her the first time he saw her, and he was always sorry it was me and Whippy Bird that saved May Anna from falling down the glory hole instead of him.

◉◉◉

Butte may have had sulfur fumes and smelter grime, but it still was the best place in the world to grow up in. You had to be tough to make it, and we were tough all right. Boys had a better time of it in Butte than girls, who had to spend their vacations tending kids and washing clothes. Boys like Pink and Chick, who were as close as me and Whippy Bird, ducked out of the house the minute they finished breakfast and didn't come back until suppertime and maybe later. They never helped out at home. They just spent their time raising hell—which they did a good job of until the day they died, and maybe even after that. Me and Whippy Bird being the youngest in our families and May Anna being an only child, we had more time to play than most girls.

Buster liked having May Anna around, but she wouldn't run with his gang unless we could go along. She told us it wasn't proper. May Anna always had standards, even after she turned out. She was a member of your high class of hookers. Me and Whippy Bird and May Anna wouldn't do a lot of things the boys did, like we never stripped down and went swimming naked or pledged the oath, which means you had to pee on somebody's foot. And me and Whippy Bird and May Anna refused to step barefoot in cow pies—even though we knew that if you did, you could go barefoot all summer without even getting a blister, not to mention lockjaw and die.

We did other things like run along the railroad tracks and hang around the livery stable and the garages, since by then there were more cars in Butte than horses. And we made money. We collected maggots from the dump at the slaughterhouse and covered them in cornmeal and sold them to fishermen.

There were days when we went over to the smelters with a bucket to pick up coal that we took home to use. Sometimes a workman on top of a coal car threw down a bucketful because he understood about hard times. If nobody was around, one of the boys climbed on top of the railroad car and tossed the coal down to us on the tracks. Looking for coal just kind of became second nature to kids in Butte. Even now, when I see a chunk of coal lying someplace, I'll lean over to pick it up if I don't think to stop myself.

When he got older, Buster organized a raffle for a ton of coal with the money going to the gang, and we all sold tickets. The first year, May Anna's mother won, which surely did please May Anna because they could use that coal. The second year, by "coincidence," May Anna's mother won again. After Buster fixed it so she won the third year, too, people stopped buying tickets, and the gang had to find another way to earn money.

One summer when my pop worked up top at the Badger, we would take his dinner over to him almost every single day. We'd bring two buckets, one for him and one for us, then we'd sit outside on the old slag heap and eat in the sun. That was one of the nicest times in my whole life, sitting there on the slag pile, me and Whippy Bird and May Anna and Pop. Sometimes we had sandwiches, but mostly we ate pasties, which is what the Cornish people always ate for lunch.

You can order pasties at the Jim Hill, but they come with canned gravy, and unless Whippy Bird makes them, you might get hamburger inside. Real pasties—that's "pah-stees" with the emphasis on "past"—are little piecrust envelopes filled with meat and vegetables, leftovers mostly.

Sometimes the tourists at the Jim Hill who don't know any better ask for "paste-ees," which is what strippers wear. If Whippy Bird's behind the counter, she says, "Honey, you're in the wrong place. You want me to give you directions to the red-light district?" If the tourist has a sense of humor, she gets another two-dollar tip.

I expect you know there was another reason for taking two dinner buckets to the Badger. Like most of the other miners, Pop did a little high-grading. Pop picked up a chunk or two of high-grade ore in the morning, then slipped it into the dinner bucket before we left. Some people think that's stealing, but we thought of it as part of your pay.

One time we got searched—me and Whippy Bird did, that is. We were carrying one dinner bucket, and May Anna had the other. That old boy took our lunch bucket apart, but he never even looked into the one May Anna was carrying. It didn't bother us since we didn't have any ore that day, but after that, whenever we did, we made May Anna carry it. She never did get searched.

Sometimes, we collected frogs at the swamp and sold them to Frenchy's down near Venus Alley for frogs' legs. He gave us fifty cents a dozen. May Anna said it was the first money she ever made in the District, and that's how she got started—hooked on frogs' legs.

Whippy Bird said "hookered" on frogs' legs was more like it. As you can tell, Whippy Bird surely is a card.

In the beginning when we tried to sell those frogs' legs, me and Whippy Bird caught the frogs while May Anna pulled off the legs, but Frenchy wouldn't buy them. He threw them on the trash heap and said we had to bring in whole frogs. Whippy Bird said that was so he could keep the legs in pairs. "Those customers don't want a big right leg and a bitty left one like a crippled-up frog," she explained to us. As usual, Whippy Bird was right.

The first day we became aware of the power May Anna had over men was a day we were hunting down frogs. We were nine or ten. It was summer, one of those good summers you like to think back on like you were Tom Sawyer in the book, when the air was warm and yellow from the sun. Like a lot of places that are winter most of the year, Butte summers were special, and we lived every day of them.

We'd already learned to hate school. Our teacher that year was Illa Vedshmik, and May Anna said she was older than God. Me and Whippy Bird had never heard anybody say that before, and it became our favorite expression all summer. May Anna picked it up from one of Mrs. Kovaks's boyfriends, the one that drove around in the Reo and played golf.

May Anna used to imitate that teacher, wrinkling up her nose the way Old Lady Vedshmik did when she smelled something bad. May Anna was good at imitations. One time *Motion Picture* said if she hadn't been so beautiful, May Anna could have been a great character actress. That was early in her career, and as you know, she did go on to become one of your all-time most highly respected personages of the screen.

Anyway, we'd gone after frogs' legs to the pond where the boys kept their rafts. It wasn't much of a pond, because it was mostly filled with water from the mines, but the boys liked it because it was dangerous and they'd been told if they ever drowned, their bodies would be lost forever. Whippy Bird claimed that's because the pond really was a glory hole, and it went down a thousand feet. Maybe even to China, May Anna said. The boys also liked that pond because it was used as a garbage dump, and it stank to high heaven, which kept most people away. Kids had to be tough to go there.

The rafts weren't much. They were older than God, built by some boys who were grown men by then, and every year new gangs claimed them.

When me and Whippy Bird and May Anna showed up at the pond, Buster and Chick and a bunch of the gang had taken one raft, and they were diving off it into the water—J. Bare Nuddy, as the fellow says. They didn't notice us for a while, so we stayed there and stared at them. All of a sudden Pink Varscoe spotted us, and he yelled, and all those boys dove for their clothes. All except Buster, who stood there staring straight at May Anna. I never did know whether he was too surprised to move or was just showing off. Whatever it was, May Anna was impressed. Me and Whippy Bird turned away, but May Anna kept looking. "He sure looks swell standing there with that thing hanging out," she said.

Me and Whippy Bird just giggled, then May Anna yelled, "Hey, Buster, you going to let us come on board?"

"Sure thing!"

"You going to get your clothes on or you got other ideas?" Buster's brother, Toney, asked. Buster jumped down at that, and Whippy Bird always said he didn't even know he was stark naked. He was just so happy to see May Anna that he stood there like a statue. After all the boys were dressed, they pushed over to us, and we got out on the raft, which Buster and the boys named the *Happy Warrior*. We must have been there two hours, sailing along through the dump singing "Red Wing" and smoking Fatima cigarettes, happy as the queen of England. Toney passed around a fruit jar with whiskey in it, though he wouldn't let the girls have a taste. He wouldn't let Buster have any either since Buster was the captain of the raft and had to keep a clear head. That was OK with Buster. He always did what Toney said.

There we were, having the best old time, me and Whippy Bird even then sitting next to Pink and Chick, when all of a sudden a gang of Bohunks across the pond climbed on another raft, called the *Pirate,* and took out after us. They were big boys, too, fourteen or fifteen years old. Their leader was Pig Face Stenner, and me and Whippy Bird and May Anna were scared.

There was good reason for that. Those Bohunks hated our guts because we were Cornish. They were always ambushing us and lobbing ore chunks at us. Once they hit Chick in the head with a brickbat that made such a bad cut, his mom had to sew it up with a needle and thread. He had that little bare place on his head for the rest of his life. "Chick sure is tough. He has more fight scars than Buster," I told Whippy Bird once.

"Tough or dumb," Whippy Bird said. "He never learned footwork."

May Anna had an extra reason to be scared of Pig Face. He was not only a drip, he was mean. Buster was sweet and worshipful, but Pig Face would hit May Anna on the arm to get her attention at school or spit on the floor right next to her feet. May Anna said once when she was walking along down the street by herself, he jumped out at her from behind a fence with his pecker in his hand. Instead of running, May Anna just stood there as cool as could be and said, "I never saw anything so teeny-weeny." Being little girls didn't mean we didn't know about boys.

After that, I guess, Pig Face had it in for May Anna. Once, when

May Anna's mom put her hair in long curls for a special program at school, Pig Face cut one of them off. If it'd been me, I'd of cried my eyes out, but May Anna never, never cried unless she wanted to.

Buster surely must have known about that long curl because there wasn't much about May Anna he didn't know. I suppose he was just itching for a fight, and here was Pig Face—with May Anna there to watch.

Pig Face and his gang pushed their raft out into the middle of the pond and challenged us. So our boys pushed our raft over toward the *Pirate*. When we got to the middle of the pond, right up next to them, we didn't know what to do. Were we all supposed to jump on their raft and fight or just sit there and yell insults? "Why the hell did you have to let the girls get on?" Toney asked Buster, which was what I was wondering, too.

"May Anna wanted to," Buster answered. That was reason enough for Buster to do anything.

Like I said, this pond was a garbage dump, and Pig Face's gang had found a whole crate of rotten tomatoes somebody had thrown away. We didn't know that, of course. But once we got out in the middle where we were defenseless, Pig Face let loose with a tomato that hit Buster and squashed on his bare chest. "Bull's-eye, chump!" Pig Face yelled. Before Buster could move, he got hit with half a dozen more. We didn't have anything to throw back, so we called a retreat and tried to maneuver the *Happy Warrior* back to the bank where we could at least make mud balls. That was Pink's idea, and he usually had a pretty good noodle.

No matter how fast we pushed toward the bank, the *Pirate* stayed right alongside us, with those boys throwing tomatoes. Me and Whippy Bird and May Anna were scared.

"You get behind me, Effa Commander. I'll protect you," Pink said, sounding big, but he forgot I was there, and when he moved, I got pelted. The boys got the worst of it, though. With their bare arms and legs covered with tomatoes, they looked like spaghetti drowning in sauce. The only thing that saved them was that Pig Face's gang ran out of ammunition. That and Buster McKnight.

What set Buster off was Pig Face when he wound up and threw a huge rotten tomato that hit May Anna square in the face. That was the first hit on her. Pig Face threw it so hard, he knocked May Anna flat on her back.

Buster took one look at her, then growled, "You're dead, Stenner!" Shrieking like a wild Indian, he leaped off the *Happy Warrior* onto the *Pirate* and lit into Pig Face. It wasn't a pretty fight like you came to expect from Buster later on when you could watch him dancing around and almost see him planning his next hit. Buster hadn't even developed his special punch then. All he did was plow into Pig Face like an ore car. He hit Pig Face with a right to the stomach, then a left to the head. Buster kicked Pig Face in the knee, then hit him with another right to the stomach. Pig Face keeled over. You have to understand Buster had not got his full growth like he did later, and he was a foot shorter than Pig Face and twenty-five pounds lighter, but that didn't bother Buster. He was a regular Jack Dempsey. He fought from the heart that day like he always did. It was his first knockout.

"Push him overboard," Buster told Pink and Chick when he was finished. "He can sink to the bottom and stay there for all I care."

"Ah, come on, Buster. He didn't mean nothing," one of the Bohunks begged. "If you push him off, he'll never come up again."

Buster being the nice person he always was thought it over for a minute, then said, "All right, I'll leave him there but only if May Anna says so."

"If I let him live, he has to promise never to talk to me again," she said.

"Is that a deal?" Buster asked the Bohunks, who nodded. At that, Pig Face groaned and opened his eyes. "Next time, I'll kill you," Buster told him, and Pig Face never doubted it.

Pig Face Stenner wasn't much of a fighter after that. May Anna says he learned to pray while Buster beat him up, and that's why he turned out to be a priest. May Anna, who was a papist herself, never would go to him for confession. "How can you ask for forgiveness from somebody named Father Pig Face?" she asked.

Buster won that fight, but he was plenty hurt. As soon as he jumped back onto the *Happy Warrior*, May Anna fussed over him, wiping the tomato splat and blood away. "I'm so proud of you, Buster," she said. She dipped her lace handkerchief, which she carried all her life, into that awful pond water and rubbed off the stains on his chest and his face.

Pink and Chick looked at me and Whippy Bird like they expected us to do the same thing. I said, "Sorry, Pink, no hanky."

"No knockout, neither," Whippy Bird added to Chick.

When she was all done, May Anna kissed Buster right on the lips. Me and Whippy Bird had never seen anybody do that except in the pictures, and it surprised us more than seeing Buster without his clothes on. Buster's eyes really bugged out of his head. It came to me and Whippy Bird then that May Anna had power over men. She could inspire them to protect her and hand out the rewards when they did. We weren't jealous as you might think we'd be. We always thought May Anna was special. She was one of the Unholy Three, and that meant she was our true friend for life.

CHAPTER

3

Life was hard for most people in Butte, but May Anna had it harder than the rest of us. That's because of the way her mother lived and because she didn't have a father.

In the beginning, of course, we thought Mrs. Kovaks was glamorous. We called her The Merry Widow. Our mothers were plain and had long hair that they wound around their heads, and they were as round as saffron buns. Not May Anna's mom. She was slender and wore rouge and smoked Chesterfield cigarettes. She was the only woman we knew who smoked, except for us, of course. Mrs. Kovaks's hair was marcelled, like it was set in wet cement, and her skirts came to her knees.

"Your mother's a flapper," Whippy Bird told May Anna one day. We thought that was swell, and May Anna took the compliment just the way she did later when all her fans cheered her at movie premieres, tucking her chin down and looking up with her glory hole eyes and that little wisp of a smile with her hand over her mouth. Even though me and Whippy Bird thought Mrs. Kovaks was the cat's, we thought she was a dumb onion, too, with men always giving her the shove. Still, she was nice to May Anna and to me and Whippy Bird, too, letting us wear her old gardenia corsages and put on her perfume.

When May Anna's mother cooked, it was never corned beef and cabbage or meat loaf, but things like Oysters in 1920 Sauce. Of course, she didn't cook much, which is why May Anna ate with me and Whippy Bird lots of times.

Mrs. Kovaks served cocktails when she entertained men. May Anna said her mother got out gin and lemons and a siphon, though she let May Anna chip the ice for her. We thought having cocktails was a lot more elegant than sitting on the front stoop in your undershirt drinking a bucket of beer the way Pop did on Saturday night.

We liked watching Mrs. Kovaks get all gussied up in shiny dresses with fringe that jiggled when she walked. Sometimes she tied little beaded ribbons or rosettes in her hair. She wore real silk stockings, and when she finished putting them on, she always said to me and Whippy Bird and May Anna, "Now, you look, girls, are my seams straight?" We looked up and down her silky legs, but her seams were hardly ever crooked.

When her stockings got too many runs, Mrs. Kovaks gave them to May Anna. "When I get rich, I'm going to have new silk stockings every day of the year and never wear a pair with runs," May Anna told us. She did, too, only by then they were nylon.

We liked to be there when Mrs. Kovaks's dates came to take her out. They were snappy, just like Mrs. Kovaks, and wore two-tone shoes and fedoras. When they drove up, they tooted the horn and called, "Come on, kiddo. Shake a leg." Sometimes she went uptown to meet the traveling men who set up their displays in the Sample Room at the Cash Saloon. Later on, of course, we realized most of Mrs. Kovaks's men friends were married.

May Anna's mom worked at the Finlen Hotel as a maid, cleaning

rooms and changing sheets. She told us the sheets and pillow cases
were starched as stiff as a bone, and they snapped when she shook
them out to make up the bed. She said it was the best-paying hotel
job in town, but me and Whippy Bird think the real reason she liked
to work there was she met men.

One time, Mrs. Kovaks took me and Whippy Bird and May Anna
to lunch at the Finlen Hotel for May Anna's birthday. Mrs. Kovaks
said we'd have a jolly good time, and we surely did. "Jolly good" was
something one of Mrs. Kovaks's boyfriends said. We had creamed
chicken on toast and peas and ice cream and cake. When they
brought in the cake, everybody in the place sang happy birthday to
May Anna. We all said it was the jolliest time we ever had.

After May Anna became a star, she told us that she celebrated her
birthdays in the most expensive restaurants in America. Once Tyrone
Power even came to one of her parties. But she always said her
all-time favorite was the one with her mom and me and Whippy Bird
in the Finlen Hotel. Me and Whippy Bird were proud when she
added, "That's because it was family."

Mrs. Kovaks's boyfriends brought her presents all the time, like a
bottle of perfume or a heart-shaped box of candy with a satin ribbon.
Sometimes, they sent her stuff that she kept on a little whatnot in
the corner of the living room, which May Anna dusted every Saturday. It was filled with the most interesting knickknacks, like a big
seashell that was pink and smooth as a baby. When you held it up
to your ear, you could hear the ocean roar (that's what Mrs. Kovaks
told us anyway, but Whippy Bird said that was as damn fool an idea
as digging to China, which we had come to realize was a con that
May Anna pulled the first time we met her). There was a little blue

glass shoe with bumps all over and a sterling silver spoon with an Indian and HOT SPRINGS, ARKANSAS on the handle. Also, an ashtray with melons painted on it that said MELON PILE, ROCKY FORD, COLO. Mrs. Kovaks had quite a collection of picture postcards, too, that she pasted in a book so you couldn't read the writing. That was OK because mostly they said dumb things like "Keep your shirt on till you see me, Toots." And they all ended in "Ha! Ha!"

If she was going to be out late, Mrs. Kovaks sent May Anna over to our house to sleep. Sometimes she stayed for three or four days before Mrs. Kovaks came back. May Anna said her mother liked to go to Helena or Billings on the train, and once she went to Ogden for a week. But mostly she went out just for the evening to one of the roadhouses around Butte. She liked to drink whiskey and dance.

When May Anna was twelve, Mrs. Kovaks kept company with a man named Straight Back Billy Higgins, who had a little black Ronald Colman mustache, real silk handkerchiefs, and a battered old Maxwell. Me and Whippy Bird thought he was handsome in a mysterious and evil way and we liked to sit on the running board of his car and make up stories about him. May Anna told us he was a railroad bookkeeper, but me and Whippy Bird knew better. He was a bootlegger. You could tell right off because of his pink hands and his oily hair parted in the middle. What's more, he gave Mrs. Kovaks a bottle of hooch every time he came to town. Sometimes he offered May Anna a drink of it.

Straight Back called May Anna "snooks" and "girlie," and tried to hug her or make her sit on his lap. He brought her dumb jewelry like a Scottie dog pin, which her mom made her wear to school. May Anna lost it. "I guess the clasp broke," she told us.

"It'll do that when you throw it down a glory hole," Whippy Bird told her.

Once, Straight Back sneaked up on May Anna when she was home alone. He walked right in the house calling for Mrs. Kovaks, though he went into May Anna's bedroom, and he surely knew that was not where Mrs. Kovaks slept. May Anna was asleep, but when the bed-springs creaked, she woke up to find Straight Back, buck naked, climbing in beside her. "I got a real nice surprise for you," he said, but it was Straight Back that got the surprise.

May Anna screamed only once before Straight Back clapped his hand over her mouth, but that scream was loud enough to bring the one person who would walk through fire to save her, and that person was Buster McKnight. May Anna said it was just her good luck that Buster happened to be passing by. Hanging around like a lovesick dog is more like it, Whippy Bird says.

The next thing Straight Back knew, he was rolling backward down the Kovaks stairs into the street. Standing over him was Buster with his fists up and May Anna holding him back. "You come here again, I'll kill you, you creep."

"Let me get my stuff," he whined.

"You hear me, sap?"

Straight Back was so flustered, he shook his head no. Buster started for him, so he shook his head yes and scampered into the Maxwell, still naked as the day he was born, and drove off. May Anna threw his clothes on the porch in case Straight Back decided to come get them, but he never did. Mrs. Kovaks gave them to a tramp.

After that time with Straight Back, Buster always had this way of knowing when May Anna was in trouble. The two of them didn't date then. None of us did. We were too young. We went around in a gang together. But Buster was always next to May Anna. Even when he wasn't, May Anna knew Buster could come out of nowhere to protect her.

I guess all the women in Centerville knew how Mrs. Kovaks got by. There were plenty that gave her the cold shoulder, who turned the other way when she walked into the Nimble Nickel grocery. They were even rude to May Anna, which wasn't fair because she couldn't help the way her mom was. Me and Whippy Bird laughed at how the women who snubbed her were the ones who claimed they were like a second mother to May Anna when she became famous. I know the way they treated her hurt May Anna, but she never let on.

Sometimes Buster got even for her. "Here, give this to your mom," he'd say, slugging some poor kid whose mother stuck up her nose at May Anna.

My mother wasn't like the other women. Neither was Whippy Bird's. "You play the hand you get dealt, and Minnie Kovaks makes the best of what she has, which isn't much," Ma said. Besides, she added, it was hard being without a man. After all, Mrs. Kovaks tried to be a good mother to May Anna, and you couldn't ask for more than that.

Ma sent up saffron cake and potato soup when Mrs. Kovaks was sick, and she told her to send May Anna to stay with us any time she felt like it. Ma was always sewing on buttons and letting down hems for May Anna or cutting down Mrs. Kovaks's frocks for her. Whenever she made my underwear out of Lyon's Best flour sacks, Ma made a pair for May Anna, too.

Ma wouldn't hear a word against either May Anna or her mother from the other women. I remember once when Ma was hanging out wash, Mabel Molish next door remarked that she didn't know why Ma would do laundry for the daughter of a fancy woman, and they ought to run her out of the neighborhood. "You got inside information about fancy houses?" Ma asked her. Mabel Molish always got into other people's personal business. She hinted to Ma that Pop was stepping when he was out of town on union business. Ma finally told her, "If he don't step, he's a fool. If he does, he's a son of a bitch, and if I catch him, I'll kill him." She put the clothespins into the bag she kept hanging on the line, then added, "I'll also kill anybody who tells me he steps."

Even after May Anna turned out, Ma kept an eye on her. When May Anna took sick with pneumonia one time, Ma sent a note to her saying she was to take a taxi to our house and stay with us so Ma could look after her. May Anna did, and not once did Ma say a word about what she was doing for a living. In fact, when my brother, Little Tommy, kidded her that somebody might take us for a hookhouse, Ma told him he could get out if he didn't mind his manners with a guest. What gets me is how Ma knew May Anna had pneumonia. Even me and Whippy Bird didn't know that.

May Anna wasn't the type of girl to forget a kindness. Once, for no reason, she sent Ma an ermine scarf from Hollywood with a nice note that made Ma cry. Ma never wore the scarf, of course. Where would she go with it? Instead, she kept it wrapped in tissue in a box along with a *Photoplay* picture of May Anna wearing that exact scarf at a movie premiere. Ma nearly wore out that fur taking it out of the box to show people. Every Mother's Day, May Anna called Gamer's and had them send Ma a five-pound box of candy, wrapped in copper foil with a picture of Butte on it.

As she got older Mrs. Kovaks's looks started to go, and she got thick around the middle. She wasn't as careful about her appearance, going around with messy lipstick and chipped nail polish. Whippy Bird says she was always sort of hard-looking, but we just didn't see it that way when we were kids.

The men she picked up then weren't as nice as they used to be. Sometimes they smacked her when they got drunk, and her face was red and swollen for days. Or they took her out then ditched her, and she had to beg for a ride home. She took to drinking during the day and sitting around in an old bathrobe with a cigarette stuck on her lip. Finally, she lost her job at the Finlen and got to hanging around bars, picking up just anybody. By then, we knew what was going on, and we felt bad for May Anna. But that was much later—after Jackfish Cook. When Mrs. Kovaks met Jackfish, she was as spiffy as any woman in Butte.

Jackfish—Mrs. Kovaks's boyfriends always told me and Whippy Bird and May Anna to call them by their first names—set charges at the Neversweat, which was a mine on the Hill. It was cool as a cucumber in the 'Sweat, which is how it got its name. Jackfish didn't work there all the time. In the summer he hunted for gold, since his true calling was being a prospector. When he met Mrs. Kovaks, he'd just come down out of the hills.

At first, we didn't see that Jackfish was different from her other boyfriends except he had the brightest red hair I ever saw, brighter than Whippy Bird's. He was Irish, and he got drunk and whooped it up on Saturday nights so that he always woke up on Sunday mornings with a damn fool hangover. He had to have a couple of beers before he even got out of bed to get ready for church. Jackfish always made May Anna go to church with him. He said Mrs. Kovaks was a grown woman and could make up her own mind about religion. If she wanted to be an atheist, that was all right with him. "If May Anna's going to be an atheist, it has to be her choice. That means she has to know what she's turning down," he explained.

Jackfish did it right, too. He went to Hennessy's and bought May Anna a Bible and a rosary, and every Sunday he took her to the Blessed Sacrament Church, which Whippy Bird called BS. Whippy Bird always has been a cutup. If Jackfish was nursing an especially bad hangover on Sunday morning, he would sneak out to the Pekin Noodle Parlor for Chinese food. He claimed Chinese food was the only true cure for a hangover. Even better than the body of Christ. Me and Whippy Bird never noticed that Chinese food helped our hangovers much, and we never tried the body of Christ.

A few months later, May Anna had her first communion. Her mother bought her a white dress and a veil. May Anna, being thirteen, was a head taller than any of the other girls walking down the aisle to kneel by the altar, and she looked silly in that white dress with the bow in the back. She didn't mind, though. It was one of the proudest days of her life. Me and Whippy Bird were there, and we prayed we could become Catholics, too.

Jackfish took pictures of her with his Kodak. We used to give history writers copies of the picture of May Anna in her communion dress, which is my favorite picture of her, but people don't want that one. They ask for pictures of May Anna when she was a hooker. There are plenty of them around, only people don't recognize her. I think your historians expect May Anna to wear satin dresses and fishnet stockings like saloon girls in the Gay Nineties and to stand in front of a sign that says CATHOUSE. In most of the Venus Alley pictures we have, the cathouse looks like a funeral parlor, and May Anna has on anklets.

Sometimes, after school, Me and Whippy Bird went to the Catholic church with May Anna to pray. We all knelt down on those little wooden benches, then put a penny in the slot and lit a candle. Once the three of us lit all the candles and didn't pay a cent, and May Anna said we would fry in hell. We surely liked BS. You could go in there even during the week and smell incense and listen to little chimes or people chanting. Me and Whippy Bird were Methodist, and every time we went into our church the only smell was furniture polish, and the sound was somebody running the vacuum.

May Anna thought about being a nun, which just about drove Buster crazy. But it only lasted two weeks—until she found out Pig Face Stenner was called to become a Catholic priest of God. That was the end of it for May Anna, though she did play a nun in *The Lord's Chosen*. Buster told me once that keeping May Anna from being a nun was the only decent thing Pig Face ever did.

After he knew Mrs. Kovaks a month or two, Jackfish moved in with her and May Anna. That was the closest May Anna ever came to having a real family. Mrs. Kovaks stopped drinking, and she started cooking regular meals, though she never was much good at it. "If it's smoking, it's cooking. If it's black, it's done," she explained to Jackfish and May Anna, but they never minded. They told her it was just the way they wanted it. The important thing, May Anna said, was she tried.

Sometimes at night, Jackfish read books or magazines or even anarchist newspapers. Pop said there wasn't anything Jackfish didn't read. He caught him in the Nimble Nickel once reading the labels on tin cans.

Jackfish and Pop were good friends because they were both union men. That didn't keep them from arguing all the time. Sometimes it was politics or prize-fighters or just about anything, sitting there on Mrs. Kovaks's front stoop in the summer. Mrs. Kovaks lived in a fourplex, one of those places you see all over Butte, two up, two down, hooked together with a staircase shaped like a wishbone. I have a snapshot that Hunter Harper tried to swipe for that book of his of all of us lined up on the staircase.

When he sat out on the steps after shift, Jackfish would give May Anna a big graniteware bucket and a quarter and tell her to go around the corner to the saloon for a bucket of beer. May Anna greased the bucket before she left so she wouldn't get half suds. Once me and Whippy Bird went with her, taking care to go to the back door and knock, of course, since it wasn't right for little children to go in the front. On the way home, we all took a sip or two of that beer, and by the time we got back, it was half gone. "Holy Jesus," Jackfish said when we handed him the bucket almost empty. "Holy, holy, holy." That was when we became the Unholy Three.

Sometimes Jackfish and Pop drank in the Big Mug after shift. If they felt flush, they ordered a shot with a beer chaser, which is called

a Shawn O'Farrell or a Shawn O, but mostly they just drank beer—
and argued. The Irish and the Cornish argued all the time.
The Irish were big like Jackfish, and most of the Cornish were
small, like Pop, but strong. I expect Pop could have beat up Jackfish
even though Jackfish outweighed him by a hundred pounds. But they
never fought. Each other, that is. The fish eaters and the Cousin
Jacks beat each other up just about every day in front of the Big Mug.
All it took was for somebody to call a Cousin Jack a "petticoat,"
which is not a flattering term for your Cornish people, and the fight
would start. Whenever anybody threatened Pop, Jackfish stood up
with him, and ditto with Pop for Jackfish.

Jackfish liked to sing, too, and since we had a piano, Jackfish
brought Mrs. Kovaks and May Anna to our house of an evening,
and he and Pop sang harmony. Mrs. Kovaks sang, too. She had the
sweetest voice. May Anna didn't inherit it, though. She sounded
like a crow, and in her musical picture, *Debutantes at War*, the
studio had to dub May Anna's voice for the singing parts. Jackfish
sang old Irish ballads that made him so sad he cried, especially
"Danny Boy." May Anna cried, too, but that was just to please
Jackfish.

Jackfish took May Anna to the St. Patrick's Day parade. He said
you couldn't be a good father if you didn't take your kid to a parade,
though that didn't explain why he took me and Whippy Bird, too.
In Butte, we celebrated St. Patrick's Day for about a week because
that's how long it took to do all the singing and dancing and drinking.
Then it took another week for everybody to sober up. The Cornish
celebrated St. George's Day, but it wasn't as exciting as St. Pat's

because there were more Irish in Butte than anybody. On St. Patrick's Day, everybody in Butte is Irish.

What we liked best about St. Pat's was the parade because we wore big green bows in our hair and marched down the street with Jackfish, who was a Hibernian. Afterward, he took us to an Irish supper where they had corned beef and cabbage and soused mackerel. "Jackfish was the most soused of all the fish," Whippy Bird told us. That's because he drank about a hundred schooners of green beer, then washed it down with Irish coffee. You make Irish coffee with coffee and sugar and whiskey with whipped cream on top. Jackfish usually did without the coffee and sugar and whipped cream.

In the winter, me and Whippy Bird went to May Anna's after dinner and sat at the kitchen table and played Authors or listened to Jackfish tell stories. Sometimes, he turned out the light. Then in the dark he spun spooky tales about the banshees and the Little People. The Little People are like Tommyknockers except they're Irish, not Cornish. Me and Whippy Bird would get so scared that Jackfish had to walk us home, taking May Anna along for company. Walking down the dark streets was scary, too, because Jackfish stopped and peered around corners, looking for ghosts. If there was a storm, he disappeared in the falling snow, and we couldn't find him. He could see us, though, and if anybody came along, like a tramp, Jackfish loomed up out of the dark, big as a horse, to protect us. Next to Buster, who was probably out there keeping watch, too, Jackfish was May Anna's biggest protector.

The thing Jackfish liked best was surprises. He bought May Anna a string of pearls that she wore even after she got rich. She never wore any other pearls, even the genuine pearls some big producer gave her.

She said pearls always reminded her of Jackfish. He brought both
Mrs. Kovaks and May Anna Whitman's Samplers for Valentine's,
and one day, he gave me and Whippy Bird a great big box that was
all wrapped up. When we got the paper off, the box said CHOCOLATES,
and we were so excited, we pried that lid off as fast as we could. Well,
it wasn't chocolates at all, it was a big spring with an ugly face on
it that popped out at us like a jack-in-the-box and nearly scared us to
death. Did me and Whippy Bird ever feel like a pair of damn fools
when Jackfish and May Anna hooted and called, "April Fools!"

Maybe the best time May Anna and Mrs. Kovaks ever had with
Jackfish was that last Christmas. Jackfish had been living there over
a year, and it looked like it might take, so folks began calling May
Anna's mom Mrs. Cook. Once or twice, May Anna even called him
Dad. Me and Whippy Bird told her that wasn't right, since it went
against the memory of her own father, who had been killed in the
mine accident in Arizona. That was when she told us there never was
a Mr. Kovaks, that her mother made it up. I felt so sorry for May
Anna that every time we lit candles at BS, I prayed Jackfish would
marry Mrs. Kovaks and become May Anna's father.

Christmas was special back then, with lots of old country tradi-
tions, and we always had a good time. Us being Cornish, the Unholy
Three made circles out of evergreen boughs and put candles at the
bottom and hung them on the front door and in the windows. Then
we made extra to carry with us when we went caroling.

Ma made her currant ring and saffron buns, which she called
nubbies, beef-and-kidney pie, ginger cookies, and, of course, suet
pudding, so heavy it sank right down to your toes. She got out her

best silver as well as the cloam, the heavy old china her mother had brought from Cornwall and given her when she got married.

It was a tradition to invite May Anna and her mother for Christmas dinner, and after Whippy Bird finished eating at the Birds', she came over with her family, too. Even Buster showed up. Jackfish got hold of some sweet cherry wine from Meaderville, and me and Whippy Bird and May Anna were allowed to have a drink of it. It was the strongest stuff we'd ever tasted.

Bummer Bird brought his cornet, and we all sat around the table drinking cherry wine and singing. The Cornish have the best voices in the world, and we were all Cornish except for Jackfish, who was Irish, of course, and they are the second-best singers. You can imagine we sounded good. When it got dark, we lit the candles on the evergreen circles and carried them all over the neighborhood, singing Christmas carols. Hunter Harper wrote that up in his history book, about it being a Cornish tradition in Butte. At least he got one thing right.

Late that night, Jackfish took May Anna and even Mrs. Kovaks to Christmas Eve mass at BS, but they were late, and the church was full, so they had to kneel outside in the snow. It was as cold that night as it ever gets in Butte, cold seeping up from your feet and in through your fingertips, and I expect coming in through your knees, too, if they were planted in the snow, but May Anna said she never felt it. She said she felt like the Holy Family.

That Christmas, Jackfish gave May Anna a music box. It was the prettiest little thing, all polished wood, and when you opened it, a tiny brass cylinder turned, and it played "Sweet Rosie O'Grady." May Anna was so happy, she just played and played and played that thing, even when we were singing Christmas carols. That was the Christmas Jackfish gave Mrs. Kovaks a dusty rose velvet dress. It was the same dress she was buried in.

That music box still works. May Anna left it to me in her will. She left Whippy Bird the pearls, which she wears a lot at the Jim Hill. I don't know whatever happened to the Bible and the rosary. I expect they disappeared, since May Anna didn't make any mention of them in her will. She said the music box and the pearls were special, and only me and Whippy Bird would understand. People said May Anna was hard. Or what they said was Marion Street was hard. But me and Whippy Bird knew the real May Anna Kovaks.

What broke up Jackfish with May Anna and her mom was prospecting.

Some men are prospectors through and through, and Jackfish was one of them. He worked in the copper mines in the winter only because he couldn't pan gold through five feet of Montana snow. Working winters was the way Jackfish could build himself a stake. As soon as spring came, Jackfish went. He spent the whole summer poking holes in the mountains.

There were a lot of men like Jackfish who were after a find. Pop said it wasn't getting rich so much as it was being independent. You were free out there with no shift boss to order you around. There are some men who'd rather be inside the earth instead of on top of it, Pop said, and that's why there'll always be underground mining. But Jackfish told him, "Being inside the earth is natural only for rats and moles and Cornish."

That first summer with May Anna and Mrs. Kovaks, Jackfish was torn. Mrs. Kovaks was scared if he went off he'd fall down an old glory hole and never come back. "I'll go back to the Finlen, and with you at the 'Sweat, we'll make more money than any old gold mine," she said. She went back to the Finlen, too. And May Anna caught more frogs and maggots than me and Whippy Bird put together. Those two really wanted Jackfish to stay on.

In the end, what they did was compromise. Jackfish said he'd go for a couple of weeks. It would be like a vacation for all of them. Mrs. Kovaks and May Anna could have the house to themselves and play cards and not have to worry about cooking for him. He'd have a few days off by himself in the mountains to fish and look around for a gold mine. He said Mrs. Kovaks didn't have to worry about him because he'd agreed to partner with Ernie Latina, who had a Chevrolet.

Early one morning, Jackfish and Ernie headed southeast of Butte into the Tobacco Root mountains, picked a spot, and started panning the gravel. Right off, they found a few gold flakes. Jackfish told us later he thought he was going to strike it rich for sure, but he was wrong. They must have dug up half that mountain, but all they found was a nugget the size of a pea.

That didn't discourage them, though. Two weeks later, they still thought they had themselves a gold mine, so they headed back to Butte for dynamite and lumber for sluices. There had been a cloud-burst, and Buffalo Creek was up. Ernie tried to ford it in the Chevrolet and got stuck in a pothole right in the middle.

Water kept coming up over the running board until finally the seat and the engine were drenched. The water and the mud got into their clothes and their prospecting equipment and even into the little leather bag where Jackfish kept the nugget. It washed that tiny bit of gold right out. Ernie was so mad, he swore off prospecting and said if Jackfish cleaned the mud out of the car, he could have anything he found. So as soon as they hauled the Chevrolet back to Butte, Jackfish got out the gold pan and shoveled all that muck into it, then ran the water on it and panned. Sure enough, he found that nugget. He gave it to Mrs. Kovaks, who had a little loop put on it and wore it on a chain around her neck. She left it to May Anna, who left it to me in her will, but the lawyer said he never found it. Me and Whippy Bird think he knew it was a valuable gold specimen and kept it because May Anna never would have let it go.

With Ernie bailing out like he did, it was too late for Jackfish to go prospecting on his own. Besides, Jackfish believed in omens, and said he never saw a more likely message from God that he was to stay home. May Anna was so happy she spent all her frogs' legs money lighting candles at BS. All fall and winter and spring, they were a family again, playing jokes and singing carols at Christmas.

Jackfish was different the next summer, though. Pop said he was becoming too domesticated, that Jackfish needed to get out for the sake of his soul. I guess Jackfish thought so, too. No matter how much Mrs. Kovaks pleaded, Jackfish said he was going prospecting.

"It's not like I'm stepping," Jackfish told her. Pop said Jackfish liked the women, but when he lived with Mrs. Kovaks, he never stepped. That didn't make Mrs. Kovaks feel any better though.

The day Jackfish left, Ma gave him a currant ring, and Pop gave him a bottle of real Canadian whiskey, and Mrs. Kovaks and May Anna hugged him and hugged him. Mrs. Kovaks sat on the porch with a handkerchief to her eyes while me and Whippy Bird and May Anna stood on the steps waving until Jackfish was out of sight.

We didn't see him again or even hear about anybody running across him the whole summer. Mrs. Kovaks had gone back to the Finlen to work again. May Anna said they needed the money, but we knew her mom was lonely, too. She couldn't sit around the house all day by herself. Then, after Jackfish had been gone three months, she started stepping. One night, she didn't come home until almost morning. May Anna never said a word to me and Whippy Bird. But we knew. You always know about stuff like that.

Pretty soon Mrs. Kovaks was going out every night and coming home drunk. We knew May Anna was worried even though she told us her mom was only making friends. Once when me and Whippy Bird went to May Anna's we heard them arguing.

"If you keep acting like this, Jackfish will throw you out," May Anna pleaded with her. Mrs. Kovaks said Jackfish couldn't throw her out because it was her house.

"What if he doesn't come back, then?" May Anna asked her.

"I already made up my mind he won't. He's dead," Mrs. Kovaks said. "He fell off a mountain or got eaten up by bears."

When May Anna came out to us, she was pale, dabbing at her eyes with her hanky. "He'll come back. I know he will. It doesn't matter, though, because it's over," May Anna told us. May Anna stopped working on her mother. Instead, she started being as mean as she could be to Mrs. Kovaks's boyfriends, hoping if she wasn't nice, they'd go away. But it didn't work. She even got Buster to threaten Bear Meat Canonia, who was keeping company with Mrs. Kovaks, and though he never came back, Mrs. Kovaks found another man to

take his place. Me and Whippy Bird tried to be extra nice to May
Anna because we knew she was aching inside.

It got worse and worse. In the fall, when it looked like Mrs. Kovaks
was right about Jackfish being dead, Splooks Shea, a bartender from
the Blue Parrot, moved in with her, and they spent most of their time
together either drunk or getting there.

Jackfish came home in October. Pop saw him first and called to
me and Whippy Bird to come and see. Jackfish was trotting down
the middle of the street, pushing a jack as hard as he could because
he was in a hurry. The jack didn't go fast enough, so Jackfish ran
ahead of it and took the stairs at Mrs. Kovaks's two at a time. He burst
into the house calling for May Anna and Mrs. Kovaks. Then he saw
Splooks sitting there in his underwear and Mrs. Kovaks in her slip,
both of them having a drink. We never knew what they said or if they
said anything at all. It wasn't a minute before Jackfish came right
back out. Pop grabbed his arm and said something about Mrs. Kovaks
being a good woman despite how it looked. "Don't throw away your
family, you damned pig-headed Irishman!" he said. But Jackfish
pulled away and ran down the street.

That was when me and Whippy Bird heard May Anna. She ran
out on the stairs and called out "Jaaaackfish!" in the most pitiful voice
I ever heard. Even in *Her Man* when John Garfield ran out, she
didn't sound as mournful as she did that day on the steps of her house.
She yelled only once, but you could hear it echo all over Centerville,
sounding back and forth like a bell ringing. There was no other sound,
just "Jackfish" echoing fainter and fainter. Jackfish never looked
back.

The reason Jackfish stayed out so long was he had struck it rich, exactly as he planned, though May Anna didn't care much about that. She just wanted Jackfish back. It wasn't a big strike, but it was big enough. It would have put the three of them on Easy Street. Whippy Bird said if Jackfish had moved back in, May Anna never would have become Marion Street, so maybe it was for the best. But then again, maybe not.

Jackfish sold out for a hundred thousand dollars. He went to Europe and mailed May Anna picture postcards every month or two. He never wrote anything, never even signed his name, but May Anna knew they came from Jackfish. After he spent all his money, he came back to Butte and worked as a miner until he got his back broke in a cave-in. Then he went on the dole. May Anna was in Hollywood when Jackfish had the accident, but we wrote her right away and told her about it. She sent Jackfish money every month until he died.

Me and Whippy Bird stopped by to see him from time to time, taking him fresh currant ring, which was his favorite. He said we'd turned out to be regular Cousin Jennies, but his heart wasn't in teasing us anymore. He came to our house only once after that. It was when Pop died, and he was laid out in the parlor. Ma told me to go to bed since a friend would sit up with Pop that night. I couldn't sleep, and when I heard somebody talking, I crept downstairs to see who it was. "I shoulda listened to you, Tommy. I'm here to say you were right, and I was a hard-headed damn fool." I sneaked back up to my room so Jackfish wouldn't know I'd heard him.

Whenever we went to opening night at one of May Anna's movies in Butte, there was Jackfish in the audience. You couldn't miss the red hair. Once I saw him coming out of the theater with tears streaming down his face, and the picture wasn't even sad.

CHAPTER
4

Buster McKnight turned pro the night somebody spit on Toney McKnight's shoe. I remember it because it was also the night Pink Varscoe kissed me for the first time.

It was Miners Union Day, and a bunch of us decided to go out to Columbia Gardens. Toney had a fight there that night, and he wanted us to go and cheer for him. Even then, I think he liked Whippy Bird and wanted to impress her, though Whippy Bird says back then he was twice as old as her, and Mr. Bird would have killed him if Toney had so much as put a finger on her. Mr. Bird felt that way about every boy Whippy Bird went out with, especially her husbands. She says Toney just wanted to show off, which he surely did like to do.

Toney'd been a fighter for a couple of years. He started punching as a union thug, beating up miners who spoke out against the union. Then he lined up a few bouts to see if he could make money at it. He wasn't very good, but he fought dirty, hitting where he wasn't supposed to, so he won more times than he lost.

He had a heap and said he'd drive all of us, so we didn't mind if we went. There was me and Whippy Bird and May Anna, Pink Varscoe and Toney and Buster. Whippy Bird says don't forget Chick

O'Reilly. I remember thinking we were snuggled in like honey in a comb, because I kept telling Pink to mind his own beeswax whenever he put his hand on my knee.

It was a busy night. Any night in Butte used to be busy. Sometimes the sidewalks were so crowded you had to walk in the street, even at 4 A.M. But on Miners Union Day it was busiest of all because everybody in Butte went out on the town. The saloons were full and the restaurants, too. Even the hotels were packed because people came in from out of town for the parade. The reason we were glad to get a ride in Toney's jalopy was the streetcars were so crowded, it would take forever to get to the Gardens even though they were right at the edge of Butte.

The Gardens were one of the finest things Butte ever had. There was a roller coaster and a merry-go-round and a nice zoo with a bear pit and even peacocks that sometimes got loose and wandered uptown. I always wondered what would happen if one of those birds fell down a mine shaft. The miners were superstitious, and I bet meeting a peacock underground could make them think it was a sign from the devil that their time had come. I'm surprised nobody ever stole one of those birds and took it underground. The sound of a peacock screeching in the stopes would have sounded like a banshee for sure.

The thing I always liked best about the Gardens was the gardens. There were always flower displays. Sometimes the gardeners spelled out COLUMBIA GARDENS in different colored flowers that they grew in their own greenhouses. It was swell, all right. There was grass and lots of trees, too, something we didn't have in Centerville or most any other place in Butte.

And the smells! Who could forget that about Columbia Gardens.

The popcorn and the fried grease smells. In Butte it stank of the smelters and that electric smell that came from streetcars. You got the aroma of garlic and onions and Italian sausage from Meaderville or those funny pungent spice smells from the Chinese restaurants and herb shops. At Columbia Gardens, though, you smelled flowers. It was like perfume. Roses and hyacinths and pansies.

The pansies are what I liked most about Columbia Gardens. There was maybe a whole acre in pansies. When we were little, they'd let us kids loose in there for ten minutes, and we could pick as many pansies as we wanted. Sometimes when I can't sleep, I think back to when I was a kid in the pansy garden. I think heaven is being let into that garden by yourself with as much time as you want to pick the flowers.

We weren't out to pick posies that night, of course, although Pink snitched a rose for me from one of the flower baskets. The night was pretty. Lots of drapey flowers like ferns hanging from the light poles, and there were Chinese lanterns strung up over the sidewalk, too. Whippy Bird says there never were Chinese lanterns at Columbia Gardens, but this is my story, and I'm telling it my way.

We had plenty of time to walk around and go on the rides before the fight. Pink took me on the roller coaster and said he'd hold on to me if I was frightened, but I told him that was stupid. If I was scared, I wouldn't go. If I wasn't, I didn't want him hanging on to me. Besides, if I wanted to fall out, there was nothing he could do to stop me. May Anna told me you were supposed to make men feel like big, strong protectors, even though you knew you didn't need them. She could do that just fine, but I couldn't, which is why she went out with Robert Taylor and I didn't, I guess.

So there we were, smelling the flowers, going on rides, and stuffing ourselves with hot dogs and cotton candy. Except for Toney. He wouldn't eat anything before a fight for fear he would throw up in the ring, so Buster didn't eat anything either. I guess that was moral support. You have to say for Buster and Toney, they always backed each other up.

We were standing around the refreshment stand, and Toney said it was about time for him to go suit up for the fight when that guy spit on his shoe. I don't think he meant to. He took a swig of something that was wrapped in a brown paper sack. It must have been bad because he spit it out on the ground. Only it got all over Toney's shoe. It was a nice two-toned leather slip-on with a white top, and that man left a big brown stain on it.

That made Toney mad as hell because he spent most of his money on clothes, and he always looked spiffy. He might have thought getting spit on made him look bad in front of Whippy Bird, too. So he grabbed the guy by the tie and said, "Hey, pal, wipe the shoe."

If Toney had just asked the man to say he was sorry, he might have said okeydoke and done it, but nobody's going to lean down and clean bad whiskey off your shoe, especially a drunk, dough-faced Bohunk who looks meaner than a mule.

"Clean it yourself, you lousy petticoat," he told Toney, though I, myself, never thought Toney looked Cornish. He was too big.

"You want to fight, chump?" Toney asked him, putting up his dukes.

Before any of us saw it, and especially before Toney saw it, that Bohunk hit him in the head and knocked him backward. Of course, it took more than that to hurt Toney McKnight. Still, he was surprised and stunned some, and him being a fighter, he was plenty mad at not having his defenses up. He hit that man's chin with his right, then gave him a left to the stomach, and the Bohunk caved in like his brown paper bag.

That set off the chump's friends, and they started closing in on Toney—until a couple of cops showed up. They took one look at the man lying on the ground and asked who started the fight. The Bohunks pointed to Toney so the cops cuffed him right there.

"Hey, I'm supposed to fight," Toney told them.

"You just did, bud," the cop told him right back.

"Not here, over at the ring, you dumb ox."

I always thought Toney was a goofy thinker when he was mad, and Whippy Bird says that was surely right. She says he wasn't such a swift thinker when he wasn't mad either, but she's just kidding.

"Who you calling dumb ox?" the cop asked Toney.

Well, right there Toney could have apologized, and Buster might have ended his days as just another retired miner.

"You, you stupid bastard," Toney answered.

Buster didn't have a temper like his brother, and he tried to explain that Toney was scheduled for a boxing match, but the policeman told him to shut up. "We're taking him in to cool off," he said.

By then, Toney realized what he'd done, but it was too late. The cops were dragging him away. "You fight for me," Toney told Buster.

Buster just stood there with his mouth open. It was like Toney had hit him, too.

"Go on, kid," Toney called over his shoulder. "Nobody'll know the difference." Which was true enough since the two of them looked pretty much alike even though Toney was older.

"I can't fight!" Buster called back, shaking his head.

"You bet you can!" The cops had taken Toney half a block, one dragging him and the other pushing him along with a nightstick in the back. We were following. "Kid," Toney pleaded, pulling up short, "I'm in real trouble if I don't show. You gotta do this for me."

That's the only reason Buster fought. He never in his life gave a thought to being a professional fighter before that night. He just always assumed Toney would be the boxer in the family. Buster said he learned fighting just to protect himself, which I already said is not the case. He learned it to impress May Anna. But I think it's true he hadn't thought about being a professional.

The cop kept pushing Toney along with his nightstick, and when Toney tried to stop, he gave Toney a chop in the kidneys. "Get going!" he said. That must have been why Buster agreed right there he'd fight.

"Don't you worry, kid," Toney yelled. "You just get in the ring with him. It's only four rounds. Protect your head. You can do it."

Buster stood there watching Toney until he disappeared in the crowd, then he turned to Pink with kind of a helpless look. "Where's Toney's trunks?" he asked.

That made us all laugh because we thought Buster would say something like he couldn't do it or he was scared or try to bluff and say he would beat the hell out of the other fighter. He didn't do that. He was cool like he always was, in the ring or out. That was one of Buster's strengths. In his early matches when the other fighters didn't know him, they'd say mean things to Buster to get him flustered, like call him a petticoat. It never worked, though.

The only way anyone ever successfully baited Buster was to tease him about his girlfriend being a hooker. It always backfired since it didn't fluster Buster; it just made him vicious. Like the time Morrie the Mauler told him, "I'm gunna finish you, then celebrate with the blondie in Venus Alley." Buster didn't say anything, didn't even bother to set him up. He just took one step forward and slugged Morrie in the mouth. Morrie went down for the count. Usually, Buster was known as a gentleman. In fact, one or two writers called him the Gentleman from Butte, but he could be mean when it came to sticking up for May Anna.

We were all excited about Buster fighting. Pink and Chick raced over to Toney's car to get his trunks as well as his shoes, which turned out to be too small for Buster. That's why he crow-hopped all over the ring that first time, making the sports writer who was there think this was some new kind of foot technique. But then that writer thought the fighter was Toney, not Buster. Toney fought under the name "Kid McKnight," so nobody knew what his real name was. The two McKnights looked so much alike, nobody could have told you which one was in the ring anyway. Except us, of course.

Nobody cared either. Toney didn't have many followers except for Buster and Chick and Pink and a few girls you could count on hanging around him because he was such a flashy dresser. Toney was not exactly the biggest fighter in Butte. That's why he was doing a four-round exhibition match at Columbia Gardens at the same time there was wrestling and foot races going on. You fought for "exposure," the Gardens said, which is another way of saying the purse wouldn't pay for more than two rounds of Shawn O's for Buster's gang.

I never knew why Toney fought, whether he just liked the attention or whether he actually thought he had a chance at something. Whippy Bird said it was a way to keep out of the mines. He never liked getting his fancy clothes dirty. Everyone said he was "high-toned," which is where he got his name, of course. May Anna said he was the toniest dresser she ever met, and she would surely know. Toney could have been a bouncer or a bartender or, in fact, the bootlegger he was. He didn't have to be a fighter. Maybe he didn't care about it much because he never stood in Buster's way, never made him feel he'd taken anything away from Toney. I expect Toney knew he ended up with more glory being Buster's brother and manager than he'd ever have got as Kid McKnight.

Buster went off to the boys' room to change clothes, then he came back, looking as fancy as Toney in those purple silk shorts.

"Why, Buster, you're elegant," May Anna told him. It was the first time I ever heard her purr. Buster looked just like a Columbia Gardens peacock when she said that.

Then he started shadowboxing and doing warm-ups like he'd seen Toney do, though I don't know if it helped him. May Anna helped him, though. Just before he headed for the ring, she planted a kiss on his mouth and said, "I'm proud of you, Buster. I'll be watching." Old Buster, he walked down that aisle like he was already a champ.

Chick acted like his trainer and got the water bucket and the towel and the mouth sponge, though he didn't know any more what to do with them than the rest of us. Buster was the only one who knew fighting, and that was only because he helped Toney train and used to hang around the Centerville Gym.

I never knew the real name of the man he fought. He was called the Butte Bomber. Buster said he was just some bum, but he looked dangerous to us. He was bigger than Buster, who was no peaweight himself, and he had a broken nose and flappy ears like cartoons you see of prize-fighters. He climbed through the ropes and sneered at Buster, then said so everybody could hear, "Where do they get these kids?"

Like I said, Buster never got flustered, even in his very first fight. He stood there, quiet, just like a gentleman, while Chick laced up his gloves.

May Anna was cool, too, though me and Whippy Bird were sweating buckets. She just smiled sweetly at Buster, kind of like a Madonna, with her hands folded in her lap, her head high. It was the first time I noticed May Anna had a neck like a goose. I think she'd already started practicing being an actress.

Pink sat down next to me. He was sweating, too, with little beads of perspiration standing out on his face. It was as hot there as it ever gets in Butte, but it wasn't only the heat that got to Pink. He found out the Butte Bomber just about killed somebody in his last fight, and Pink being the damn fool he sometimes was, he told us all about it, so we were scared for Buster. Whippy Bird said if he told that to Buster, she personally would kill him. May Anna wasn't frightened though. "Buster will take care of Mr. Butte Bomber," she said.

We weren't as sure as May Anna. Buster came out of his corner quiet, not looking scared, but not looking like he was out for a fight either. He never glanced at us, not once, but I was sure he knew right where May Anna was sitting. When the fight started, he danced around with the Bomber for a few minutes in those tight shoes. Meanwhile, we were hoping and praying Buster could just keep doing that for four rounds without getting killed.

After dancing for what seemed like an hour, the Butte Bomber lashed out at Buster. Buster dodged him, and they went back to sidestepping. It didn't start as much of a fight, them just moving around, making little swipes and dodging each other. A couple of times, the Butte Bomber connected, and once he knocked Buster down for a count of two. We were worried when that happened, but Buster hopped right up. He told us later the only reason he fell was because of those tight shoes. It was a pretty boring start, the boys said, and they knew more about it than me and Whippy Bird. It was so boring, in fact, that when the second round ended, people booed.

I think that was what got Buster going. Up to that time, he was just trying to get along without being hurt. But the crowd booed Kid McKnight, and Buster was responsible for Kid McKnight's honor. That meant Buster had to do something. So when the second round ended, Buster sat down on his little stool and whispered to Chick, "This is it. I'm gunna knock him out. You just watch me." Chick told us Buster didn't even sound excited, just said it like you'd say I'm going to go get a glass of beer and a cigarette. He meant it, though. When Buster came out for the third round, he was a fighter.

You couldn't tell from looking at him. He was still crow-hopping in Toney's tight shoes and looking dumb as a Bohunk. Then the Butte Bomber took a poke at him with his right, and Buster moved in and damn near killed him. Buster countered with his left, hit with his right, then his left, and went in for the finish. He slugged the Butte Bomber with the most powerful right anybody ever saw in Columbia Gardens. The Bomber was out for five minutes. When the referee held up Buster's hand and named him the winner, we leaped up on our chairs, yelling and hollering. May Anna was the loudest. So much for Miss Cool Movie Star. We clapped and whistled and hugged, and then Pink Varscoe kissed me. That was the start of serious things between me and Pink.

May Anna ran over to Buster, when he was climbing through the ropes, and kissed him. Then Chick kissed Whippy Bird. There was more kissing that night than May Anna ever had in any of her movies.

It turned out, Toney watched that fight. As we were leaving we turned around and saw him standing in the back of the room. He'd talked those cops into letting him go but not soon enough for him to fight, so when he got there, Buster was already in the ring. You'd think Toney would have been cheering, too, but he wasn't. He was just studying his brother, quiet and collected the way Buster usually was.

Like I say, it wasn't much of a fight. We were cheering like crazy, but nobody else was. As far as the crowd was concerned, they were just watching a couple of dumb turnips take pokes at each other, hoping to see blood. It didn't matter to them who won. The people there didn't know they were in on the ground floor of boxing history. It's funny when me and Whippy Bird remember about that night, how we never knew something of importance to the world was happening. I bet *Life* magazine would pay about a million dollars for a picture of May Anna giving Buster a kiss after his first fight.

Maybe the *Montana Standard* sports writer knew. He gave Buster two paragraphs on the sports page the next day, saying Toney McKnight had perfected a new step that allowed him to knock out the Butte Bomber with a lightning right. He wrote that Kid

McKnight was a power to watch on the Montana boxing circuit and predicted he would one day play in Salt Lake City. Maybe even Spokane.

"So, I won," Buster told Toney when he caught up with him. Buster still had on those little purple pants, and May Anna was hanging around his neck. Buster wasn't so cool you couldn't tell he was proud of what he'd done and wanted Toney to be proud of him, too.

Toney nodded but didn't say anything. Now, you may think Toney acted that way because he was jealous. Or you might think, like we did later, that Toney was giving a lot of thought to Buster's future. I have to tell you both of those are true thoughts, but me and Whippy Bird decided there was something else going on in Toney McKnight's head, too.

We think Toney was supposed to throw the fight that night. That's why he sent Buster in when the cops dragged him off. That's why he told Buster just to take care of himself. He didn't give him any instructions about hitting the Butte Bomber because he never even thought about Buster winning the fight. He was just supposed to show up. Me and Whippy Bird think he got paid to take a dive, maybe by some of those bootleggers he hung out with. So at the time Buster came up to him, Toney was worrying was he going to get killed by somebody for a double cross.

When I first told that to Whippy Bird, she said if Toney was going to lose, why did he want all of us to go along and see it. That made sense, and I thought about it for a time. Then I pointed out how she always got soft and cried when anybody was hurt. Maybe Toney figured she'd put out for him since she wasn't dating Chick yet.

When Whippy Bird thought about it, she said it made sense to her, too. Me and Whippy Bird believe that's another reason Toney McKnight never fought again; he didn't dare.

Of course, by the time we figured that out, it was too late to ask Toney, though Whippy Bird would have been the one to do it, and I'm not sure she would have.

Even if we were right about Toney worrying he was going to get brained, we know he was thinking about something else, as well. That was Toney for you, always hustling. This time he was scheming about how to make a buck for himself out of Buster's powerful right arm.

Buster and Toney looked at each other for a long time, Buster wanting Toney to say he'd done a good job. Next to May Anna, Toney was the one Buster admired most. Toney knew that, so after a minute or two, he broke into a big grin, and he and Buster hugged each other and pounded each other on the back.

"Buster, you get out of my pants and uncurl your toes, and we'll all go over to Meaderville and celebrate. I'll get the purse." So me and Whippy Bird and May Anna and everybody else climbed back into Toney's heap, and he drove us to the Rocky Mountain Cafe to spend Buster's first prize fight winnings.

Even after all that junk we ate at the Gardens, we'd worked up an appetite yelling for Buster, so we all ordered ourselves dinner. We were drinking Shawn O's, too, except for Buster, who almost never drank. He paid for a round, then he changed his winnings to silver dollars and went over to a slot machine and put in a few. Before you knew it, the bell went off, and there was all this noise just like when Buster floored the Butte Bomber. He won himself fifty dollars.

Buster just couldn't lose that night—which is what me and

Whippy Bird told May Anna when we found out Buster didn't take her home until 5 A.M. We would have been killed if we'd ever stayed out that late, but I doubt that Mrs. Kovaks ever knew what time May Anna got in.

"Buster," Chick told him, "I never saw anybody throw a punch like that. You are the new Butte Bomber."

"Butte Bomber, hell, you're the new Jack Dempsey," Pink said. They were falling all over themselves to flatter Buster.

"You aren't the new anybody," May Anna said. "You're better than anybody. You're you."

"You're the champ," Chick said.

"He's no such thing. He won one fight against a bum," Toney said.

It sounded like Toney was pouring cold water on Buster's win, and we didn't like that. Even Buster looked unhappy.

"You won one fight in your whole life," Toney said again. Toney liked the sound of his voice, and he may have realized just then that he wasn't going to get attention from fighting anymore, so he'd have to get it from talking. "But," he said, pausing to make sure he had our attention, "you could be a champ."

We cheered at that. Those Shawn O's surely had taken effect. We would have cheered to see Buster tie his shoes.

"I know something about fighting," Toney said, and he stopped, maybe hoping somebody would say you bet you do, Toney. Nobody did, though, so he continued, "And I have never seen a right arm like that."

Chick pounded Buster on the back, and Pink slapped me on the knee and said, "Natch."

"If you would be willing to take some instructions from me as your manager and train the way I tell you, I think you can make it as a boxer." Toney sat back looking important.

Pink called for another round of Shawn O's and paid for them out of the silver dollars Buster piled up on the table.

Then Toney got serious, like he was finished talking big. He ignored us and turned to Buster. "Kid, I know I can never amount to anything as a fighter. I can win a few bucks and have a little fun, but I don't have the power. You got the power. You got the cool head, too, which is something else I ain't got. The thing I don't know about is do you want to be a fighter, and will you train?"

Buster looked down at his hands and didn't say anything. The McKnight boys forgot about the rest of us, and we pretended we weren't listening, though of course we were.

"Well, why not?" Buster said. "What the hell else is there for me in this boob town besides going down in the mines for the rest of my life? You really think I can make it Tone? No shit now."

"Yeah. But you got to work at it. Every day. I can tell you how. I can even show you some of it, though I never cared enough to work at it much myself. If you're not going to dedicate your life to it, you say so now so I won't waste my time. You do it, and you'll be a champ."

"He'll do it," May Anna said. She put her little white hand over Buster's big mitt.

Things had got serious all of a sudden. Only a few hours before we had gone down to the Gardens to see Toney fight. Now we were hearing Buster's decision to be a champion fighter of the world. We all felt strange and didn't know what to say. Then the waitress brought our dinners and took our orders for a couple of bottles of

wine to follow all those Shawn O's. Today, wine's for pansies, but
during Prohibition, that Meaderville wine was stronger than whiskey,
so we had a high old time. In fact, it was our first high old time, since
me and Whippy Bird and May Anna were sixteen years old and still
in high school. We were too young to drink that night even if
drinking was legal. But who thought about that? It was Prohibition,
and drinking wasn't legal for anybody else either.

While we were all sitting around being serious, I'll tell you what
Pink Varscoe was thinking about, and that was trying to kiss me
again, but I didn't want him to, so I said, "Pink, don't you think you
ought to propose a toast."

Pink raised his glass. "To the Unholy Three," meaning me and
Whippy Bird and May Anna.

"You jackass," I told him. "Not to us. To Buster!"

So Pink toasted, "To the new Kid McKnight! Bottom's up!"

Buster shook his head. "Kid McKnight's Toney's."

"Take the name. It's yours if you want it. Jack Dempsey got his
name from his brother. You can get yours from me." Buster said no,
Kid McKnight was Toney's name, and if he didn't use it, the name
should be retired. He wanted his own ring name.

So we ate spaghetti and drank wine and got serious again, thinking
up championship names. We suggested the Kid from Butte and the
Centerville Kid and the Butte Killer. Chick said what about Slug 'em
McKnight. Pink thought up the Butte Buster then Buster Knockout,
which we all liked. Even Buster liked that one, though after he
thought it over, he decided it was too cute. He wanted something
classier. We mulled over the Montana Mauler, which had a snappy
ring, and Pride of the Copper Camp, and the Butte Bull. Then Chick

suggested the Fighting Miner, but Buster wasn't a miner, so that wouldn't work.

Buster said he'd think about all those names, but you could tell none of them was quite right as far as Buster was concerned. May Anna said they weren't stylish enough, and Buster cared what May Anna thought.

We sat there studying on it when all of a sudden Whippy Bird looked at the clock, jumped up, and said, "My God, it's midnight, Buster. We have to get out of here!" None of us had been paying attention to the time. Now me and Whippy Bird were in serious trouble.

We jumped up and started for the door, all of us except for May Anna. She just sat there with a little smile on her face, quiet as a statue. She put up her hand in the way she had that made everybody stop and pay attention to her. No matter if there were a thousand people having a Roman orgy, all May Anna had to do was put up her pale little hand and everybody stopped and listened.

"I have it, Buster." Her voice was quiet, but we could hear it above all the noise in the Rocky Mountain.

"Have what, May Anna?"

"Your name."

"Huh?"

"Your new name. Courtesy of Whippy Bird," May Anna said. Then she stood up very slowly and looked at us with her glory hole eyes and held up her glass in a toast and said, "Ladies and gentlemen, meet the new heavyweight champion of the world. Ladies and gentlemen—Mr. Buster Midnight."

CHAPTER
5

Of course, nobody but us knew about Buster Midnight for a long time. We thought he was king of the hill, but so what? Fight promoters didn't exactly beat a path to his door, and Buster more than anybody, even Toney, knew he had a long way to go to be a major prize-fighter.

As time passed, we got used to Buster practicing to be a boxer, taking it in stride and not paying him any mind. After all, Buster wasn't much different from the other boys who left high school to go into the copper mines—which was the first thing Toney told Buster to do. Get the heaviest, dirtiest job he could in a mine. That kind of work would build up his body, Toney claimed. Strength wasn't all Buster needed. Strength wouldn't save you if somebody got to you before you had a chance to draw on it, Toney said. Buster had to be quick, too. So he learned to run and dance around and dodge and chop and jab and develop a good one-two.

Toney made him jump rope for his footwork. Me and Whippy Bird and May Anna used to sit by him on the front porch of the little McKnight house in Centerville, keeping him company while he jumped up and down like some halfwit, grinning or talking to anybody else who stopped by. He even skipped rope at May Anna's house while she sat on the stairs and talked to him. You'd think people would laugh at that big man jumping rope, but nobody did it more than once. I remember the afternoon when Pug Obie was coming off shift. "Hey, honey," he called to Buster. "Where's your dolly?"

After Pug got up off the street, though, it was "Hey, bub, can't you take a joke?" Mostly, people knew Buster and knew he was in training, and they admired that. The gang could tease him but not anybody else.

Sometimes Toney would get a broom and wave the handle around fast in front of Buster's nose. "Hit it, Buster! Hit it!" he'd yell. And old Buster flailed back and forth trying to hit that broom, punching and slugging. Before long, he got so good at it that Mrs. McKnight told them to use a stick or else Buster could sweep the house with what was left of the broom. That was a funny idea, all right. Big Buster hunched over, sweeping the house with a broom on the end of a twelve-inch handle.

When he waved that broom around, Toney said mean things to Buster, like calling him "she," or telling him he was a dumb petticoat or some others (which I would not want you to know about now that Toney's deceased) to make Buster mad.

There was a reason for Toney saying mean stuff. He wanted Buster to learn to control his temper in the ring. Buster, as I said before, already was a cool customer, but Toney knew there were things that would make Buster mad—mad enough to lose his temper. Getting rattled could make Buster lose a fight. So Toney trained Buster to deal with anything anybody said—inside the ring or out. Toney said a boxer had to be careful not to get into fights outside of the ring because he would be in big trouble.

Toney also gave him a rubber ball to toughen up his hands, and when Buster wasn't working in the mine, skipping rope, or hitting the broom, you could find him at home reading the sports page with his hands going squeeze, squeeze, squeeze, on that red rubber ball.

Now that reminds me of something I want to say. During the murder trial in Hollywood some of those reporters said Buster was a dummy, that he couldn't even write his own name. Hunter Harper put that in his book, which is another reason why I don't like him and why I'm writing this down so you'll know the truth. Buster read all the time, maybe not your major works of literature like *Forever Amber,* but he read the newspapers and the fight magazines. What's more, he always carried pulps with him, which he read on the train or in the dressing room. Sometimes when he was traveling and staying in a hotel room with nothing to do, he even read the Gideon Bible.

The reason that talk got started about Buster being an illiterate was Buster and Toney were fooling around once, and they posed Buster for a funny picture. Buster put on Toney's coat, which was too small for him, so when he buttoned it, it pulled in the front. They put a hat on his head that was so tiny it just perched there, with Buster's ears sticking out under it. Finally, Buster stuck out his tongue, crossed his eyes, and grabbed the *Montana Standard* from the porch and turned it upside down just as Toney snapped the picture. It was the kind of silly Kodak everybody takes. Buster probably gave it to May Anna, but somebody got a hold of it later on during the trial, and the California papers printed it. The wire services even picked it up. That's why the story went around that Buster was a pumpkin head. And that is a lesson not to take damn fool snapshots.

There were other things Toney taught Buster. He made him practice his punches in a shed out back that was so low Buster couldn't stand up straight. He had to squat down, and that developed his crouch, Toney said.

To build up his speed, Buster ran. He ran to work then back home at night. When he wasn't working, he ran foot races against the horses that pulled the delivery wagons on Montana Street, but he got so he always won. Then he went to Columbia Gardens and ran around the race track. When they took out the horses to exercise, Buster raced against them.

Sometimes we went down in Toney's machine and watched Buster run against the thoroughbreds. "If you don't make it as a boxer, at least you can fill in at horse races," Whippy Bird told him.

"May Anna can be the jockey," Pink smirked. He said it under his breath so Buster wouldn't hear. Me and Whippy Bird did, though, and Whippy Bird punched him in the ribs.

"Or you can be a mine mule," I yelled, and I was just about right. Not long after that when one of the mules in the Mountain Con where Buster worked was sick, Buster pushed the ore cars himself. For a time, he was called Mule McKnight, but that name never stuck. Probably because Buster insisted that everybody call him Buster Midnight. We insisted on it, too. That was the classiest name I ever heard, even better than Marion Street. I guess me and Whippy Bird can pat ourselves on the back for helping to invent two of the most famous names in America.

Not everything Toney made Buster do was so great, though. He told him to chew pine resin that he dug out of trees. Me and Whippy Bird tried it once, and it tasted like hell, worse than near beer. That pine gum was tough as leather. Toney said it helped Buster toughen up his jaw. He told Buster to chew garlic before a fight, too, but Buster never did that. He wasn't against breathing garlic fumes on the other boxer, which was the reason Toney told him to do it, of course, but he sure didn't want to stop those kisses he got from May Anna every time he won a fight.

There was one other thing Toney had Buster do that was crazy, and that was get beef brine from the Hutchinson Brothers Packing Company and soak his hands in it. He even rubbed it on his face. Buster claimed it made his hands tough as ore—"hard-rock hands," one of those sports writers called them.

All that was just the start. In addition, Toney arranged for Buster to work out at the Centerville Gym. Toney hustled up some kind of deal, as he always did, probably providing free bootleg. It let Buster practice there for nothing as long as he was a sparring partner for the other fighters training at the gym. That was good because Buster learned about fighting from other people besides his brother. Toney didn't know everything there was to know about fighting—even though Toney thought so.

It's odd when you think about it. There was Toney, only a so-so fighter who didn't care enough to train himself, but still, he was the best trainer in Butte for Buster. He was harder than anybody else ever would have been on Buster, too. "You think I'm tough?" Toney would say when Buster complained. "You just step in that ring with somebody who knows what he's doing. You'll find out what tough is, Buster Kid Midnight." Toney always got Buster's ring name mixed up. I think that's because he still hoped Buster would pick up Toney's old Kid McKnight name and bring it glory.

After he'd trained for a couple of months, Buster told Toney to line him up a fight. Toney wouldn't do it. "You fought a bum," he told Buster. "You connected with a lucky punch. You might not be so lucky the next time. What if the other guy gets lucky instead? What if you go in the ring with somebody who kills you or even worse, ruins your career? How many hits you think you're gunna take if you get matched up with a real powerhouse?"

Toney told Pink he was afraid if Buster got beat bad in a couple of fights, he'd lose his confidence, and that was the worst thing that could happen to a beginning boxer. He didn't want Buster to quit before he got started. He also told Pink he didn't want to waste his own time on a second-rate fighter. What me and Whippy Bird think was Toney wanted to make a big splash with Buster. Every time Buster stepped in that ring, it was Toney in there fighting, too.

After a while Buster got bored and said he wasn't going to run horse races all his life, and if Toney didn't get him a fight pretty soon, he'd give it up. So Toney looked around for some tanktown bouts. Butte was a big fight town. Toney wanted to wait on Butte until Buster Midnight was somebody.

So he lined up a fight in Billings, which was just an ordinary town. Toney and another trainer put it together. They rented an Elks hall one Saturday night and sold tickets, agreeing to split the take, no matter who won. I expect it was right then that Toney decided he would manage Buster's winnings—if managing is what you call it. He managed them just about as well as he did the Columbia Gardens purse that we spent on Shawn O's and dinner in Meaderville.

That's part of the reason Buster never had any money left over

from his fighting days. But then who ever heard of a fighter that got
rich doing anything but running a restaurant? Buster didn't fight for
money, anyway. He wanted to be somebody. For May Anna. And
that was the way it worked out.

We went to Billings with Buster and Toney to watch that fight,
of course. It took half a day to get there, so me and Whippy Bird
got permission to spend the night in a hotel, which was as exciting
as seeing Buster fight. Pop said I could go if Whippy Bird did. And
Mr. Bird said Whippy Bird could go if I did. May Anna's mother
didn't care and probably didn't even know that she was gone.

Toney took us over in his new Studebaker President Eight, which
had window shades and a backseat that held about two dozen people.
He had gotten big-time in the bootlegging business in those days,
making runs to Canada every week or so, and that's why he ditched
the heap for the Studebaker car—and why he had ten or twelve
bottles of Canadian whiskey tucked under the seat.

You have to realize back then, though the boys were out of high
school, me and Whippy Bird and May Anna were sixteen and not
as familiar with liquor as we were later on. Me and Whippy Bird
especially. We were so green we still thought you got drunk mixing
an aspirin with a Coke. That day we knew for sure we could get drunk
drinking Canadian—and right out of the bottle since Toney didn't
pack glasses in the Studebaker President Eight.

"Toney, don't you have no ice?" Pink asked, leaning over the front
seat. "You can't ask these ladies to swig from the bottle."

Toney, without taking his eyes off the road, said, "I got ice, all
right, just no glasses. If you want to hold the ice in your hand and
pour this good whiskey over it, then suit yourself."

"Or use Whippy Bird's shoe," said Buster. "Her shoes are too small for a bird," which is the truth. She is the only grown woman I ever knew who wore Thom McAn little girls' shoes, and that's because she has a size three foot. Today she wears little kids' sneakers from Sears.

All of us were drinking except Buster because Toney wouldn't let him. Me and Whippy Bird passed out, which wasn't such a bad idea since that is a long, boring drive. When we woke up we were sober though it took me a little while before my mouth felt like it was part of me again.

May Anna was better about drinking since she just sipped a little every now and then. I remember waking up while she was singing. Her voice sounded good to me, which is why I knew I was still drunk. She said the whiskey kept her warm, which was no little thing since it was winter. You never knew anything as cold as winter in Montana. The wind blows straight down from the North Pole with nothing to stop it except barbed wire fences with the gates open. (I read that in Hunter Harper's book and thought it was catchy, which is why I'm using it. He shouldn't complain since he got most of his stories from me and Whippy Bird.)

In Billings we stayed at a big hotel on Broadway, which I remember almost as much as I do that fight. I'd seen fights before, but I'd never stayed in a hotel until then. The only other times I'd ever been away from home were when I stayed with Whippy Bird or May Anna or if I went to my grandmother's house in Anaconda. In fact, the only other time I could remember being a paying guest in a hotel was when Mrs. Kovaks took us to May Anna's birthday lunch at the Finlen in Butte.

We had a big iron bed painted white that was swaybacked and sagged in the middle, just like home. Me and Whippy Bird and May Anna drew straws to see who had to sleep in the middle. Whippy Bird lost, but it didn't matter because May Anna slept somewhere else. I bet you can guess where.

When we got to Billings, Buster and Toney disappeared inside the Elks hall while we checked into the hotel and checked out the town, which was not one of your more exciting places. We were in a position to know because we were from Butte. People talk about mining towns being rough and ugly, but they're exciting, too. Billings was dull, and we felt like hot stuff around those hay farmers and cowboys.

The Unholy Three had grown up quite a bit by then even if we were still in high school and didn't know much about liquor.

May Anna's hair wasn't platinum blond yet, but it was getting lighter. It wasn't that mine runoff color anymore. She'd shot up some in height, too. Willowy was what the movie magazines called it. She was willowy in Billings.

Me and Whippy Bird weren't so bad either. Whippy Bird was still little—she is still waiting for her growth, which is a little joke we have—but she looked perky with all those red curls. She never got the freckles your redheads usually get either. Me, I was tall, and I wore my hair in a bob, and I was skinny—but skinny was fashionable just then. Pink told me I looked like Tillie the Toiler in the funny papers, but then he always flattered me. Still, we were lookers, if I do say so myself. We surely cut a picture of fashion there in Billings among all your ordinary people. We sure knew it, too, walking around

in our high-heeled slippers, chewing Wrigley's Doublemint, and setting fire to Camel cigarettes, as May Anna liked to put it.

Whippy Bird says shut up, Effa Commander, you're bragging, and
I surely am. She says we weren't that cute, but I distinctly remember
we were. She says May Anna looked like a goddess, and we looked
like Mutt and Jeff in knee garters.

The setup for the fight wasn't much. Toney and the other manager
put a bunch of folding chairs on the floor of a meeting room. The
hall was decorated with flags and streamers left over from some
dance, and there were stuffed animal heads around with the hair
falling out. The ring itself was just a platform raised up about a foot
or two off the floor, with ropes about as thick as clothesline. There
were two little rickety stools with the paint coming off for the fighters. I remember when Buster stood up once to start a round, there
was a big paint chip sticking to him that looked like a hole in his
pants.

The hall was already filling up when we got there. We were so late,
the boys thought we were lost, though the truth was we'd stopped
at a soda fountain. I ordered a black cow, Whippy Bird got a muddy
river, and May Anna had a lime rickey. Whippy Bird says how can
you remember what you ordered fifty years ago, Effa Commander.
But you remember the things that are important. Besides, I have
been a professional food person all my life, and my mind works that
way. Then we got to flirting with the cowboys and forgot the time.

Pink and Chick saved us places in the front row. Of course, May
Anna just naturally sat in the middle.

"Where the hell have you been?" Chick asked Whippy Bird.

"That's for me to know and you to find out," she snapped. You never could fence in Whippy Bird. When I heard that song "Don't Fence Me In," I said they wrote that one for you, Whippy Bird.

The boys were puffed up, acting like they were big-time Butte prize fight fans who blew in especially for the match. They talked in loud voices about this new fighter, Buster Midnight, and what a natural he was. The boys put down quite a bit on Buster, who didn't look so good by the odds. It took me and Whippy Bird a long time to learn the big money in prize fighting wasn't the purse but the bets. Of course, you had to bet right, which is something we never thought about. We just bet on Buster. But then that meant we always came out right.

I gave Pink five dollars and told him to place it on Buster for me, but Pink said he'd give me a piece of his bet, if I was good to him. Pink was always saying things like that. I just told him I'd rather put out five dollars than put out for him, if you know what I mean. Whippy Bird says I put out plenty in my time when Pink and I were going around together, but that is not any of your business.

This being the first professional fight of Buster Midnight, we all felt important. The boys had cigars that they kept chewing and lighting, and then chewing again. Me and Whippy Bird and May Anna chain-smoked the Camels, leaving little bits of red lipstick on the ends, which we thought looked swell. May Anna had learned to hold her cigarette between two fingers so that her nail polish showed, and she used her little fingernail to pick the bits of tobacco from her tiny crooked teeth.

After everybody sat down and the hall filled up with a cloud of cigarette and cigar smoke as thick as the Butte sky, the referee climbed through the clothesline and called everybody's attention. First he introduced the Billings fighter, who fought under the name the Finnish Cowboy. He was big, of course, and blond, and dopey-looking. He had a face that looked like it was made up of little blocks of stone stuck together.

Everybody clapped and cheered The Pride of Southeast Montana, which was another thing the Finnish Cowboy was called, and people stamped their feet and whistled while that Finn ox-lumbered down the aisle and into the ring. If size could win, Buster would have been dead right there.

Then the announcer said the second fighter was the Dynamite King of the Butte Mines—Buster Midnight. I don't know where they got that dynamite business because Buster never set charges. He was just a mucker.

There were some boos from the Billings crowd, but we cheered and hollered, and so did some other people. That's when me and Whippy Bird realized we didn't own Buster Midnight. That night we discovered Buster Midnight had fans. In fact, right there, with Buster running down the aisle to the ring in Toney's old purple silk shorts, Whippy Bird turned to me and said, "Remember I told you this, Effa Commander. Buster is going to be a famous person." I did remember because I almost never knew Whippy Bird to be wrong.

We all yelled and made a nuisance of ourselves, but Buster and Toney weren't paying attention. They tended to business. They never even looked at us. Even Buster never looked at May Anna. Toney whispered things to him, and Buster nodded. Then Buster did a funny thing. He stood up tall, raised his arms over his head and smiled at the crowd. Then he made a couple of little punches at people in the audience and grinned. The crowd loved it.

"Buster learned right at the beginning that boxing is show business. That's why he was always so popular," May Anna said later on. "Buster McKnight was just a shy, nice guy, but Buster Midnight was a showman." Who in the state of Montana would ever dispute a fact about show business with May Anna Kovaks–Marion Street?

The Finnish Cowboy looked at Buster like he was a nitwit. Then he glanced over at his trainer in a way that said, "This is going to be easy." You couldn't blame him for underestimating Buster, who did look a little dopey himself. The Finn would find out about him soon enough.

The bell sounded, and Buster and the cowboy came into the ring, skipping around and making little swipes at each other. For a man as big as he was, the cowboy had a funny way of fighting. He crouched over and kept his head down and his shoulders hunched up, like a turtle. Every now and then his head poked out of the shell and he punched at Buster. For a couple of rounds, though, neither one connected.

You have to give the cowboy credit. He was a lot better than the Butte Bomber, kind of tricky, and faster than you'd think for all that size. Finns never struck me as fast dodgers, but maybe Finn cowboys are better than Finn miners. Buster sparred, trying to find a weak spot. Toney taught him to learn all about the other fighter before he tried anything, which was why Buster was a slow starter. He told Buster nobody was perfect, that if a fighter had fists like sledge hammers, he likely had a jelly belly, too. There were plenty who could dish it out but not take it—or could take it but couldn't dish it out.

Toney told him to spend the first round or two figuring out the fighter.

The crowd didn't figure it that way, though. They thought Buster was scared. They decided he was chicken. They also thought the fight was fixed. Or at least some of them did. We found out later that the sheriff took all the ticket receipts, saying if it was a fair fight, he'd give them back, but if it wasn't, he'd return the money to the ticket buyers.

Me and Whippy Bird think Toney wouldn't blink an eye about fixing a fight for himself, but he was grooming Buster to be a champ. Letting Buster lose, especially his first fight, didn't make sense. Besides, Buster wouldn't ever agree to a fixed fight.

For a while it surely did look like all Buster was doing was trying to stay on his feet for a few rounds. The Finn thought so, too. He got overconfident. He let go with his right and forgot to defend himself, and Buster let him have it in the belly with a one-two from his hard-rock fists. That took the wind out of that cowboy. He collided with the ropes. Lucky for him the bell rang.

The Finn was plenty mad when the next round started. He charged out like a bull, which was just what Buster wanted. Angry fighters are stupid fighters, was another of Toney's sayings. The cowboy lunged at Buster, and Buster hit him in the jaw. That's the way it went for four or five more rounds. Buster just punished him. The cowboy landed a little blow, then Buster crashed into him with a fist. But every time Buster knocked the Finn down, the bell rang, and they had to start over at the next round.

We saw from the little smile on his face that Buster was having a good time. Maybe he was too confident, because the cowboy hit him with a haymaker, and Buster went down for the count of six. When he got up, we heard Toney yell to him, "OK, kid, show time's over. You ain't setting charges. No need to tap 'er light. Just finish off the cowboy." Buster got up, and headed for the Finn, but the round ended, and he went over to his corner.

Toney talked to him, but Buster wasn't paying any attention. He looked straight at May Anna and grinned. "What'll I do with him, honey?" Buster yelled.

"Put him right here, Buster," she screamed, pointing to her lap.

When the next round started, Buster came out smiling, but it was his fighting smile, the one that meant the next time you take a poke at me, you damn fool, you are on your way to hell. The Finn felt pretty good about knocking Buster down before and charged again. That was all Buster needed. He started with that little smile, looked away, wound up then hit the cowboy with a punch that came all the way from the middle of his back, a punch that was as fast and as solid as a hard-rock drill. The Finn couldn't stop it. Nobody could ever stop it. The best you could hope to do was get out of the way. That punch alone made Buster famous.

We heard it crunch into the cowboy, heard it echo back and forth through the Elks hall, heard the Finn let out all his air as he went back through the ropes and landed with his head in May Anna's lap. He didn't get up for ten minutes. By then Buster had been declared the winner, Toney had picked up the receipts from the sheriff, and May Anna had dumped the cowboy on the floor.

What people saw in Billings that night was the premiere of the strongest punch in the history of fighting in Montana. And maybe the world. Later on, when Buster was well known, every fighter in the

USA tried to copy it. Radio announcers watched for the windup to predict over the airwaves that it was coming. Sports writers called it Death in Mitts and the Concrete Glove and the Widow Maker. But anybody who follows prize fighting knows that punch has just one true name. It's still being used after all these years. Last month, in fact, Whippy Bird found an article in *Time* magazine about a boxing match that ended with a knockout. She cut out the story and put it on the wall at the Jim Hill and underlined one sentence with a red Flair pen: "The fighter let loose and connected with a regular old-fashioned Buster Midnight." Me and Whippy Bird think the Buster Midnight will go down as the most famous punch in boxing history.

CHAPTER 6

Lots of people ask me and Whippy Bird when May Anna turned out. They want us to give them the month and the day. The time would be good, too. But who remembers something like that? I guess they think we should have known it was a historic event. Maybe there was a light bulb over May Anna's head like in the funny papers, and we should have jumped up and down and written, today May Anna Kovaks became a hooker.

Well, it's nobody's business. Me and Whippy Bird always laugh at people, the women especially, who come into the Jim Hill and want to know everything about old-time prostitutes but would die before they'd sit down next to a live one. Some of them have, too, right there in the Jim Hill, where your retired women from Venus Alley come in for the senior citizen breakfast.

We probably could come up with the day May Anna joined the line, but as for the first time she got paid, how in the hell do we know? I'll tell you one thing, me and Whippy Bird weren't surprised. May Anna had been leading up to it for a long time.

Butte was wild in those days. Everybody was wild, not just May Anna and Buster. I guess me and Whippy Bird were a disappointment to our folks because we ran with a merry crowd. In fact, we were wilder than May Anna, but who'd know it to look at us now, both of us in our pants suits and members of the American Association of Retired Persons with a card that gives us a discount at the House of Sofas.

Whippy Bird was the wildest of the Unholy Three. She says you don't remember anything right, Effa Commander, but she was, and she's proud of it today, aren't you, Whippy Bird? You told me plenty about you and Chick, but I'm not going to tell because this is May Anna's story, not yours.

It may have been Prohibition in the USA, but you'd never know it in Butte. Butte was wide open. There were stills all over the mountains, and more money came out of those old gold mines after they'd been turned into distilleries than ever came out in good ore. Bootleggers knew what they were doing. Illegal whiskey was big business, with your better operators turning out hundreds of gallons a day.

They hauled the liquor into Butte and sold it to the joints for anywhere from three-fifty to fifteen dollars a gallon. The saloon keepers diluted it two-to-one, water to booze, added a little coloring, and sold it by the drink. You made good money on liquor in those days what with cheap costs and no federal taxes to pay either. Mostly, it was quality stuff. You didn't go blind on Butte hooch. In fact, after Prohibition was over, people got nostalgic for the good times when whiskey was twice as strong as the legal stuff. You could buy bootleg by the bottle, too, of course.

Some of the whiskey in Butte during Prohibition came down from Canada, and that's the business Toney McKnight was in. He sneaked across the border to Canada at night, filled up with a load of real

Canadian, then drove the back roads to Butte or Anaconda. Sometimes he was chased. Buster said Toney never knew if the guys after him were federal agents or other bootleggers out to steal his haul, but they never caught him.

Toney didn't talk much about it. He was involved with a big-time gang then, and you didn't go around shooting off your mouth. Sometimes those men killed each other. There are still bodies down in the old mine shafts today that nobody ever found.

With those connections, Whippy Bird says, Toney would have been under pressure to get Buster to throw fights. I think you have to give Toney credit for not selling Buster out.

May Anna said she met Dashiell Hammett, the mystery writer, in Hollywood one time, and he told her he once was a Pinkerton man, and he got sent to Butte. When somebody offered him money to kill a man, he got out of there fast. May Anna asked Mr. Hammett who the man was, but he couldn't remember. We probably knew him. Hell, May Anna probably went to bed with him.

With all that hooch, there were saloons and roadhouses and blind pigs, which your outsiders called speakeasies, in every block in every town in Montana and out in the country, too. You went into the bars in Meaderville and Centerville and Dublin Gulch and ordered a Shawn O' straight out. Even if you were a stranger, you got it unless you had on a coat and a tie and a badge that said US revenue agent.

Some of those places were so dangerous that you wouldn't want to go there and order anything at all. The boys refused to take us. Sometimes they wouldn't even go themselves unless they were with a gang. Pink went into a bar in Finntown and saw a man he thought was passed out on the floor drunk. "I stepped over him, ordered a beer, and got to talking to Pug Obie, who told me that fellow wasn't drunk, he was dead," Pink told us. "He got shot an hour before. Pug said the bartender was too busy to carry him out, so he just shoved him up against the wall until closing time. His pockets were turned inside out, and while I was standing there, somebody took his pants and vest. You can bet I got out of there fast."

Me and Whippy Bird and Pink and Chick used to go to a joint over by the Hot Springs called the Brown Jug that sold good liquor and had a dance floor. It was a nice place with a live band and a singer, and it did a good business. They had the first jukebox I ever saw, a Wurlitzer with a wood front just like a big console radio, and yellow and red lights. We played "Little Brown Jug" so often we wore it out. That song always makes me think of Pink.

You saw lots of cars out front, jalopies and roadsters and coupes and big touring cars with side curtains. Sometimes we saw Toney's big Reo Wolverine that he bought at Truzzolino's after he crashed the Studebaker, parked out back, so I suppose he was one of the suppliers.

Once a waiter came over with a bottle of champagne for us and said, "Compliments of Mr. Toney McKnight. Bottled it last night."

A few minutes later, Toney swaggered out, looking like the head waiter at one of those Hollywood restaurants May Anna took us to later on, and said, "You folks doing all right here?"

"You sure are classy, all right," Chick said, "sending us the aged stuff."

"Nothing's too good for my friends," he said, all puffed up, not knowing Chick was joking.

Pink had a little Marmon back then, yellow I think it was, though

Whippy Bird says they didn't make them in yellow. We usually danced for a while then went out in the Marmon and drank. Whippy Bird says that's not all you'd do, Effa Commander, but that's none of her business—or yours either.

A girl got all kinds of offers in those days. Sometimes me and Whippy Bird went out by ourselves, and there was always somebody ready to buy us a drink or to ask would you like to go outside to where there was some real good sipping whiskey. You had to be careful. Maybe they wanted to share the whiskey and snuggle up a little, or maybe they wanted something else. Every now and then you'd see a girl slink back into the Brown Jug with her hair messed up or nursing a black eye. You had to watch out for yourself, and that's why me and Whippy Bird always stuck together.

May Anna was different. She went with us sometimes, but right off, she looked the men over. Every now and then she took off with one of them, and we wouldn't see her again that night. She said she had a talent for sniffing out money, which was surely true, but she never did have much of a head for taking care of herself. Sometimes, we saw her looking like she'd been beat up, but she didn't volunteer any information, and we never asked.

Now I hear you saying to yourself, where was Buster McKnight when this was going on, and that surely is a good question.

Buster was busy making a name for himself as Buster Midnight. Toney got him fights up in Great Falls and Missoula and Helena and even down in Ogden. Then Toney took Buster on a tour to Denver and Pueblo. Buster wasn't in Butte much, and when he was, May Anna didn't like him hanging around her all the time. She got mad and told him to give her some room, which he had to do.

"As soon as me and Toney get some big fights, I'll have plenty of dough, and we'll get married," Buster promised her.

But May Anna wasn't interested. "So who wants to get married, Buster Midnight? I want to have a little fun. I'll make my own money, thank you just the same," May Anna replied.

"I should have put my foot down," Buster told us once.

"Yeah, and get May Anna's high-heeled slipper right in the middle of your instep," Whippy Bird said. There was nothing Buster could do.

Of course, Buster never liked May Anna being a hooker. You could see him watch her sometimes and know it was eating his heart out. Especially if May Anna was out on a date with a customer. If Buster ran into her then, he sat and watched out of the corner of his eye, hoping for the john to get fresh so he could step in and save May Anna. Even with May Anna giving him the shove sometimes, he felt responsible for her. May Anna, on her side, knew if she needed him, Buster would be there.

Buster McKnight was no shining white virgin himself. There were lots of girls who followed boxing, and Buster could have his pick, and he did. He always was a handsome man. Back then, there was nobody better to look at. He was big, of course, and he had black curls and his nose hadn't been broken yet. He had the best eyes, too, deep blue like the sky gets before sunset. Buster McKnight's eyes were the prettiest color I ever saw in my life.

Toney was glad May Anna turned out because he didn't want her to get her claws into Buster. As if May Anna would! He was afraid she would interfere with Buster's fighting. So he encouraged Buster to see other girls, and some of them were hookers, too. Sometimes you saw Buster's picture in the paper with a pretty blonde hanging on his arm, and May Anna would always know which cathouse she worked in.

May Anna knew them all because she had her pick of the houses in Butte. She surely had turned into a beauty and might have become a movie star on her own without being a prostitute first. She didn't have any choice in it though. She became a prostitute because of her mother. Her mother didn't tell her to do it, of course, but she was the cause of it just the same.

By the time Buster turned into a fighter, we had it figured out about Mrs. Kovaks. Things were hard for her by then. She drank all the time, and she started taking laudanum. The Finlen fired her, so she had to work in some crummy little hotel down near Venus Alley. Then she lost that job, too. So May Anna went to work after school as a waitress at the Pepsin Drugstore soda fountain, but that didn't bring in much. She figured if she could just hold out until she graduated, she would get a job at Hennessy's selling gloves or maybe as a receptionist in a doctor's office because she looked so good in white.

Then things got worse at her house. Mrs. Kovaks kept on bringing men home that she picked up, and me and Whippy Bird heard a lot of fighting and yelling over there when we passed by. Sometimes May Anna came to school with her face bruised. Chick said you'd think May Anna was big enough to keep her mother from beating her, but me and Whippy Bird knew it wasn't Mrs. Kovaks that hit May Anna. She never said anything to us, but we knew those men weren't coming home because of Mrs. Kovaks.

In fact, one day we saw a big Packard stop in front of the house, then heard the driver honk two or three times. "Hey, toots," he yelled. "Come on out." Poor Mrs. Kovaks came running with her hat and her pocketbook, but the driver waved her off. "Not you, honey. I want the young one." A few minutes later May Anna came slowly down the stairs and got into the Packard. It might seem like she was two-timing her own mother, but the truth was, those men were generous, and the Kovaks were desperate. Sometimes men gave May Anna money for going out on dates or jewelry that she could pawn.

Another time, we saw May Anna jump out of a car with her blouse mussed up and her lipstick smeared. When she saw us, she said, "Why, I don't know what got into him. He said he was taking me out for ice cream so Mom could take a nap. Men!"

"Men!" Whippy Bird agreed.

May Anna might have made it if Mrs. Kovaks hadn't gotten so sick. We always thought she took the laudanum to keep from remembering Jackfish, but that wasn't so. She took it to cover up the pain. One day me and Whippy Bird and May Anna walked into the Kovaks house and found Mrs. Kovaks all curled up on the floor, just crying from pain. I ran the block to our house for Ma, who didn't even take off her apron. The minute she saw Mrs. Kovaks, she shoved me and Whippy Bird out the door and said, "Minnie, dear, I'm sending the girls for the doctor. Did you fall?"

"Don't bother," Mrs. Kovaks whimpered. It took her a long time to get it out. "It's the cancer." I could see the tears that came to Ma's eyes. Me and Whippy Bird had tears in our eyes, too. Ma put a hand on May Anna's arm then turned to me and Whippy Bird and asked what the hell were we doing there when she'd told us to get the doctor.

Mrs. Kovaks was right about what was wrong. We didn't know how long she knew about the cancer. Maybe she just guessed. May Anna said Mrs. Kovaks's mother died of it, that it just seemed to pass down in the family.

The doctor wanted Mrs. Kovaks to go to the hospital, but she said they didn't have the money. So he gave May Anna a prescription for medicine and promised to stop in every day, which he did. Ma fixed their dinner every night. She slipped in and set it on the table. When May Anna thanked her, Ma replied, "Why it's a pleasure to have a family to cook for now that Mr. Commander's traveling on union business and Little Tommy's on the night shift. You know I never did learn to cut back recipes. You're just keeping the food from going to waste." Ma surely was a wonderful woman.

Sometimes she made special things for Mrs. Kovaks like beef tea or custard, then pretended she'd fixed them for everybody else. She told May Anna she had a little money put aside for emergencies. "I want you to take this, May Anna, since you're family. It would relieve my mind. Just pay it back when you can. There's no hurry at all. You know if you don't take it, Effa Commander will just pester me to spend it on pretties."

May Anna said thanks to you, Mrs. Commander. "We're doing just fine. We don't have any need of money, but we thank you just the same." May Anna wouldn't take it, even as a loan. She was too proud. I asked Ma why didn't she just pay the Kovakses' rent or the doctor bill herself, but she said there was a limit to how much you could interfere in other people's lives.

Me and Whippy Bird know the final straw was the food basket. Some ladies from the Blessed Sacrament Church found out about

Mrs. Kovaks and brought a food basket. They didn't just leave it on the porch and slip away. No, they got all dressed up and bustled up to the front door where everybody could see them. Me and Whippy Bird were there with May Anna when they rang the bell and handed the basket to her like she was supposed to fall on her knees and pretend they were the Doublemint version of the Virgin Mary.

One of them said, "My dear, we like to do this for those less fortunate. We hope you appreciate it and are grateful to the Lord. The Lord is only punishing her for her sins, but He will be merciful."

Then the other woman looked May Anna up and down like you do a used car and added, "I'm looking for a kitchen girl and might consider you."

Me and Whippy Bird were so mad, we could have knocked them down the stairs. The Kovakses needed that basket. We thought May Anna would either say thank you very nicely or else scream at them to get the hell out, but she did something me and Whippy Bird would never have thought of.

"Why, ladies, whatever is this about?" she asked. "Mother and I have no need for a food basket. You must be mistaken. But won't you sit down? My friends and I were about to have tea." So those women had to sit right down there in May Anna's house and drink tea and be in her debt then slink back out with their basket. Even in *The Sin of Rachel Babcock,* May Anna was never as gracious and as much a lady as she was pouring tea for those two busybodies that day.

When they left, May Anna stood there clenching her fists, her face white. "I'll never take charity," she said. "Never! Never!"

Later on, when we saw *Gone With the Wind,* Whippy Bird asked, "Do you think Scarlett O'Hara would take a charity basket before going hungry again?" It wasn't more than a week after those two biddies called that May Anna was working out of a house in Venus Alley.

Ma tried to talk her out of it. She went to see her and invited the Kovakses to live with us until May Anna finished high school. May Anna shook her head and said her mother was her responsibility, and she'd made her decision. Then Ma hugged her and said she loved her and she was always welcome at our house, anytime. May Anna told her that was the nicest thing anybody ever said to her, and it probably was. May Anna said Ma was a saint. When Ma died, May Anna sent Pig Face money for enough candles to burn down Blessed Sacrament.

A few days after she'd gone to work for Nell Nolan, who was the biggest madam in Venus Alley, me and Whippy Bird ran into May Anna on the street. It was over by where the Ben Franklin is now. She worked all night, then she came home during the day to be with her mother. Or sometimes she worked the day shift so she could be home at night. "You know what I'm doing now," May Anna said. "You can pretend you don't know me. I'll understand."

Me and Whippy Bird looked at her like she'd gone crackers. "See here, kid," Whippy Bird said, "just because you've got a job don't mean you're better than me and Effa Commander. We're still the Unholy Three whether you like it or not."

May Anna laughed and laughed and said she was the luckiest girl in the world to have two best friends like me and Whippy Bird. Then she got serious and said, "Whippy Bird and Effa Commander, you've got to help me out."

We told her we surely would though we didn't have much money. Then she said, "Not money. A name. I need a new name. All the girls have them." She thought maybe a movie star name. Since we'd just seen *Rio Rita*, we thought Bebe Daniels would be nice, but she said there already was a Bebe Daniels who worked up the alley. I liked Mary Miles Minter, who was also a movie star, but May Anna asked what drunken miner could say Mary Miles Minter and make himself understood? Barbara La Marr was another favorite, but May Anna didn't think men would want to go to bed with somebody named for a dead person. That was when me and Whippy Bird looked at that street sign and before you knew it we had named the woman who would someday be one of the brightest stars in Hollywood.

After May Anna turned out, the Unholy Three was mostly me and Whippy Bird. We still saw May Anna as much as we could, and she was always our friend. Sometimes when she was working at Nell Nolan's during the day, me and Whippy Bird walked down Venus Alley just like it was any other street. If May Anna spotted us and she wasn't busy, she tapped on the window, which was a signal she would meet us at Gamer's in five minutes for a coffee break. Even during the day, the street that ran along Venus Alley was as busy as Broadway after shift since the high school boys liked to cut through there on their way to the football field and bang their helmets on the doors.

Mrs. Kovaks died six months later, which Ma said was a blessing and we thought was a relief. She sure wasn't pretty to look at, and at the end you could hear her screaming at May Anna all over Centerville. Ma said she was just crazy from the pain.

There weren't many at the funeral, just May Anna and Buster and the Birds and us. May Anna saved up her money to buy a nice stone

that said REST IN PEACE MINERVA EVANS KOVAKS. Then after asking
Ma to give Mrs. Kovaks's things away to a poor family May Anna
gave up the house and moved into Nell Nolan's full time.

In May, me and Whippy Bird graduated from high school. I went
to work for Gamer's as a waitress, and Whippy Bird got a job at the
power company as a professional secretary. She came into Gamer's
two or three times a week for lunch. Gamer's, which had its own
bakery, was one of your better Butte establishments. I remember one
Saturday we baked twenty wedding cakes. We made our own candy,
too. Babe Gamer ran a confectionery in the basement with seven girls
making candy and packing it to mail all around the world. At Valentine's and Mother's Day you'd have your miners lined up five deep
in front of the counter to buy those big copper-foil boxes.

We ran into May Anna on the street sometimes or in the store.
Or May Anna came into Gamer's with some of the other girls from
Venus Alley. They were always real nice and left good tips, too.
Sometimes at night, the girls called and asked would we bring over
a pastie or a chicken potpie, and if I wasn't too busy, I'd run it over.

You read about your hookers being mean or else having hearts of
gold. I suppose there were both, but the ones me and Whippy Bird
knew in Butte were like anybody else. Unless you knew they worked
on the line, you never guessed it. They weren't all hussies with
low-cut dresses or thick makeup. In fact, me and Whippy Bird always
wore more makeup than May Anna except that May Anna liked
bright nail polish.

Where we'd see May Anna most of the time was if we ran into
her out on the town. In fact, that is how we happened to be maids

of honor at May Anna and Buster's wedding. It wasn't a legal wedding, of course, but it was good enough for Buster.

Pink and Chick took me and Whippy Bird to the Jug one night. A few minutes later May Anna blew in with another girl and Buster and Toney. Buster had just won a fight at the Knights of Columbus gym, and they'd been drinking plenty. Even Buster was feeling fine, which was unusual for him. They ordered some more at the Jug because that's the main reason you go there, then they came over and joined us.

"Buster Midnight has just successfully won his two hundredth fight," May Anna said, slurring her words because she was drunk.

"Aw, May Anna, I never fought that many fights."

"Including Pig 'Puss' Stenner," she said. May Anna was surely drunk as a lord. "What is more, this is Buster Midnight's birthday, so we are going to have a special celebration."

"We already have," Buster told her.

"No, Buster. This night I want to do something special. Like lunch at the Finlen Hotel."

"It's already eleven-thirty at night," he said.

"Then I'll order a birthday cake. Effa Commander, go down to Gamer's and bake Buster a cake."

"The bakery's closed," I told her.

May Anna pouted for a minute, then she said to Buster, "What have you always wanted besides lunch at the Finlen and a birthday cake from Gamer's?"

"He's always wanted to marry May Anna Kovaks," Chick said, and we all laughed.

"There is no May Anna Kovaks. There is only Marion Street," May Anna said.

"I'll take what I can get," Buster said.

"All right, we'll get married. Pink will be the priest, and Toney will be the best man, and you will be the maid of honor," she said, pointing to me and Whippy Bird.

"Who?" we asked.

"You," she said. "Whippy Bird and Effa Commander."

Toney got everybody at the Jug in on it, moving chairs aside to make an aisle for the wedding march and turning a table into an altar with a red and white tablecloth for the altar cloth. May Anna found a white crêpe scarf for a veil, and me and Whippy Bird got down a bunch of crêpe paper flowers that was pinned to the wall for a bouquet. They were dusty, but May Anna didn't mind. Then Pink stood up in front of the bandstand and picked up the baton and told the band to play "Here Comes the Bride."

They played it five or six times while we took May Anna into the little girls' room and stripped her down to her white satin slip, which was as plain and elegant as a cocktail dress. We draped the scarf over her head, put the bouquet in her hand, and when we finished, she looked more like a nun than a bride.

Buster stood up in front of Pink with a picture of a flower pinned to his suit. He'd torn it off a cigarette advertisement hanging over the bar. Chick and Toney were behind him waiting to be the best man. Then we marched—staggered is what Whippy Bird says—from the bathroom to the bandstand and stood right under the cutout wooden jug that was the symbol of the place. Pink, who'd never been to a wedding and didn't know what a preacher was supposed to say, just waved the baton and announced that Marion Street and Buster Midnight were man and wife.

Buster picked up May Anna and carried her outside to that black deuce roadster of his while we threw popcorn. Then the two of them drove off, drunk as coots, to spend their wedding night at Nell Nolan's. Mrs. Nolan didn't think it was so funny, even though later on she got to calling May Anna Mrs. Midnight. She made Buster pay for an all-nighter.

CHAPTER
7

It wasn't long after May Anna "married" Buster that she went to Hollywood, and you can thank President Franklin Delano Roosevelt for that—except that he was Governor Franklin Delano Roosevelt then.

He came to Montana to get us to vote for him for president of the United States. Not me and Whippy Bird because we were too young to vote then, though we voted for him the three other times he ran. Vote early and often, that was always Butte's motto.

There were ten thousand people who turned out to see Governor Roosevelt speak at the courthouse, which was our pride, better than the state capitol. The capitol has a copper dome, but our courthouse has copper doors and marble columns the color of melted strawberry ice cream. We took the day off and met Governor Roosevelt at the train along with most of the rest of Butte.

"There he is," Whippy Bird said when the dining car slid by, but I told her she was a damn fool because everybody knew he was in the last car. Whippy Bird was right once again, though. He was there in the diner eating his ham and eggs with nobody but Whippy Bird recognizing him.

A long time after that, May Anna met President Roosevelt at the

White House when she went there for a dinner with her famous
actress friend Faye Emerson, who was married to one of the Roose-
velts. May Anna told President Roosevelt she remembered him visiting Butte when she was a girl. By then May Anna was lying about
her age. Hell, by the time she was ten miles out of town she was lying
about her age. She said she went with her two best friends, and that
we were known as the Unholy Three, which made me and Whippy
Bird proud, you can bet, to think that President Roosevelt in the
White House knew about us. Whippy Bird says maybe he told Mrs.
Roosevelt. Now wouldn't that have been something?

May Anna met Mrs. Roosevelt, too, but she just shook her hand
and said pleased to meet you, so she wouldn't know about us unless
the president told her later on. It's just as well May Anna didn't say
anything to Mrs. Roosevelt because she was a smart cookie and she
would have known May Anna was lying. When Franklin Delano
Roosevelt came to town, it was just me and Whippy Bird standing
at the station. May Anna didn't go along. She was too busy selling
her services to the men he brought with him.

The hookers always liked it when the bigwigs came to town because they brought lots of men with them, but never their wives. The
men had just one thing in mind, and that was getting a little, as the
fellow says. May Anna said it made you wonder what their wives were
like, though May Anna never had anything against wives. She said
that's what drove men to Venus Alley. "If it weren't for married men,
we'd all starve to death," she told us.

I can tell you where she told us that. We were having coffee in the
Chequamegon on North Main, which we always called the "chew-
quick-and-be-gone-again." Only we weren't chewing anything, just

drinking coffee. May Anna ordered tea. She thought tea was more genteel. Once when me and Whippy Bird visited her in Hollywood she took us out for coffee at some restaurant decorated with pink ducks and palm trees, and I remember the waitress bringing her coffee, and May Anna saying in her sweet little voice, "Oh, would you be so good as to bring me tea instead?" May Anna always said "would you be so good," even before she went to Hollywood. Me and Whippy Bird picked that up from her and used to say things like "Would you be so good as to bring me the can of Crisco?" or "Would you be so good as to buy me a roll of toilet paper when you go to the Nimble Nickel?"

Whippy Bird says would you be so good as to stay on the subject, Effa Commander. You must be old, the way your mind wanders. Well, I'm not any older than you are, Whippy Bird. When you point a finger at somebody, there are three more pointing back at you.

There were all those big government men lined up in Venus Alley waiting for the girls, and there was May Anna, still at Nell Nolan's, earning her living as fast as she could. One of her newly arrived customers was a little man with hair like Richard Dix and a tiny mustache, one of those thin ones that men you don't trust wear.

May Anna was making conversation and asked him what he was doing in town. He replied he was with a Movietone News crew taking pictures of Governor Roosevelt. You might think that would be hot stuff in Butte, but we weren't nincompoops. Even me and Whippy Bird wouldn't have fallen for that, and May Anna knew a lot more than we did about that kind of line. She just hooted and said, "Sure, honey. The governor left at one P.M. You miss the train?"

He didn't like that. He argued he was in there taking moving pictures of Mr. Roosevelt to show in the newsreels they used to play in movie theaters along with the previews and the cartoon. He claimed he stayed on to shoot an extra day or two. May Anna said, "If you say so, honey." He kept insisting he was telling the truth, and May Anna kept agreeing in that way you do so the other person knows you don't believe them—and all the time May Anna was taking care of business. His business, if you know what I mean.

It didn't matter to May Anna what that man did as long as he paid and gave her a tip, but he just had to have May Anna believe him. He said if she went up to the Finlen at 8 A.M., she could watch them set up their newsreel cameras. May Anna said she wouldn't be going to bed much before 8 A.M. so she sure wasn't going to get up that early. Then he said to come at noon, and if she did, he'd put her in the Movietone News. He took more time arguing than he did on his business, so May Anna said sure because Nell Nolan was knocking on the door to say that time was up.

What me and Whippy Bird never figured out was why May Anna met him at all. Maybe she believed him or maybe she thought she could turn another trick. Whippy Bird thinks May Anna was angling for lunch at the Finlen Hotel, and that was why she got all dressed up. Dressed up for May Anna, even then, was elegant. Of course, May Anna never looked like a hooker—even though there must have been people at the Finlen who knew she was.

May Anna remembered every single thing to tell us later. She showed up the next day, dressed so fine she just knocked the socks off that little man when he saw her. He was standing in front of the Finlen with three or four other men operating one of those great big cameras on a stand with lots of cords draped all over the sidewalk.

They were taking pictures up and down the street, and May Anna walked up there, cool as you please, held out her little hand, and said, "How do you do. So nice to see you again."

She was some sight in Butte, dressed all in white like the day she took first communion at BS. Nobody in Butte wore white because of the dirt and smoke. What was surprising was she was some sight to the little mustache man and his crew, too, and they were used to movie stars dressed in white dresses and shoes and purses. It wasn't just the clothes, though. It was May Anna. Seeing May Anna every day, me and Whippy Bird just overlooked that in the four years she'd been a hooker, she had turned out to be one of the most beautiful women of the world.

Those men stood there like she was some vision. The mustache man stuck out his chest like a peacock at Columbia Gardens and took her hand, as if he thought she was Fay Wray instead of a hooker from Venus Alley.

"So good of you to come," he said, then he whispered, "What was your name again?"

May Anna almost gave him the shove at that, but she was already an actress, so instead she gave him her closed-mouth smile that didn't show her crooked teeth and purred, "Marion Street." She purred very professionally by then.

May Anna liked it when men fell all over themselves for her, so she was having as good a time as that man—May Anna said she never did know his name. He showed her the big newsreel camera and all the other stuff they had spread across the sidewalk. With his mustache and a beret, he looked like pictures you see of movie directors.

He also looked like a damn fool in Butte, which made people laugh at him when they stopped to look.

It was just like an accident when one person stops to see what's going on, and before you know it, there's a crowd. So in about ten minutes there were lots of people around May Anna and the mustache man. They were laughing at the man and gawking at May Anna when a little girl came up to her and asked for an autograph.

May Anna was as surprised as if somebody had handed her a thousand-dollar bill instead of the back of an envelope. She looked up to see who was pulling her leg, but there was just the little girl. Behind her was a woman who was beaming at May Anna and pushing the little girl toward her. May Anna thought it was a joke but wrote "Love, Marion Street" anyway, expecting any minute now the mother would recognize her and turn red and tear up the paper. But the mother said thank you kindly. Then somebody else asked for her autograph. May Anna said she signed her name at least six times.

Some little kid asked her, "Are you a famous actress?" and you'd of thought the jig was up. Not May Anna. She smiled as sweet as she could and said, "Why bless you, no. I will be someday, though, so you just keep that piece of paper." I expect if that kid did, it would be worth five or maybe ten dollars today.

We always knew May Anna planned on being somebody, though we didn't know who. Maybe she didn't either. She said acting never entered her mind until that little kid asked. Maybe she went there to turn a trick but found she had a chance to better herself. May Anna was not one to let opportunity slip by.

With all those people watching, the little man acted as important as Cecil B. DeMille. He waved his arms and pushed people away and told May Anna to go up by the power company, walk across the street, and ignore the camera. She did, just strolled along looking fine. Then he said go back and do the same thing only look into the camera, and she did that, too. Then he ordered her to walk a diagonal across the corner of Broadway and Wyoming. Finally, he said walk away from the camera up toward Granite Street, just slow and easy, and she did that and became a movie star.

Something else that never occurred to me and Whippy Bird before was that May Anna had quite a backside. When she swung that caboose in her tight skirt, men just naturally fell over in the street with their tongues hanging out. Whippy Bird says, now, Effa Commander, how would you expect us to notice something like that?

May Anna walked up and down that street about two hundred times. The little man was hoarse from yelling instructions, and May Anna's feet hurt something awful. Still, she kept right on walking. Later on, May Anna told Hedda Hopper that she believed in pushing herself hard, and that her motto from the time she was a little girl was "Beauty knows no pain," which is a crock of applesauce. We never heard her say that, and what's more, May Anna was no beauty when she was a little girl. She did have a way with words, though. A way with lies is more like it, Whippy Bird says, but she means it in a nice way.

About the time May Anna's heels were worn down and her feet were bleeding, this big man with a cigar came out of the Finlen and stopped to watch. He stood there for five minutes before the little man saw him and turned red and said, "Vic, hey, we thought we'd get a little man-in-the-street action, show the local yokels gawking at the big guy."

The man with the cigar said, "Yeah, good idea. You going to show just one local or this burg got other people?"

"Right, Vic. Right. Just want to make sure we got this one down," he said, leering at May Anna.

The man with the cigar looked him right into the ground. So the mustache man called to May Anna, "Thanks a lot, honey. See ya in the Movietone News." He started packing up the camera, making little motions to May Anna to be on her way, but she was having too good a time. She never even looked at the big man, but you can bet she knew he was there, and she knew he was somebody. She stood quietly in that way she had so she's the center of attention, then held out her hand to the little man and said, "Thank you so much. It's been great fun." Then she began walking away.

She took half a dozen steps, when Vic called, "Hey, sister!" May Anna didn't stop for even a second. She kept right on going. It always surprised me how May Anna could look like she was walking fast but never get anywhere.

"Honey!" he called. May Anna kept on walking. By then she must have been half a block away. There was just May Anna and Vic on the sidewalk, since people were standing in the street, out of the way, thinking this was part of the movie.

Finally, Vic puffed up the street after May Anna and grabbed her arm and said, "Hey, I'm talking to you." May Anna didn't look at him. She looked down at where his hand was clutching her little white arm, turning it red, and in a second Vic let go.

"Yes?" May Anna said. She looked at him like he was a stray dog.

Vic was flustered. When he saw the mustache man watching them, Vic scowled at him until the little man scurried around like a chicken, gathering up all his wires. When Vic turned back to May Anna, she was giving him her bored look. "So," Vic said. May Anna didn't answer.

"You want to be an actress, do you?" Vic asked.

"Not especially," May Anna told him.

"Then how come you're walking up and down the street in front of the cameras?"

"Because the gentleman asked me to."

"You always do what gentlemen ask?" He stood back and looked her up and down. His eyes kept coming back to look at her chest, which had grown a good deal more than the rest of May Anna since the day we first met her at the Little Annie glory hole.

May Anna flashed him an angry look and said, "Did you want something?"

That stopped him. May Anna said every time people like Vic went anyplace, they ran into pretty girls trying to get into the movies. He didn't know what to do around one who didn't care about going to Hollywood. Though, as you can guess, after her experience with the newsreel camera May Anna had decided she wanted to be in the movies in the worst way. She was playing the professional part of hard-to-get. Vic was playing the chump.

"Well?" May Anna asked. Right there if Vic had said, well, nothing, May Anna might be sitting in the Jim Hill today with me and Whippy Bird. Her whole career was held up on that "well." Could have been sunk in that well, Whippy Bird says. Whippy Bird's sure a wiseacre, all right.

"Well," Vic said. "I, ah, wanted to thank you for helping us out back there and ask if there's some place besides the Finlen where a man can get coffee and invite you to join me. As a way of saying thanks. Or maybe you'd like lunch?"

"Coffee would be fine," and May Anna gave him her hand-over-the-mouth smile. One thing you had to say for May Anna was she wasn't a gold digger. Too smart, Whippy Bird says, and maybe that's so. Too smart to try to take old Vic for lunch when she was going for something bigger. Still, May Anna never tried to get anything from me and Whippy Bird when we were kids. Or Buster either. She never had Buster buy her jewelry and sweaters and perfume, and she could have. He'd have bought her anything she wanted.

May Anna brought Vic down to Gamer's, where I was working, and she sat right down at my booth, giving me a kind of warning look so I wouldn't say anything. I'd gotten used to May Anna bringing in johns. I knew better than to give her away. "Good afternoon," I said to her. I sounded like a Butte girl putting on airs instead of fancy like May Anna, so I cut out the high-toned talk and turned to Vic and said, "Hiya." He sat next to May Anna on the seat even though most people sit across from each other. He was a big man, so May Anna was pushed into the corner.

Vic ordered two coffees, but May Anna asked if I would be so good as to bring her tea instead. "Yes, ma'am," I said. "Coming right up."

Before I left she held out her little hand to Vic and introduced herself. "My name is Marion Street," which was another high sign to me that she was on the job and not to give her away. When she wasn't working, she was still May Anna Kovaks.

Vic shook her hand like it was a piece of ice and said, "Pleased to meet ya, Marion. You live in this burg? You seem too fancy to hang out in a dump like this."

May Anna knew I would jump in at something like that since me and Whippy Bird have always been proud of Butte. "Lemon, if you please," May Anna said to me, giving me the scoot sign with her hand.

So I scooted, and when I came back with their order, May Anna was telling him about the history of Butte and all the society families, just like she was from a mansion over on West Broadway instead of a Centerville fourplex.

"So what do you do besides walk down streets?" Vic asked her.

"Oh, this and that." May Anna was not going to tell him that "this" was hookering, and so was "that."

"And you don't want to be in the movies?"

"I just was."

"Oh, that. That's just a newsreel. It'll end up on the cutting room floor."

May Anna pouted.

"I guess I could look into it. Sometimes these things can be arranged. After all, I'm in charge here, see."

May Anna brightened.

"So, you don't want to be in the movies?" Vic said again, like a stuck seventy-eight rpm record.

"It would be fun, of course . . ."

"Aha. I knew it."

"But you hear such awful things about actresses."

"Like what?" Vic was starting to leer.

"Like loose morals."

"Nooo," he drew out the word like he was shocked.

"I'm not a prude, but . . ." May Anna waved her hand. She squeezed the lemon in her tea, but it squirted in Vic's eye, so she pulled out a lace handkerchief and told him to look up while she wiped his eye. He looked down inside her blouse instead. May Anna saw him do that, and she decided it was time to move in. "How does one become an actress?"

I wondered how Vic could believe anybody was that dumb, but he was hooked. I moved all my checks to the counter across from May Anna and pretended to add them up so I could listen, but I could have stared flat out for all the attention he paid me. Even from there, staring across the stand of fudge brownies with lemon icing all piled up, I could see his eyes glisten.

He licked his lips and put his hand over May Anna's. "I could try you out. You know, give you a screen test, see."

"But I just had one."

"Where?" He sounded suspicious.

"Right out there on the street."

"Oh, that." He'd moved his hand up her arm. By then poor May Anna was sitting in about six inches of space. "Why, honey, we have to see if you can read lines. Then we got to photograph your face and your body." He leered at May Anna's chest and reached up to unbutton her blouse. That is not proper behavior in Gamer's Confectionery, and I was ashamed for May Anna.

May Anna could take care of herself, though. She put her little

white hand up to her blouse and gave old Vic such a nasty look that
he backed off. He slid back so far on the seat, he almost fell on the
floor. I had to hold my hand over my mouth to keep from laughing,
it was that funny. I was afraid I'd mess things up for May Anna, but
nothing could keep me from hearing the end of this.

"Sorry, honey," he said.

May Anna gave him her little smile, and he cheered up. "I'm not
trying to offend you or anything," Vic said. "The thing is, you're a
pretty girl, and we like to photograph pretty girls in low-cut dresses.
You know how it is."

May Anna was still smiling, and Vic kept on going. "Maybe it
would be better if we was to find a place in private. You know, this
joint ain't the sort of place to talk over business. I could explain to
you what we need and maybe take some pictures. You might have
a real future in the movies."

She thought that over for a minute then nodded. "Where?" she
asked.

"You got a place? Or maybe you live with your folks. We could
go to the hotel. Yeah, that's a good place. I got a room there. Real
private. We could talk, ya know. You don't mind taking off your
blouse, do you? So I can see how you'd look in a bathing suit."

For a long time, May Anna just looked at Vic until he flushed and
these little drops of sweat popped out on his forehead and the top
of his head, where it was bald. Finally, May Anna gave him her best
come-on look and tilted her head. "Of course not, the price is the
same."

"Huh?" Vic said. "We don't pay for screen tests."

"Same price," May Anna repeated. "Ten dollars. Your hotel room or my place—Nell Nolan's in Venus Alley."

I thought Vic would drop his teeth, which May Anna said he might have done because they weren't his. Then he started laughing and pounding on the table. "A hooker!" He was so loud that I was glad for May Anna's sake the place was almost empty. "You sure fooled me, honey."

"In advance," May Anna said.

Vic got up, still laughing, and May Anna put out her hand, just like a lady, so he could help her up. "Here I thought you were after a screen test," Vic said.

"I am," May Anna said. "I just proved to you I can act."

Vic slapped her on the backside and shook his head. "You sure can do that, toots."

They were almost out the door before I realized he hadn't paid the check. "Sir," I called. "You forgot this." They stopped, and I handed him the bill. It was twenty cents. When he reached in his pocket, May Anna whispered to him. I don't know what she said, but he handed me a ten-dollar bill and told me to keep the change.

May Anna never told me and Whippy Bird much about what went on in that hotel room, but we didn't have to be too smart to figure it out. The next morning, when she came up for air, she told us that Vic was just like a Shawn O'Farrell: every time he had the main event, he wanted a chaser. Me and Whippy Bird and May Anna had a big laugh over that. Even though Vic turned out to be Victor Moskovy, the famous director who you've heard of, we always called him Shawn.

When May Anna got back to Venus Alley, Nell Nolan was sore
that she'd skipped out on the night's business, leaving Mrs. Nolan
shorthanded or whatever you call it, with all those important people
in town. She threatened to fire May Anna, but it was too late. May
Anna had come back to get her things. She told Nell Nolan that Vic
was taking her to Hollywood on the North Coast Limited.

Nell Nolan tried to talk her out of it. "He's just using you," she
said. "You'll never be a movie star, Mrs. Midnight. He'll throw you
aside for somebody else, and you'll be a marked woman."

"So what's different from Butte?" May Anna asked, and Nell
Nolan had to admit she was right.

May Anna came to tell us first thing. Old Shawn was busy that
night so she treated me and Whippy Bird to a farewell dinner at the
Pekin Noodle Parlor, which was one of our favorites because it had
little private rooms with shower curtains in the door so we could
giggle and talk without anybody listening. Me and Whippy Bird still
go there for the sweet-and-sour shrimp, shrimp chow mein, and
shrimp fried rice, which is a number eight and costs $6.75, including
tea and soup.

May Anna was excited, and so were me and Whippy Bird, but we
were sad, too.

"Here's to the Unholy Three," Whippy Bird said, holding up her
cup of green tea, which we had mixed with gin from a bottle May
Anna brought. We all carried big purses back then when we went
out.

"Holy, holy, holy," May Anna said, drinking up. "Jesus, I hate
tea."

"The end of the Unholy Three, you mean," I said.

"The hell with that," May Anna said. "There'll never be an end to the Unholy Three. Till death do us part." She took another drink.

Whippy Bird stuck her head outside the shower curtain and called the waiter. "Would you be so kind as to bring more tea?" We all giggled.

"Have you told Buster?" I asked.

May Anna stopped talking and looked into her cup. It was one of those round ones without a handle. Today, the Pekin serves tea in coffee cups and gives you stainless-steel knives and forks so you don't have to use chopsticks and spill food down the front of your dress. You get saltines in cellophane packages with your soup, too. Back then, though, we had real teacups from China. Back then, also, you had your Chinamen working in the noodle parlors instead of divorced mothers with kids to support.

"No," she said at last, and I had to ask, "No, what?" because she took so long I'd forgotten I'd asked her a question. "No. I haven't told Buster. How could I? Buster and Toney are in Great Falls all week. They won't be back till Sunday."

Me and Whippy Bird didn't say anything. After all, that was May Anna's business. "It's got nothing to do with Buster anyway. I can do what I want. I don't have to ask Buster."

"That's surely true," I said.

"He'd try to talk me out of it, and it's none of his business."

"That's not what this is about," Whippy Bird said. "It's about your saying good-bye to Buster."

May Anna was eating pork fried rice, trying to pick out the pieces of pork from the rice with her chopsticks. "I know, damn it. I can't face Buster. I'd rather sneak out of town than face Buster."

"Buster loves you," I said.

May Anna put down her chopsticks. "I know he does. I love Buster, too. I don't love him as much as he loves me, though, and I'll never love him enough to stay here in Butte. I'll never love anybody that much. Now's my chance, and I'm not going to let Buster stop me."

"He wouldn't stop you," Whippy Bird said. "Buster would let you do anything you wanted. Buster McKnight would die for you."

"You ought to tell him. Even if you write him a letter," I said.

"I know. But what would I say?" Me and Whippy Bird shrugged. "You write it. You'd know what to say. Please."

"Buster would know we wrote it," Whippy Bird told her.

"No he wouldn't. Please. I don't want Buster to be hurt." She had tears in her eyes. We knew they weren't real, but if she cared enough to try to fool us, how could we say no?

So that is how come me and Whippy Bird wrote that letter to Buster the next day. We worked on it a long time. It wasn't very good, but it was better than not getting a letter at all. This is what it said:

Buster, darling, I have an opportunity to go to Hollywood. Don't follow me. We'll be together someday. Wish me luck. I love you.
Love
May Anna
P.S. I hope you win the Great Falls fight.

We didn't want to let May Anna go, but she said she had to meet Shawn at the hotel. The Chinaman brought our bill and three fortune cookies, and we took turns reading them. Whippy Bird's said:

FORTUNE IS JUST AROUND THE CORNER. Ha! Whippy Bird never did get a fortune. Mine said: TONIGHT IS FOR LOVE, which wasn't true either, since I went home by myself and didn't see Pink for almost a week.

Then May Anna broke open her cookie: COMES PLEASURE, FOL-LOWS PAIN. May Anna laughed and handed her fortune to me. "You keep it, Effa Commander. I'm not going to pay any attention to a fortune like that." I kept it as a memento of May Anna. It's in my memory box.

Me and Whippy Bird walked her over to the hotel and left her. That's when it sunk in that May Anna was going away, maybe for good. We never thought about the Unholy Three being separated before. We were going to miss our best friend. Along with that, we were feeling bad about telling Buster May Anna was gone. Me and Whippy Bird decided we couldn't let him find out from just anybody. He was our friend, and we owed it to him to tell him first ourselves. So we hung around outside by Buster's house all day Sunday, waiting for him to come home from Great Falls, listening to the train whistles and thinking about May Anna going farther and farther away. When their car came down the street late that afternoon, Buster saw us right off and gave us the victory sign from the open window. "Hey, I won! Let's go celebrate!"

Me and Whippy Bird jumped up on the running board before he even got the door open and hugged him. Then Toney got out of the car, and we hugged him, too.

"We'll pick up May Anna and go over to the Rocky Mountain. She don't work Sunday."

"This dope made me drive seventy miles an hour to get here. We could of got ourselves killed." Toney stopped when he saw we were not smiling. "What's up, kiddos?"

Me and Whippy Bird each hoped the other would tell, but the quiet was deafening. "May Anna's gone," we finally blurted out together.

"She take a little vacation?" Toney asked. Buster just stared.

"She went to Hollywood," Whippy Bird said. "She's going to have a screen test."

"Oh, hell . . ." That's all Toney could get out of his mouth before Buster turned and stomped into the house.

"Hey, Buster! Wait up," Toney called, running behind him to catch up. But Buster didn't answer. He slammed the screen door so hard, it broke off the top hinge.

The next time me and Whippy Bird and Buster and Toney saw May Anna was in the Movietone News, swinging her backside up toward Granite Street.

CHAPTER
8

We didn't see May Anna for a long time after that. And except for letters every now and then, we didn't know what was happening to her. Later on, of course, we knew everything about May Anna because we read about her in the movie magazines. But you can't believe everything you read in them.

Shawn dumped May Anna not long after they got to Hollywood, though May Anna, being the generous person she was, always gave him credit for discovering her. She told *Silver Screen* she was a high school girl walking across the corner of Broadway and Wyoming in Butte when Victor saw her and asked her mother could he give her a screen test—which contains about as many lies as you'd ever find in one statement.

Shawn did give May Anna a screen test, but nobody signed her up because of it. So she got her first important job in Hollywood as a cigarette girl at one of the big nightclubs. She wore a short skirt and a little pillbox hat with a strap under her chin like Johnny in the Philip Morris advertisements and carried a box with different brands of cigarettes and little packages of matches that went with them. They sold for plenty, and most of the men gave May Anna big tips, though you'd be surprised at who would try to stiff her. She said the

ones you thought would be cheap, like Jack Benny, were always the
nicest.

The biggest tips came from the men who wanted to pick her up,
and there were plenty of them. May Anna said in that man's town
your hairdo was more important than your virtue. Whippy Bird says
so what was new for May Anna; her hairdo was more important in
Venus Alley, where she made her living from not having any virtue.

Some of the men who made passes at May Anna had connections,
but most of them just wanted to take off her clothes. Hollywood was
not the fine place you might think. There were men who took
advantage of young girls. Some of those girls who went to Hollywood
to break into pictures ended up as drunks and even junkies. You
might think we just discovered cocaine and heroin in America today,
but me and Whippy Bird know better. Growing up in Butte, we
already knew about the opium and happy dust you bought in China
Alley. May Anna learned real early to just say no to drugs. She also
learned to just say yes to enough right men so that a year or two after
she went to Hollywood, she was modeling in advertisements.

I remember the lunch hour Whippy Bird opened the *Collier's* and
found a picture of May Anna in a Catalina swimsuit. She was reading
the magazine in a booth in back, waiting for me to take a break and
join her. Then she turned a page and screamed so loud, everybody
in the restaurant looked up, including me. "Effa Commander! Look-
it here!" she called. I rushed to the booth, along with Babe Gamer,
who wanted to know what was going on.

"That's our friend. That girl in the Catalina swimsuit," I told her.

"You know, I could swear I've seen her someplace," Mrs. Gamer said. "Maybe here." Then she remembered who May Anna was and smiled. "Nice to see a local girl make good."

Whippy Bird went out and bought up a dozen *Collier's* and gave them to Buster and Toney and even dropped one off for Nell Nolan. We wrote May Anna we'd seen the ad, and May Anna wrote back she'd gotten twenty-five dollars for posing for that picture. Me and Whippy Bird thought that was small change compared to what May Anna made in Venus Alley, but maybe there was more competition in Hollywood than on Butte's row. After that, me and Whippy Bird were always opening up *Woman's Home Companion* and the *Delineator* and seeing pictures of May Anna whipping up Jell-O or putting on Hinds Honey & Almond Cream or taking the Armhole Odor Test for Odorono. Once we saw her in an upsweep hairdo advertising Modess. You couldn't tell us that May Anna hadn't made it.

It wasn't long after that May Anna got her first part in a motion picture. She was so excited she sent us a telegram: LANDED MOVIE ROLE STOP GANGSTERS ON PARADE STOP SPEAKING PART STOP SEEUN PICTURES STOP LOVE MAYANNA. It was the first telegram me and Whippy Bird ever received, and I have it in my memory box. Toney had to explain to me and Whippy Bird what all the "stops" meant.

May Anna wrote us later that a director spotted her in a Spencer corsets ad and said she'd be nice in the part of the woman who got strangled in the movie. You probably never saw *Gangsters on Parade*. Nobody else did except me and Whippy Bird and Buster. It played at the American in Butte, and it even got top billing with a big sign

on the marquee that said BUTTE GIRL STARS, which wasn't true. You
saw May Anna for about five seconds, saying, "No. No. Ahhhhh."
That was the speaking part. Then she slumped to the floor with her
tongue hanging out of her mouth.

We'd seen May Anna play a lot of parts, looking cow-eyed at
Buster or carrying on with Shawn at Gamer's. But sitting at the
American watching May Anna get killed, me and Whippy Bird knew
she would be a Star of the Silver Screen.

We got Pink and Chick to take us opening night. After that, the
boys wouldn't go again, so the two of us went by ourselves. We spent
every night and every day off at the American watching May Anna.
Me and Whippy Bird memorized every word of that picture—as well
as *West of the Pecos,* which was on the same bill. I got so tired of
that movie, I never liked westerns after that, but we had to sit
through it so we could see May Anna's picture again. If we left, we'd
have to pay to get back into the theater.

Buster was always at the American, too. He sat there waiting for
May Anna to get killed, then left after May Anna's part and had to
buy another ticket to get back into the American to see her get killed
the next time. Buster always did waste money.

For a while we used some of those lines we memorized, like
"Forget it, you cheap crook" and "Where's the loot?" so our time
wasn't wasted. Whenever I asked Whippy Bird to do something she
didn't want to, she replied, "No, no, aahhhhh." And every time a
woman customer at Gamer's was snotty, I'd mutter, "I'll ice the
dame," under my breath, which was what the killer said before he
murdered May Anna.

We didn't say that stuff around Buster, though, because he took

May Anna's acting very seriously. "Nothing's going to stop May Anna from getting what she wants," he said.

Well, we took it seriously, too. Who else did we know who'd made it big like that, except Buster, and he wasn't big yet. We could see May Anna was doing just fine because it seemed like every time we saw a movie after that, there would be May Anna. She was never in the main feature, just the B pictures, the kind where the men keep their hats on inside. She didn't get many good speaking parts like in *Gangsters on Parade,* but she worked steady, and that is a major accomplishment in Hollywood where so many of your starlets had to work as waitresses or prostitutes. May Anna said she never had to work as a prostitute in Hollywood. Whippy Bird says that's how you put it when you don't get paid cash.

The next big break for May Anna came in *Tough Man,* where she was a supporting actress and got a screen credit, too. She played the girlfriend of a gangster named Mad Dog, and got shot in a getaway car. May Anna got killed a lot in the early days.

Tough Man was the first time we noticed May Anna had high cheekbones and that "luminous" skin everybody wrote about when she was a sex goddess. Whippy Bird says we sure were a pair of nitwits never noticing all the good parts of May Anna before. I remember when the robbers were in the bank vault and one of the gangsters struck a match that lit up everybody's face. May Anna glowed like a Madonna with a halo, so you didn't even notice the others. That's why when she was a big star, the director always had her stand under a street lamp with a lot of fog blowing around her. Everything was black except May Anna's shining face. Or you saw her in a dark nightclub smoking a cigarette with smoke swirling over her head and her face shining through it. She must have smoked about a million cigarettes in the movies. Whippy Bird says she is sorry about tobacco causing cancer because she liked to see those scenes in the movies with champagne glasses and cigarette smoke.

May Anna wasn't the only one doing exciting things. Me and Whippy Bird had plenty of news that you'll be interested in. While May Anna was getting established in Hollywood, me and Pink decided to get married. Had to get married, Whippy Bird says, and that is surely true though we had planned on it anyway.

Some boys might have run out on you when they found you were pg, but when I told Pink I was in the family way, he was so excited he hugged me and said we'd run off to anyplace I chose that very night. But I wanted a wedding with Whippy Bird as my maid of honor. Pink said I could have the biggest wedding in Butte, but I just wanted it quick since I knew people would be counting.

We got married a week later. I was fretting that Pink wouldn't show up, which would ruin my life, but Whippy Bird said there wasn't a thing in the world short of death that would keep Pink away. I guess that was right. Buster stood up with us, too, and he made sure Pink was there even though he was nursing the worst hangover you ever saw. Buster and Chick took Pink to the Jug the night before the wedding, and they got him drunk, and I don't know what else. I didn't want to know. All that mattered was that Pink was there, even though he did have to say the words three or four times to get them straight. That was just the hangover, though. When the minister pronounced us man and wife, Pink kissed me for three minutes, until the minister drummed his fingers on the cross. Chick reminded Pink that he was paying by the hour, and we could kiss for free at the Rocky Mountain Cafe.

That's where we had our reception. Toney made about a hundred toasts to our happiness. He even toasted the Unholy Three. Pink, as an old married man, advised Chick to take the plunge himself. Then as we were leaving on our honeymoon to Ogden, Utah, Buster gave me a hug and said, "Babe, you got a fine man. And Pink's one hell of a lucky guy." I told Buster I surely hoped he found happiness, too, one day.

When we got back from the honeymoon, which was only three days, Pink went to the mines; he worked at the Mountain Miser then. I went back to Gamer's, but things weren't right with me. I was sick all the time, not just morning sickness but something else. I'd never been pregnant before, but I knew there was something wrong with that baby. Two months later I lost it.

I always thought I failed Pink that way. He was so excited about us having a baby, but he never said a cross word to me about losing it, and I loved him even more for that. He was the love of my life, just like May Anna was for Buster. Losing that baby was one of the sorrows of my life, and Pink's, too, bless him.

It took me a long time to get well. I had to stay in bed for two months. Pink never complained. He took care of me like I was a little blown-glass ballerina. He cooked and cleaned the house after he got home from work, which is not something your average Butte miner would be pleased to do. Pink told me the only thing in the world he wanted was for me to recover.

Even with all those doctor bills to pay, Pink brought me flowers. The first time I got out of bed and ate at the table, he pinned an orchid corsage on my bathrobe, lit two big candles, and put on a record of "Little Brown Jug." You'd have thought we were celebrating with plank steak at the Finlen Hotel instead of eggs and hash browns in the kitchen. Whippy Bird says I was the luckiest girl in the world to be married to Pink Varscoe, and she is surely right.

Sometimes Buster stopped to cheer me up, which was especially nice because right then Buster didn't have much to be cheerful about. His career was going nowhere. In fact, me and Whippy Bird wondered if Buster was finished as a boxer.

When May Anna left, Buster McKnight acted fine, but Buster Midnight went to pieces. I had to laugh when Hunter Harper wrote that the effects of too much fast living caught up with Buster. That's hogwash. The rest of us were the fast livers. Buster took care of himself. What put him in that long, slow tailspin was May Anna going to Hollywood.

Buster lost his first fight in history a couple of weeks after she left. It was a dinky fight against a punch-drunk old bum who wasn't good enough to be Buster's sparring partner let alone face him in the ring. The fight was held in the Knights of Columbus hall. Me and Whippy Bird and Pink and Chick went, and it was the sorriest fight I ever saw. Buster just asked to get beat up. There was no sign of the famous Buster Midnight punch. In fact, Buster didn't punch at all. He got hit and hit again. People booed, but Buster still didn't get any better. In one round, the other fighter knocked Buster down, and the only thing that saved him was the bell.

When the fight was over, Buster lost the decision. We booed at that and told Buster he was robbed. But we knew it wasn't so.

Losing one fight wasn't bad, but Buster lost five in a row. All of a sudden he was washed up. We didn't see the other fights, since they were out of town, but Toney said Buster was just as bad. After that Toney had a hard time rounding up matches in Montana for Buster.

"He's got no heart no more," Toney said. "It makes me madder than hell that that broad did this to him."

We were down at the Rocky Mountain Cafe doing our best to get rid of a couple of bottles of red while we fed the slot machines.

"Don't you blame May Anna. God didn't put her on this earth to work Venus Alley so Buster could beat up people," Whippy Bird told him. She was always quick to defend May Anna, just like she is now.

"Hell, it's Buster's fault," Chick said, agreeing with Whippy Bird. "Maybe he's not as good as we think."

"He's good all right," Toney said. "The best in the business. But he ain't going to last long at this rate."

"Maybe he just has to get out of Montana," Chick told Toney, who was brooding, dropping ashes from his Old Gold on top of his spaghetti. "Where else could you set up Buster? What about Colorado, all those mining towns?"

"Hell, Colorado mining towns are dead. Besides, that ain't far enough away," Toney said.

"What about California, since that's where May Anna is," I asked.

"Right out of the frying pan into the fire," Toney said. "That's the dumbest idea I ever heard."

Pink didn't like Toney saying that. "You shut your mouth. Don't you talk like that to Effa Commander," he said.

"Sorry, Effa Commander. I didn't mean it. I know you're trying to help. It's just that I see Buster's whole career falling down a glory hole." I bet he was thinking about his own career taking a dive down a glory hole, too.

"So take him where there aren't any glory holes. Take him to New York," I told Toney.

He put out his Old Gold in the spaghetti and thought for a long time. "Just maybe I will," he said finally.

Buster didn't think much of the idea. When he showed up later, Toney was all excited, telling Buster he was wasting himself on a bunch of burgs when what he really needed was a shot at the big time. "Hey, Kid Midnight. It's city lights for us. Me and you is moving up in the world. I'll get you fights in New York and Chicago and all the big cities. Next time you see Butte, you'll be head of a parade."

"Naw. I been thinking about trying to get on at the Badger. They're hiring."

That was the worst thing Buster could say. It made us all feel miserable. It was OK for Buster to work in the mines when he was on his way up, but he quit mining to work full-time as a fighter. Going back meant Buster was giving up.

"Oh, come on, kid. We'll have a hell of a time." Toney slapped him on the back.

"No, Tone. I'm sorry to let you down. That's the way it is now."

They argued back and forth like that. Buster wouldn't budge. We figured Toney would get him to come around, and we were right. He never did start at the Badger. In about a week, Buster and Toney were on their way. Pink asked him why he'd changed his mind, and Buster said he'd gotten a telegram from May Anna, though he never told Pink what it said. Me and Whippy Bird were surprised because May Anna never mentioned anything in any of her letters about sending

Buster a wire. Whippy Bird says you're batty, Effa Commander, if
you still think May Anna sent that telegram.

So Buster and Toney were on their way but not to New York and
not with any style. They didn't have any money since Toney couldn't
bootleg with liquor legal again, so they decided to ride the rods. Now
any kid who grew up in Butte knew how to hop a ride on the
cowcatcher or the death woods under the boxcars. That was the way
you got from Butte to the smelter at Anaconda. Toney figured with
them being broke they would hitch a ride to Chicago to look things
over then go on to New York.

But Toney never rode the bottom of a train before, and from the
bottom of a transcontinental railroad car, he couldn't tell what direction they were headed. That's why he and Buster wound up in Salt
Lake City, Utah, instead of Chicago. They rode all the way on the
steel rods beneath a Pullman car, and Buster said he never would do
that again even if he had to walk. They had to tell stories all night
to stay awake because if you fell asleep on the underside of a freight
car, which was only a few inches above the track, you were dead.
Toney was all for keeping on to Kansas City, but Buster said no.
Besides, a hobo traveling alongside them said Salt Lake was a prosper-
ous town because the cigarette butts around the tracks were only
half-smoked.

So Toney went around and got Buster a fight in an old gym where
there were pictures of Jack Dempsey. It wasn't a big fight because
Buster didn't look like much of a fighter with a couple days growth
of beard and an inch of railroad dust on his clothes. The promoter
figured he was just a bum who was willing to get beat up for a few
bucks. Still, he signed him up. Then Buster won. Toney said Buster

didn't just win. He won by a knockout in the second round, bringing them twenty bucks. The promoter wanted to sign Buster on for more fights. Toney wasn't Buster's manager for nothing. The price went up, and two weeks later, they had enough money to afford tickets to ride inside the Pullman instead of under it. You'd think they'd ride coach and save the money, but not Toney and Buster. When they had it, they spent it.

After he won a few fights, Buster started to get his confidence back. It didn't hurt that Toney called May Anna long-distance and told her she owed it to Buster to write him a letter every now and then. So she started writing Buster letters of his own instead of telling me and Whippy Bird to say hello to him for her. Toney didn't want him to go into another slump, so he decided to skip the big cities where he might get beat and book fights for Buster in places like Denver and Kansas City. Toney worked out a regular itinerary of Buster Midnight fights, and Buster won them all. Most of them with knockouts. He fought for a couple of months then came home to Butte to rest, knocking off a few bouts at the Centerville Gym and the Knights of Columbus for the hometown folks. Then he headed out on the circuit again. Pretty soon, Toney was talking about Buster being a champ again. The old Buster Midnight was back.

He surely was a more serious Buster Midnight, though. Toney didn't have to tell him to work out. That's all Buster did. What was driving Buster, Whippy Bird said, was the need to prove he was good enough for May Anna, now that the two of them were back together—by letter anyway. The only way he could do that was to be a champ. As usual, Whippy Bird was right.

. . .

Now I'm going to tell you about what happened to Whippy Bird. She
and Chick got married, though they took the longest time to make
up their minds. Whippy Bird says to say she didn't have to, but that
was just luck. Luck and three days because Fred Commander
O'Reilly was born nine months and three days after the wedding. We
called him "Moon" because when May Anna saw his picture she said
he looked just like Moon Mullins in the funny papers.

If you didn't know, it would be hard to tell who Moon's parents
were because me and Pink cared about that baby just as much as
Whippy Bird and Chick. I still do. Moon once said to me, "I sure
was lucky, Aunt Effa Commander, that God gave me two mothers."
He has never once missed sending me a card on Mother's Day,
though when he was little, I know it was Whippy Bird who bought
them for him to give me.

The four of us took little Moon everywhere. Chick finished making
the cradle he had started for our baby and put it up in our living room
so Moon could sleep there. I never saw Pink get excited the way he
did the Christmas we gave Moon a scooter. Of course, it took him
a while before he could use it, since he was only six months old.

We were all together with Moon when we heard May Anna on
the radio the first time. We caught the show by accident.

Me and Pink were eating at Whippy Bird's house, and we were
right in the middle of Radio Pudding, which is the worst dessert that
was ever invented, when *The Jack Benny Program* came on the radio.
We had been kidding Whippy Bird about how she forgot to bake the
Radio Pudding and that we were going to get heartburn because it

was so heavy. That made Whippy Bird laugh because she knew she
was no cook. She was laughing harder than any of us when the
announcer said, "Why here's one of Hollywood's brightest stars."

We didn't pay any attention to Jack Benny until we heard May
Anna's voice say, "Why, hello there, Mr. Benny." Hearing May
Anna say "Why, hello there" sounded so natural that Pink turned
around to see if May Anna was at the door before he caught himself
and realized her voice was coming from the radio. Me and Whippy
Bird sat there with our mouths open while Pink and Chick poked
each other, swelling up like they were part of the show.

Mr. Benny and May Anna did a skit where May Anna purred and
talked sexy. When he asked if she'd like to go to the movies, she said
she'd bring her mother along.

"As a chaperone?" he asked.

"No, as your date," May Anna told him. "I'd ask my grandmother,
but she's busy."

She surely was good. When the skit was over, Jack Benny thanked
May Anna for coming to the show and said to be sure and see her
in *Mobster Madness.* Everybody clapped, including us. Then at the
end of the show, the announcer read her name again, and we
cheered.

"You hear that, Moon?" Whippy Bird said to little Moon, who
was clapping, too. "Your Aunt May Anna–Marion Street is going to
be a rich actress and send you to college," and we laughed, though
we did not know then what a true thing she said.

After that, we heard May Anna on the radio all the time. She
played the same part over and over—the Visiting Starlet Marion
Street. In its "Radio Section," *Time* magazine talked about how May

Anna was becoming a popular radio guest, calling her the "purr-fect cinemactress Marion Street."

After I told Buster about listening to May Anna on Jack Benny, he went to the furniture store and bought the biggest Emerson radio they had. When May Anna was on the radio, Buster turned the Emerson up so loud you could hear it all across Centerville. Later on, Buster gave me that radio, and I still have it to listen to the Oakie O'Connor show, live from Butte, Montana.

CHAPTER

9

May Anna was like a shooting star. She went from "no, no, aahhhhh" parts to speaking words you could understand like "Honey, let me fix you something to eat?" Then she became what they call a supporting actress. Mostly she was in gangster pictures, but that was all right because we liked them, and so did most other moviegoers. You could slaughter dozens of people in the movies back then, killing them right and left with machine guns and car accidents, and nobody minded. People didn't worry about little kids going bad from watching movies the way they do now. Me and Whippy Bird always took Moon to gangster movies, and he didn't grow up to be an axe murderer.

It was no surprise that May Anna's looks were the reason for her success at first, though she had talent, too. She was so pretty and vulnerable up there on the screen people just naturally liked her. She made them laugh, and she made them sad. One night, me and Whippy Bird went to the Montana Theater to watch her in *Death Mob*, the movie where she went off the cliff in the car, when we heard a lady behind us crying. We looked at her, then me and Whippy Bird looked at each other, and it hit us. She wasn't watching May Anna like we were. She wasn't seeing somebody she knew playacting. She was watching a poor dumb blonde she felt sorry for go over the edge and die.

May Anna had a few other things going for her besides her looks and her acting ability. *Photoplay* said she had a photographic memory. She read her lines once, and she knew them. That's all it took. You heard about your movie stars holding up shooting schedules and costing studios lots of money because they didn't know their part, but you never heard that about Marion Street. She was a professional. Maybe that came from her training as a hooker. Whippy Bird says memorizing was not what May Anna learned being a hooker.

May Anna was in a lot of movies then because Hollywood turned out a lot of pictures. Everybody we knew went to the movies once or twice a week, and it was always a double bill. The studios filmed a B movie in about a week. That meant you couldn't make many mistakes—and May Anna with her good memory didn't—because they liked to get things done in one take. The studios also made movies cheap. There wasn't much scenery, and they never went on location the way they do now.

May Anna wasn't supposed to play Stella, the lead, in *Mobster Moll.* She had the part of the younger sister who got electrocuted. But the actress who was picked to play Stella—me and Whippy Bird don't think it's right to tell you her name though you probably know anyway—was doped up that week and hadn't learned her lines. May Anna knew them, though. By the time that actress had her head cleared up, the movie was in the can, which is the way they say it in Hollywood, and she was canned, which is what we say in Butte. And May Anna was a star. When we saw *All About Eve,* Whippy

Bird said do you think they used May Anna as the model for Eve?

It didn't matter to me and Whippy Bird how May Anna got the part. We just cared that she did. *Mobster Moll* wasn't such a great movie, but people in Hollywood go to your B movies to look for talent, and John Elmoor, the famous director, spotted May Anna, which is how she got to play in *Evil City* with Arthur Lowe. Before he offered her the part, though, Mr. Elmoor went back and watched some of May Anna's other movies, and he told her she died better than anybody in Hollywood, which was one of the nicest compliments May Anna ever got up to that time.

That's why he gave her the part. He was a good director, and May Anna's best death scene of her career was the one with Mr. Lowe. You could just see the tears in his eyes when May Anna forgave him for shooting her by accident.

Evil City was a big hit. Of course, most people went to see it because of Arthur Lowe, but May Anna got her share of publicity. She was on the cover of *Modern Screen,* and there were articles about her in all the other movie magazines. They weren't just pictures of May Anna taken at a party, but real articles about her. That was when me and Whippy Bird learned you can't believe everything you read. There were stories about May Anna's happy childhood in Butte and about her being discovered by a news crew on Broadway in front of the Finlen when she was a high school girl planning to go to college. One article said that May Anna hoped to retire from the screen some day and go back to Montana and live on a ranch and have a family, which is about as false as anything ever written about May Anna.

The one that made me and Whippy Bird laugh out loud was a story about how May Anna loved to cook. There was a picture of May

Anna all made up and wearing high heels and a strapless cocktail dress covered by a little organdy apron, standing in front of the stove with an eggbeater in her hand. Me and Whippy Bird wondered how she knew which end to hold on to. The only thing May Anna could operate in the kitchen was a can opener. The other pictures showed her stirring batter in a big bowl and taking a pan out of the oven, and finally there was one of May Anna sitting down to eat what she'd cooked. There was even a recipe for Marion Street's Nut Loaf, but it wasn't May Anna's recipe. It was mine. May Anna called me long-distance and asked me to send a recipe quick because she had promised to write down one for her fans. She promised to tell them it came from me, but that didn't get printed. The only thing May Anna ever cooked was Campbell's Pork & Beans. Whippy Bird says one of the attractions of working in a hookhouse for May Anna was that the meals came with.

When Pink saw that recipe in the movie magazine, he said he bet May Anna never knew you could break up nuts and put them into a loaf of bread, ha ha. But I was proud. One of the pictures showed May Anna feeding a piece of my nut loaf to Donald O'Connor, and I got a swelled head because May Anna told me after they finished taking the pictures, Mr. O'Connor asked her could he have another piece.

Because of *Mobster Moll* and *Evil City,* May Anna got a contract with Warner Bros. They planned to develop her into a blond Bette Davis and star her in what May Anna called weepers. May Anna wrote us that one of the Mr. Warners called her the broad with the platinum blond halo. They also gave her a nice salary so she could move out of the hotel where she lived into a deluxe apartment that she shared with another Warner Bros. movie starlet, Anne Bates. Me and Whippy Bird see Anne Bates on the television today selling diapers for senior citizens.

May Anna wrote us that the two of them had twin beds, which made her the first person we ever knew who slept in a twin bed. They also had a blond dressing table with a big round mirror, which we thought was swell. I wanted a blond bedroom suite in the worst way after that, but me and Pink never could afford it. He surely would have bought it for me if he had the money, because that man never denied me a thing. May Anna may have had millions of men falling at her feet, but I had Pink Varscoe. Whippy Bird says Pink never would have bought me twin beds though. I guess you can tell why without me explaining.

It was the Warner Bros. publicity department that brought May Anna and Buster back together after Buster went to New York and became famous.

Buster had been doing just fine himself. He was on his way. People knew about him, and a Buster Midnight fight drew a big crowd from as far away as St. Louis.

That year Buster fought Killer McGillis in Spokane just before election day. As the two of them slugged away, somebody yelled, "Kill the Democrat son of a bitch!"

Then another fan yelled, "Clobber the Republican bastard!"

Before you knew it, everybody in the audience took sides and yelled for the Democrats or the Republicans and slugged it out with each other, too. The only thing was, nobody knew which one of the fighters was the Republican or the Democrat—or whether they belonged to the same party. That didn't matter. When Buster won, both sides claimed him. For the record, as the fellow says, Buster was a Democrat.

That was also the fight where Toney sold about twice as many tickets as there were seats, and the men who didn't get in talked mean. After that, Toney decided it was time to take Buster to New York. He was talking Madison Square Garden. And this time Toney and Buster got on the right train.

We went to see them off, and so did some of the local fight fans and a couple of newspaper reporters and a bunch of girls that you always see hanging around prize-fighters. Toney knew it was important to get publicity, so he was in good with the writers and photographers. They took pictures of Buster mugging with the girls and another with his mits up like he was getting ready to fight. The one the *Montana Standard* printed, however, was Buster giving me a good-bye kiss. The caption read: BUSTER BUSSES HOMETOWN GIRL BEFORE MONTANA PUGILIST HEADS FOR BIG TIME.

We all laughed at that when it appeared in the paper. Chick and Whippy Bird joked with Pink that his marriage was on the rocks. "Didn't I see you in Venus Alley?" Chick kidded me. Pink didn't care. He thought it was a big joke on me, and he even went down to the *Standard* and got a copy of that picture and gave it to me, framed, on my birthday. It still sits on my living room mantel today though I recently got a new frame for it. I picked the frame that had a picture of Glenn Ford in it because he was a friend of May Anna's.

Whippy Bird sent a copy of the *Montana Standard* picture to May

Anna with a letter saying Buster was two-timing her with me. May Anna sent me a telegram back that said: ANYTHING MINE BELONGS UNHOLY THREE STOP   LOVEANDKISSES MAYANNA.

Buster loved that trip to New York. He said one of the benefits of being a famous fighter was riding across the country on a stream-liner, watching the world go by and eating bread-and-butter pudding in the diner. They rode coach on that trip, but later on, Buster had a private compartment. When he was the champion, he rode in private railroad cars that rich boxing fans loaned him. Buster liked that. They were as sleek as the Jim Hill Cafe. There was always a waiter in a white jacket to fix drinks or broil a steak, and he was allowed to invite all the friends he wanted to come along.

Buster ran with a fast crowd that liked the parties he and Toney threw, which is one more reason the two of them never had much money. When they had it, though, they surely did have a good time. You'd think me and Whippy Bird would have been mad at them for not being sensible about their money, but we weren't. Maybe that's because they spent it on us, too. Buster never forgot us during those years. He was just as generous as May Anna. I remember the Christ-mas when he sent Moon boxing gloves and a punching bag, and me and Whippy Bird got red fox fur wraps. We went to lunch at the Finlen just to wear those furs and never took them off, though they got in our way and we had to eat with our arms out in front of us. Whippy Bird spilled lime Jell-O salad on hers.

Anyway, there weren't any reporters and photographers waiting at Grand Central Station in New York when Buster and Toney arrived there the first time. So as soon as they got off the train, the two of them made the rounds of the newspapers. Buster Midnight was a big deal in the West, but not many people cared about him in New York. Toney changed that fast.

People just naturally liked Toney the way they did Buster. He was friendly and generous, and he was good copy, as the reporters say. After he visited the papers they wrote articles about Buster, even using the pictures that Toney brought along that were taken at Buster's best fights. By handing out the pictures free, the papers didn't have to bother their own photographers to take snapshots.

Toney also talked to the fight promoters. Now, you might think that Toney, being from Butte, would get taken advantage of, but he was no damn fool. May Anna knew what she was doing when she walked down Broadway in front of a newsreel camera, and Toney knew what he was doing when he lined up fights for Buster in New York City. He wanted exposure, and he knew the exposure that would do Buster the most good was winning fights. After that they'd go back west and develop Buster into a contender, and that's just what happened. Toney arranged half a dozen fights, and Buster won every one, four with knockouts. Toney made sure the sports reporters were there. They wrote that Buster was a tough fighter from the hard-rock mines of the West, just like Dempsey. There was even a story about Buster swimming across Pipestone Lake in the winter to build up his stamina. Whippy Bird asked me do you suppose Buster swam under or on top of the ice?

When Buster left New York, there was a crowd of reporters and photographers at the station, and the papers all had stories about the new western contender for the heavyweight title. Even the new *Look*

magazine mentioned Buster's name in an article about future sports
stars. This was the first time Buster and May Anna were mentioned
together in print. It said:

> Every kid who grows up in the smelter smoke of Butte dreams
> of just two things—prize fights and beautiful women. For most,
> the dreams are as murky as the Copper Town sky. But not for
> Buster McKnight, a rawbones giant and latter-day Dempsey
> who fights under the moniker of Buster Midnight. Promoters
> are betting this cowboy contender will be the next heavyweight
> champion. And nobody has greater faith in Buster Midnight
> than his high school sweetheart—who is none other than
> Warner Bros.'s pure platinum dish, Marion Street, the Butte
> Bombshell.

Warner Bros. saw that article and called May Anna in and asked
was it true she knew Buster Midnight. She said she surely did. The
studio had just finished filming a May Anna picture called *Trouble
on the Waterfront*. It was about gangsters, of course. May Anna
played a school teacher who tried to clean up the waterfront, which
was run by criminals. There was a scene in the movie where May
Anna talks a washed-up boxer into fighting his best instead of throwing the fight.

When Warner Bros. heard about Buster, they thought it would be
swell to refilm that part using Buster. So they called up Toney, but
he turned them down. Toney didn't want anybody to think of Buster
as a has-been or to believe Buster would ever throw a fight. Buster
was disappointed, though he did what Toney told him to.

So Warner Bros. came up with the idea of sending May Anna to
Butte on an airplane for a publicity tour. They could hold the pre-

miere at the Montana Theater and reunite May Anna and Buster. That way, they could take plenty of pictures of the two of them together, getting both May Anna and Buster into the newspapers. Me and Whippy Bird thought it was the best idea we ever heard because it would get the Unholy Three back together again, too.

There was a big crowd at the airport that afternoon. Me and Whippy Bird, Pink and Chick and Moon, and, of course, Buster and Toney were there to see May Anna arrive. There were reporters and photographers, too. Buster was in the first suit I ever saw him wear, and he got a haircut for the occasion. You could see the skin through his hair it was cut so close at the sides. He carried a big bouquet of white roses that he shifted from hand to hand. He was nervous, all right. May Anna wrote Buster letters, and he sent her postcards, and sometimes they talked long distance, but they hadn't been together in almost four years.

"You think she'll recognize me?" Buster asked Pink.

"Probably not," Pink said, which made Buster laugh and settle down a little.

When the plane landed, everybody got off except May Anna. It was like a dramatic entrance in the movies. The stairs up to the airplane door were empty. The crowd was quiet—until May Anna ducked out the door and everybody cheered, me and Whippy Bird the loudest. She was dressed all in white with a white fox stole and a little white hat with a veil tied over her face. She waved, and Buster rushed up and gave her the roses and a big hug. May Anna was acting like a cool movie star, but you could still tell she was excited to see Buster. For a tiny minute she was May Anna Kovaks, squeezing Buster's arm and hugging him back. Then she turned into Marion

Street again, and took little dainty steps down the stairs, holding out the roses for the crowd. Me and Whippy Bird could see she was wearing silk stockings with no runs.

We were standing off to the side so May Anna didn't notice us at first. She was blowing kisses and signing autographs. Then Buster led her to the microphone, where the most important people in Butte like the mayor and the theater manager and the head of the power company were waiting for her.

All of them shook hands with May Anna, then the mayor gave a speech, and the theater manager gave another speech, but Buster didn't say anything. He just grinned at May Anna. Then May Anna, sounding like she had a mouth full of Tootsie Roll, said what a thrill it was to return to the best town in America and how she had traveled all over the United States, which wasn't true, and no place was as beautiful as Butte. She told the crowd her fondest hope was to return to Butte one day and live here.

Now me and Whippy Bird knew where the reporters got all that wrong information.

May Anna was right in the middle of talking when she spotted me and Whippy Bird. She forgot her snooty voice and yelled like a Centerville ragpicker, "Whippy Bird and Effa Commander! You come right up here! Let those girls through!" We ran up and hugged her, and everybody cheered. "These are my best friends," she said, and they cheered again. We never did find out who all those people were. Then May Anna asked where Moon was, so Chick and Pink brought him up, and May Anna kissed him and got Max Factor lipstick all over her veil. The photographers snapped away, which is why Moon was the youngest person we personally knew to get his picture on the front page of the *Montana Standard*.

After May Anna finished her speech and everybody left, her press agent came up and tried to shoo us off, but May Anna gave him a hard look. "These are my friends. They stay," she said in her gangster moll voice. So we stayed. Or rather we all went up to May Anna's suite at the Finlen and drank gin. We realized how far May Anna had come when she walked into the Finlen Hotel. She didn't have to register at the front desk or pay in advance or even wait for an elevator. They had one waiting for her.

May Anna was so busy we hardly had time to talk. There was the premiere that night then a visit to an orphanage and a ribbon-cutting ceremony and a trip to the Hill for cheesecake pictures in front of the headframes. May Anna asked me and Whippy Bird to meet her at the Finlen to go to the charity tea the next day, but we said we didn't know anything about a tea.

May Anna turned to the press agent. "I told West Point to put their names on the list." She always called Warner Bros. West Point or sometimes Sing Sing.

He shrugged and said, "I sent them to the charity dames."

"I go. My friends go. Got it?" The press agent said he'd fix things. May Anna told us they always made mistakes like that. The press agent said she was right and that he shouldn't have trusted the US mail.

When me and Whippy Bird met May Anna at the Finlen, she was dressed in white again—white silk dress, white gloves, and a hat shaped like a white soup plate. Me and Whippy Bird looked pretty snazzy, too, in matching red-and-blue flowered rayon dresses and red gloves and white rabbit capes. Whippy Bird wore her hair in an upsweep with big bangs rolled under, and I had a pageboy. To finish off our outfits, we had red linen purses and white ankle-strap shoes, and we wore the rhinestone pins May Anna brought us from Hollywood.

Me and Whippy Bird were ready to walk to the tea since it was only over on West Broadway, but your movie stars don't walk anywhere. They took us in a big white Lincoln with whitewall tires and a red sign that said WORLD PREMIERE *TROUBLE ON THE WATERFRONT* on the side. People waved to May Anna, and she waved back. Me and Whippy Bird waved, too.

The house was three stories high with white pillars and a copper roof. When we got there, May Anna sat in the car and wouldn't get out until the press agent jiggled her arm and said, "Come on, honey. Show time for the folks."

"I've never been in one of these big houses on West Broadway. I'm more nervous than at the premiere," May Anna whispered to us.

"See here, May Anna. We're right behind you. The Unholy Three. All for one and one for all," Whippy Bird said, and May Anna hugged us and got out. Your movie stars do a lot of hugging, but, of course, May Anna meant it with us.

Me and Whippy Bird had never been in a house on West Broadway either, but nobody paid any attention to us. We thought the house was ugly with all that carved furniture, and dark, too, with the heavy velvet drapes hanging in the doorways, but Whippy Bird says what did we know?

Those ladies fell all over May Anna, telling her how proud they were that a Butte girl had done so well and handing her slips of paper for her autograph. One asked her if it was true Humphrey Bogart, who was pictured with her in *Look,* beat up women. May Anna said he was so sweet he would be right at home in that very room, which seemed to disappoint them.

Me and Whippy Bird filled up our plates, then Whippy Bird asked one lady if she would be so kind as to bring her a cup of coffee instead of tea, and I thought I'd die trying not to laugh. After we'd looked over the house we sat where we could watch May Anna sip her tea from a tiny white cup that was so fine you could almost see through it. There was gold on the rim, and the handle was the shape of a question mark. May Anna answered all their questions in her new, rich, snooty voice, and you could see them drinking it all in like mules at a trough.

One by one, those ladies came by to say hello to May Anna. She shook each hand they stuck out, saying, "So pleased to meet you," as gracious as a queen. All of a sudden Whippy Bird poked me in the ribs with her elbow, making me drop my cookie. I started to say cut it out, then I saw her staring at May Anna, whose face had changed. I put down my cup and watched.

Only me and Whippy Bird could see she looked different because we knew how her face froze when she was upset. Her lips moved, but the rest of her face stopped working. Then I looked at the lady who had just said hello to May Anna. Whippy Bird whispered shut your mouth, Effa Commander. She was one of the food basket ladies who went by May Anna's house before Mrs. Kovaks died. We knew May Anna recognized her, too.

"This is wonderful of you," the lady drooled over May Anna.

"You've helped us raise hundreds of dollars for our little food basket program. We present baskets to those less fortunate, you know."

"I do know," May Anna said with a little smile.

"You know of our work then?"

"Of course."

"They do appreciate it so."

"Do they?"

"Yes. It makes us feel so good."

"I know." May Anna smiled all the time, but she put her little cup down on a crocheted doily on the table next to her. The doily was starched so stiff, the ruffle stood up two inches high.

"We'd like to make you an honorary member of our group," the lady said. She raised her voice so everyone would hear, sounding like she was giving May Anna the Academy Award.

"Oh, no," May Anna said.

"Why, we insist, don't we, ladies?" She turned around and looked at all the women, then stopped a minute on me and Whippy Bird, trying to figure out why we were there. Her look made me think that we were out of place in that room. They were all dressed in black and gray with no jewelry, and suddenly we didn't look so elegant anymore. I knew then that there wasn't any mix-up in the invitations. They didn't want to invite us.

"No," May Anna said.

The lady squinted at May Anna, not understanding. "But why?" she finally asked.

The room was quiet, and everybody watched May Anna, who stood out in her white dress just like she was under a spotlight. Her voice was sweet, and she was still smiling. I pointed to the woman and whispered to Whippy Bird, "Remember May Anna ripping off the legs of those frogs we used to catch? She's going to do it again."

"No. I don't want your membership. Just like I didn't want your food basket when you tried to give it to me five years ago. Surely you remember? You stayed for tea." May Anna's voice had become as cold as Butte in January.

The color went out of that lady's face even though she was wearing too much rouge, that maroon color that I notice the Ben Franklin is carrying again, and we knew she remembered. May Anna kept on. "You tried to palm off one of your baskets on me. You must remember?" She stopped and looked around the room, pausing just a second to make sure me and Whippy Bird were listening. "You offered me a job as a maid. That's when I went to work in . . . in Hollywood."

Later, May Anna told us she was going to tell those women she went to work in Venus Alley, but when she started to say it, she lost her nerve. She told herself May Anna, no matter how much you want to get even, that's no way to talk in a house on West Broadway. So instead she stood up like the great actress she was and looked at everybody in the room until she had their attention and said, "So nice of you broads to throw this party for my friends and me." She looked every one of them in the eye, then smiled at me and Whippy Bird and turned and walked out of the room like she was the queen of England. Me and Whippy Bird, who had learned a thing or two from our best friend the famous actress, were right behind her.

CHAPTER
10

After that trip, we knew May Anna would never come back to Butte to live. In fact, she never came back to Butte at all. It wasn't just those ladies. It was that May Anna was a big star now, bigger than Butte. There was nothing here for her. May Anna belonged to the world, Whippy Bird said.

We also knew, finally, there were things more important to her than Buster. She loved Buster, all right—he was good to her and she knew he'd always love her, and he was the only man in her life she could ever depend on. Even Jackfish left. But we knew her career was more important. May Anna may have loved Buster, but she loved Marion Street more.

Buster knew that, too, though it didn't seem to matter so much to him anymore. I guess Buster thought now that they had been reunited, he'd never really lose May Anna even if they didn't get married and live in a house in Centerville and have kids like the rest of us. "Hell," he told Pink, "me and May Anna already got married once. If we do it again, that's bigamy."

Buster was happy just being around May Anna, and Toney made sure he had plenty of chances to do that. After all the newspaper write-ups at the premiere of *Trouble on the Waterfront* in Butte and the pictures of the two of them, Toney knew May Anna was a sure ticket to fame for Buster. Not that Buster wasn't famous already, but because of May Anna, Buster got to be known by a whole new group of people who normally didn't follow boxing. "Icing on the cake," he said, and he lined up a series of fights in California.

"We're going to make him a western contender. California's west, ain't it?" Toney asked. "Besides, who wouldn't rather train under a bunch of coconut trees with May Anna Street serving up mint juleps than in a ball-breaking Butte blizzard." Whippy Bird said he had something there.

May Anna hung around Buster, all right. She went to every Buster Midnight fight in California. Sometimes she brought a crowd of Hollywood people with her and sat ringside in a white dress and a white fur coat and yelled like hell. May Anna knew plenty of things to shout, which was the result of her growing up in Butte. Also a result of working in Venus Alley. A big Hollywood producer who took her to one fight told her, "Good God, Marion, I thought those gangster dame roles were just an act. You talk like the real thing."

May Anna replied, "Thank you." When May Anna wrote us that, Whippy Bird said it was not a compliment, even though May Anna thought so.

Sometimes May Anna took Buster to Hollywood parties. At first she dragged him there because Buster didn't want to go. He said he was liable to knock something over, though like most fighters, he was not clumsy. I've seen Buster carry half a dozen full glasses in one hand and not spill a drop. Then he told May Anna he didn't know what to say to those movie stars and producers. He feared he would be tongue-tied, and everybody would think he was a dummy. That was just after the goofy snapshot of him holding the newspaper upside down was published, and some of the sports writers said Buster didn't know how to read. One called him a High Country Hick and another said Buster had the body of a buffalo and the brains of a bat. Buster wrote him a letter telling him to turn that inside out—the body of a bat and the brains of a buffalo—and it would describe most reporters he knew, but the paper didn't print that.

May Anna told Buster that compared to most of the people she met in Hollywood, he was as smart as a college graduate. She said she'd met some dumb noodles in Butte, but they didn't compare to your movie people. We never thought May Anna was such a smart piece of high grade when she lived in Butte, but when she went to Hollywood, she got a subscription to *Time*. Then, later on, she joined a book club, so maybe she was smarter than we figured. She even had every copy of *Life* ever printed. When she met Mr. Luce, who was the publisher, she told him she had the very first issue of *Life* magazine, and he said imagine that. Maybe that was why he put her picture on the cover later on.

Finally, Buster told May Anna that up there in the ring, he was somebody. Once he put on a suit, he was just a pug. When he wore a tuxedo, he thought he looked like an usher. He was afraid of people handing him their keys and asking would he park the Hudson.

Still, Buster never said no to May Anna, so he let her drag him to parties all over Hollywood. After a while, he even began to enjoy them. Too much, Toney said.

The first party he liked, Buster told us, was the one at Douglas Fairbanks's house. Buster was treated very nicely by the famous people who were guests and by the not-so-famous people there, too.

They were as friendly to Buster as anybody in Butte. Mr. Fairbanks said he was a number-one fight fan, and he'd give up his Hollywood career if he could knock out Jack Dempsey. Hell, who wouldn't, Whippy Bird said.

Mr. Fairbanks forgot about his other guests and took Buster into his rumpus room and asked him about the fights he'd been in, and did he think he had a chance at the championship, and would he show Mr. Fairbanks in slow motion how to do the famous Buster Midnight punch. Mr. Fairbanks said he could jump through the sky on ropes and fight a duel with real swords, even dive off a boat into the ocean, but he didn't have the strength he wanted as a fighter. He put Buster right at ease. May Anna said when she discovered Buster had disappeared and went looking for him, she found the two of them in the rumpus room, Buster with his coat off and his sleeves rolled up, teaching Mr. Fairbanks how to throw a punch.

"You ought to learn this, Marion," Mr. Fairbanks told her. He was crouched over like Buster with his right arm out jabbing at the air. "Buster taught me this punch. It packs a hell of a wallop."

"I already know how to punch," May Anna said. I've been watching Buster Midnight train since I was five years old. If he can knock out Pig Face, there's nobody in the world he can't lick."

Buster beamed at her. "Pig Face wasn't so tough," he said.

"Pig Face?" Mr. Fairbanks asked. "Pig Face?" Then he laughed like it was a joke. "Pig Face!"

"He hit him like this." May Anna gave Buster a little fake punch in the chin. Then she took Buster's arm and said, "Come on, You Big Lug. I've got to introduce you around." She called him You Big Lug a lot in Hollywood. There was a picture of them in *Radio Mirror* with the caption MARION STREET AND HER BIG LUG. She liked to stand next to Buster because he made her look fragile. She also liked to stand next to Buster because he got her a lot of attention. He never believed there were people who would rather meet him than Marion Street, though it was true. She said pretty girls were a dime a dozen at Hollywood parties, but people would wait in line to meet a real prize-fighter.

Buster even met Humphrey Bogart at one of those parties. He said it was too bad May Anna was right. Mr. Bogart was a gentleman, but Buster liked him anyway. He wasn't tough like he was on the screen. He came right up to Buster and said, "Hello. I saw you fight last week. Mind if I ask you a question?"

Every time Buster went to one of those parties, he ended up giving fight lessons. Toney said Buster ought to charge. He'd make more money as a boxing instructor than fighting, and he wouldn't get beat up either.

Mr. Bogart didn't care about the Buster Midnight punch, which Mr. Fairbanks did. Instead, he asked Buster about his footwork when he boxed. That was right after the stories about Buster being a dope, and while he showed Mr. Bogart how to place his feet, Buster happened to mention he was embarrassed about what the newspapers printed. Mr. Bogart told him not to pay any attention to what the papers wrote. "All you want is your name up in front of people. When it isn't, then you worry," he said. "Not everybody goes to see you fight," he added. "Some people go because you're the famous Buster Midnight, so they can tell their friends they saw you."

"They'll stop doing that if I stop winning," Buster told him.

"I guess you're right," Mr. Bogart replied. "There's not a lot of loyalty in the entertainment business."

Right then, of course, there wasn't any danger of Buster losing fights even though Toney arranged the toughest matches he ever fought. There was more and more talk about Buster going up against the champ, Clay Tom Baker, and it didn't come just from Toney. Every sports writer in America talked about Buster as the next heavyweight champion of the world. It was just a matter of time before Toney and the New York promoters signed an agreement that Buster would fight Clay Tom Baker at Madison Square Garden.

We thought Buster would train in California, but Toney felt that May Anna had already given Buster enough exposure. Besides, Toney thought Buster ought to train at a higher altitude to give him stamina. I think the real reason was Toney was afraid Buster was getting soft from going to all those parties. Me and Whippy Bird think Toney was afraid he'd lose his grip with May Anna and her famous friends around. Toney didn't want to have to fight May Anna for Buster.

So Toney set up training for Buster at Columbia Gardens in Butte, where Buster got his start. He organized a regular old-time fight camp and charged people one dollar to watch Buster work out, though me and Whippy Bird got in free whenever we went down there. Toney even had a special pass made up for Moon, who ran around the ring yelling, "Kill him, Uncle Buster. Kill him dead." Moon could shout before he could talk.

Afterward, Moon always went home and put on his gloves and hit the punching bag Buster gave him and pretended he was Buster. We

all said wouldn't it be something if little Moon followed in Buster's
footsteps. "We could bill him as the Man in the Moon," Chick told
us.

Whippy Bird said she'd rather Moon got a job where he worked
steady. Which is what he did. Moon turned out to be short and
scrawny and went to Lake Forest College and became an accountant.
"He wasn't born to fight," Whippy Bird says. "He was born to add."

We've seen some circuses in Butte but nothing compared with the
Buster Midnight Training Camp. People came from all over. Every
old boxer in Montana and plenty from outside showed up to be
sparring partners. Toney, being a soft touch sometimes, gave training
camp tickets even to the ones he turned down.

All the big New York newspapers sent sports writers to cover the
training and dig up what they call color—just like they do now when
they write about Butte's copper industry. Me and Whippy Bird must
have been interviewed fifty times about what Buster was like as a kid.
Every time we talked to a writer, some photographer sneaked up and
popped a flashbulb in our faces, so we became celebrities, too. May
Anna said she saw a picture of Whippy Bird in a Los Angeles newspaper. We became real professional at giving interviews, which is why
so many of your reporters today ask for us at the Jim Hill. The word
was out. You want color, you talk to me and Whippy Bird.

Whippy Bird told them Buster once studied to be a priest, that
he went to church every day and Pig Face always gave Buster a mass
before his fights. She said Pig Face and Buster were old friends, which
is about the funniest thing anybody ever printed about Buster. Then
she told another reporter that Buster's father was a copper king, and
he owned all the buildings uptown, which was why he was called

Broadway Buster. I guess me and Whippy Bird can't complain about reporters not getting the true facts straight.

I told them Buster's favorite thing to do was hunt jackalope, which everybody knows is a made-up animal that's half rabbit, half antelope. I invented jackalope hunting at Pork Chop John's, which is where me and Whippy Bird still go when we've got our faces fixed for a pork chop, and nothing else will satisfy it except one loaded at Pork Chop John's—Uptown, not on the Flats. We've been going to Pork Chop John's so long, we remember when they left the bone in.

I was passing the time of day with John when a man with an ugly tie and a straw hat sat down on the stool next to me and said he was a reporter from the *Herald-Tribune.* He acted like hot stuff, the way your reporters do today, and he thought I should turn cartwheels just for the privilege of being at the same counter with him. He put a Camel on his lip, fired it up, and said he was looking for a real Butte native and would I answer a couple of questions. I guess he didn't know that by then I knew the ropes.

I told him I'd answer his questions just as soon as I finished chewing on a burger made out of jackalope that Buster shot, and darn if that fool didn't believe it. He wrote a story about Buster being a jackalope burger hunter. Me and Whippy Bird thought he'd be embarrassed when he found out he'd been suckered, but all the other reporters picked it up, so he figured he got a regular scoop, as the fellow says. After Toney read that article, he called Buster the Jackalope Burger King of America. For years, people went into Pork Chop John's and ordered "jackalope" burgers. They got served the pork chop loaded, which is what they call it when they add mustard, pickle, and onion. Toney liked pork chop sandwiches so much he said once that being Pork Chop John would be about the best thing in the world.

Every store in Butte sold Buster Midnight ribbons and pins and other classy souvenirs. Me and Pink bought a Buster Midnight doll with little tiny boxing gloves and orange silk trunks for Moon. I still have my lime green rayon pillow with the gold fringe that says BUTTE, MONTANA, HOME OF BUSTER MIDNIGHT.

There were so many people crowded into Butte and Columbia Gardens for the training that they had to call in the state troopers to keep an eye on things. The law had its hands full stopping people from pestering Buster and arresting the pickpockets and the crooked gamblers. There were hookers, too, of course, but mostly the troopers let them alone. You could tell the hookers because they all tried to look like May Anna, with platinum hair and ankle-strap shoes. They walked up and down at the corner of Broadway and Wyoming where May Anna was discovered, just the way your Hollywood hopefuls hung out at the drugstore where Lana Turner got her break.

Toney never had such a good time in his life as he did when Buster was training. He slicked back his hair, which was parted just off center, and poured some kind of lime toilet water on himself. Toney was the first and only man I ever knew personally who wore perfume. He grew a little Ronald Colman mustache and wore pleated white pants and brown-and-white shoes, just like the Texans do now when they come to Butte in the summer. He tied a silk scarf around his neck, too. Whippy Bird said he looked like a pimp, though she never told Toney that. He thought he was the snazziest thing in the state of Montana, running around and yelling orders to people.

The only one who didn't seem excited was Buster. If he wasn't so big, you wouldn't have noticed him at all dressed in his old gray sweater and the baggy brown pants he bought for high school graduation. He never dressed up unless he was around May Anna. Even when he was in the ring practicing, he wore just a ratty pair of black trunks and an undershirt. Buster laughed when little kids went up to his sparring partners and asked, "Can I have your autograph, Mr. Midnight?" Buster didn't care that they mistook other boxers for him or about giving autographs, but I think it disappointed Toney that nobody ever asked him for one. Whippy Bird says that was the reason he carried around the tortoiseshell fountain pen with the gold nib that leaked blue ink all over his shirt.

The championship fight was the most exciting day I remember in Butte, even bigger than when Franklin Delano Roosevelt or Marion Street came to town. There were flags on every street post and bunting stretched across the street and BUSTER MIDNIGHT CHAMPION signs every time you turned around. Most of the stores and restaurants had life-size pictures of Buster in his famous crouch that they hung in the windows. Some of the restaurants even named dishes for Buster, like the Buster Burger—100 percent pure beef. "Tough meat is what they mean," Whippy Bird said.

May Anna took the train all the way to New York and had a private compartment, and when she ate in the diner people asked for her autograph, too. Though she didn't visit the training camp, she sent Buster telegrams almost every day and even called him long-distance. She gave interviews about how she was Buster's number-one fan and planned her filming schedule around that fight. I think she loved Buster more during that time than she ever did.

She sent Pig Face two hundred and fifty dollars to light candles for Buster, which she said ought to buy enough candles to burn down half of Butte. She didn't believe burning candles would do Buster any good, but she wanted to rub it in to Pig Face that Buster was going to be the champion. What was more, she didn't send the money to Father Joseph Stenner. She sent it to Father Pig Face Stenner.

Whippy Bird and Chick and little Moon came to our house to listen to the fight on the new RCA with the picture of the little dog on the side. Pink bought it especially for the occasion and chose the one with the biggest speaker so you could hear it all over the house. After a while though, we decided to go uptown to the newspaper office and listen to the fight with everybody else who gathered outside.

It was so crowded me and Whippy Bird each held one of Moon's little hands so he wouldn't get lost. Moon was only five years old, but being sharp like he is, he knew what was going on. He waved a little flag that had a picture of Buster on it, and kept yelling, "Bust him, Uncle Buster!" We thought that was so cute, me and Whippy Bird yelled it, too.

Chick bought us all beer and popcorn and tamales from the hot tamale man, except for Moon, who got a box of Cracker Jack, which was a disappointment to him since the prize was a bracelet made of tin. I told Moon I'd trade him the bracelet for a little toy car at the five-and-dime next time I was uptown. I wore that bracelet a few times, but the paint chipped off. Now it's in my memory box, a souvenir of Buster's big fight.

You'd think with all those people yelling, those hookers drunk, and those kids pushing, you wouldn't be able to hear the fight, but the newspaper had big speakers all over the front of the building that boomed so loud you could hear them clear up to Centerville. Whippy Bird said we should have sat on the front porch and listened to the fight. I said if we were going to do that, we should stay inside and listen on the new RCA. I think Pink was disappointed that we didn't stay home and listen, though he had just as good a time as the rest of us.

Everybody knows Buster beat Clay Tom Baker, so I'm not going to tell about it. You can look it up in the history books if you want a round-by-round account. It was a tough fight, all right. Buster developed a cauliflower ear on his right side from getting it ripped open. He got in a couple of good punches himself. Still, he didn't have a knockout, which was what we were hoping for. Me and Whippy Bird were both making deals with God for that. Buster won by a decision, and when the radio announcer said Buster was the new champ, we all went wild. Me and Whippy Bird screamed so loud, we were hoarse the next two days.

Afterward, we went down to the Rocky Mountain Cafe to celebrate. Whippy Bird wanted to take Moon home first, but I said it was a night to remember. Moon always gave me the credit for letting him stay up that night. He surely paid me back for the favor, and then some.

Chick and Pink were so excited they ordered martinis for all of us then a bottle of champagne to go with our chili. I handed Moon a silver dollar and told him to put it in the slot machine for me and I'd split the winnings with him, which means I must have been drunk because I am usually very careful with my money.

We just couldn't lose that night. First Buster won the championship, then damned if Moon didn't hit the jackpot of sixty dollars. I gave him half the winnings, and Whippy Bird told him never to play the slots again because it would be downhill from there. She gave Moon a dollar, then used the rest to start a college fund for him. The next day, just for the hell of it, Pink and I went out and bought a Plymouth station wagon with wood sides that we'd been saving for.

Me and Whippy Bird never could get over the fact we'd won so much money at the Rocky Mountain Cafe, and on that night of all nights. She always called the Buster Midnight championship fight the night Effa Commander won the jackpot.

CHAPTER

11

Since both Pink and Chick worked on the Hill in an industry that was essential to the war, they figured they wouldn't have to join up. In fact, the government sent men who refused to fight for America up to Butte to work in the mines. Pink and Chick talked for a long time about whether they ought to enlist, explaining to me and Whippy Bird it wasn't right to leave us alone if they didn't have to, especially with little Moon to take care of and a baby on the way. My baby. I was pregnant, and Pink wanted to be there because he was afraid I'd get sick again. I wanted him, too, though this time around I was sure I'd be all right. So far, all the signs were good.

At first, me and Whippy Bird were glad they weren't going, but we knew they would sooner or later no matter how much they said they wouldn't, so we talked it over on the day me and Whippy Bird took Moon up to Hennessy's to buy him a snowsuit.

After we finished shopping, we went to the Creamery Cafe to buy Moon hot chocolate and a piece of apple pie. "Chick says he'd never join the army and leave me," Whippy Bird said. She wiped off Moon's hot-chocolate mustache. "Baby, you want another marshmallow?"

"I'm not a baby," Moon said.

"Of course you're not," Whippy Bird said. "Pretty soon you're going to be the man of the family."

I put down my fork, and me and Whippy Bird looked at each other.

"Well, he's likely to be. They want to go, you know," she said. "In the worst way. Both of them. It's not the way of Butte boys to hide out from a war. I guess I've made up my mind they're going to do it."

"Has Chick told you that?" I asked her.

"No. What about Pink?"

I shook my head. "But I know Pink. He wants to go. He's just afraid for the baby."

"For you, you mean. He's scared to death something will happen, and you'll be there all by yourself."

"Well, I won't," I said. "You had a baby. I can, too."

"That is surely true," Whippy Bird added. "Besides, you've got me." She didn't have to say that. The surest thing in the world was that I could count on her. Then Whippy Bird came up with an idea that was so obvious I don't know why we never thought of it before. "You know, Effa Commander, we could live together. You've got two extra bedrooms in your house. Moon and I could move in, and we'd split the rent. That way we'd both save money and I'd be right there if you needed me."

It was the right solution, we all agreed after we talked it over. At first, though, Pink wasn't so sure. "If anything happened . . . ," he said.

"Oh, fooey. What's going to happen? I'll have two people to watch out for me instead of one. Whippy Bird and Moon."

Pink nodded. "That would relieve my mind, all right." I knew Pink had a vision of me lying dead on the bedroom floor, so I put my head on his shoulder and told him I'd rather have him there, but his country needed him, too. I was scared to have a baby without Pink, but I couldn't stand in the way of him fighting for our country.

Chick said, if Whippy Bird was staying with me, he could be sure she didn't step.

"What do you mean?" Whippy Bird said right back to him. "I'll have a live-in maid to tend Moon so I can be free as a bird."

"A dead bird, if I catch you," Chick said, and we all laughed because Whippy Bird never loved anybody as much as she loved Chick. She was the most loyal person I ever knew. Chick knew that, too.

The boys didn't give us time to think it over and back out. The very next day Pink and Chick joined the army. They figured if they signed up together, they might stay together so they could look out for each other. Raise hell together, you mean, Whippy Bird said. Die together, too, I thought, but I kept that to myself. Later on, of course, me and Whippy Bird talked about it. She'd thought that, too: if they didn't enlist together, there might be a chance of at least one of them coming home.

We were too excited then to talk about anybody getting killed though I knew in my heart I was as scared for Pink going to war as I was for me having a baby without him. The boys said they'd be back in a year, when the war was over. That's what they all said. All the men in Butte were joining up to fight the Germans and the Japs, and it got so you saw more military uniforms around town than hard hats. The depot was packed day and night with soldiers getting on trains and people saying good-bye. Every time we went out for dinner, there was somebody giving a toast to a boy who was leaving to fight for his country.

We had a big party for Pink and Chick at our house the night before they left. May Anna couldn't come, of course, but she sent a telegram saying: WITH PINK CHICK NARMY AMERICA SAFE STOP   SO IS BUTTE STOP   LOVEANDKISSES MAK. Buster and Toney came, of course, and I've never seen four grown men so drunk in my life. It's a wonder the boys got on the train in the morning.

Buster told me he and Toney ought to be going instead of Pink and Chick since they were single men. Later, the newspapers said Buster was a slacker. They wrote he pulled strings and got a deferment because he was the champion. Somebody in the United States Congress said there ought to be an investigation. What nobody ever knew was that Buster tried to enlist, but he was turned down for flat feet and being deaf in one ear, courtesy of Clay Tom Baker in the championship fight. He was so ashamed, he never told anybody but us.

Buster was down-at-the-mouth when Pink and Chick left. We knew he wanted to be on that train with them. He stood on the platform for a long time after the train pulled out, until Moon said, "Come on, Uncle Buster." Then he hit big old Buster with a little tiny Buster Midnight punch.

Buster said, "Hey, bub, don't you mess with me!" Then he bopped Moon on top of his head and picked him up and carried him to the car. Moon always did know how to cheer people up.

Nobody had the right to criticize Buster because he did everything he could for the boys in uniform. He gave exhibition matches to raise money for war relief, he taught boxing to the soldiers, and he went all over Europe to entertain the troops. Toney said some of the places Buster went were just as dangerous as the front lines. There was no doubt about it. Buster was as patriotic as Pink or Chick or me and Whippy Bird. Or Marion Street, who risked her life to entertain the troops at the battlefront.

With that easy pregnancy, I never thought anything could go wrong. I worked at Gamer's until my legs swelled up, then I quit and laid around the house getting fat. Whippy Bird wouldn't let me do any work. She sent me out to sit on the steps to watch Moon play while she cleaned the house. Other times I stretched out in a big chair reading magazines and listening to the radio. I could spend a whole day answering one of Pink's letters if I wanted to. The boys wrote us every single week from Camp Carson in Colorado, where they were stationed.

Whippy Bird made over her maternity clothes for me since she could sew. She's so short, they looked funny on me when I first tried them on, so she let down the hems and added ruffles. She even tried fixing all the meals, though I decided there was no reason for her to take on that responsibility, too. It gave me something to occupy my mind, and that was when I developed my special interest in cooking. When Whippy Bird came home at night I surprised her with a Hoover pudding or a hard-times cake, which was a good wartime dessert because it didn't use butter or sugar.

Whippy Bird worked as a typist at the Anaconda office while I watched Moon. I dressed him in his Hennessy's snowsuit every day so we could go for a walk. It was white with little ears on the hood,

and when he put it on he looked like a rabbit. We called him Moon
Bunny when he wore it. I bought him red mittens to go with it in
case Moon got lost in the snow. If we couldn't see him in that white
suit, we'd surely see those red mittens. We sent May Anna a picture
of Moon in the snowsuit, and she wrote back that his new name
should be Franklin Delano Rabbit. Whippy Bird always warned me
to be careful when I was out with Moon. She was afraid I'd fall down
on the ice and hurt the baby. "Hell, Whippy Bird. This baby is not
made of glass," I said. But maybe it was. Maybe it was.

The baby came early. We were sitting down to dinner when I told
Whippy Bird it was time. There weren't any little contractions, just
pushing pains that told me we better hurry. Whippy Bird was as cool
as could be. She told me to get my things while she ran Moon next
door and warmed up the Jackpot. It was snowing hard, a regular Butte
blizzard. Colder than hell, and snow coming down so fast you
couldn't see anything outside. But the Jackpot was as warm as toast.
That car always did have a good heater. Whippy Bird looked at the
storm coming down and said, "You want me to call a cab instead,
Effa Commander?"

No time, I told her. So she pointed the Jackpot toward the hospital, zipped in and out of the cars, ran a red light, and got us there
in fine shape. I said Whippy Bird should have signed up as an
ambulance driver during the war because she always got where she
was going.

And none too soon. The minute we arrived they rushed me into
the delivery room. The pains lasted only thirty minutes, then I was
holding that tiny girl in my arms. She was so pretty with her sprouts
of straw-colored hair like Pink's and her tiny pointed ears. Whippy

Bird said she had better cheekbones than the famous actress Marion Street.

If the baby was a girl, me and Pink decided to name her Gladys after his mother, who died when he was a boy. I was explaining this to Whippy Bird when she put her finger in the baby's tiny hand. The baby squeezed that finger so hard it left nail marks. Whippy Bird looked at the marks on her hand and the baby's little tongue going in and out of her mouth and said, "Why, Effa Commander, she's as sassy as a jaybird."

That's when the name hit me, just like the name Marion Street hit me and Whippy Bird that day we were helping out May Anna. "No," I said to Whippy Bird, "her name's not Gladys. It's Maybird. Her name's Maybird."

"Oh," Whippy Bird said. "Oh, Effa Commander." She hugged me, and I could see the tears in her eyes.

"My two best friends," I said.

"It's the prettiest name I ever heard," Whippy Bird said, and I had to agree.

"Do you think May Anna will mind?"

"Mind? She'll send her mink diapers."

When I woke up later, there was a big spray of gardenias in the ward that the other mothers thought came from Pink. When I saw them, though, I knew May Anna sent them. Whippy Bird didn't have to tell me the name on the card.

"I see you went home and called May Anna," I said. "Did you get Pink?"

"Pink!" Whippy Bird said. "Pink must be drunk under some table by now. Probably Chick's with him." She laughed. "I never heard a

man so happy when I called him. The first thing he asked about was
you. He didn't even ask was it a boy or a girl. He said how's Effa
Commander, and I could tell he was holding his breath. When I told
him you were all right, and he had a little girl, he started to cry. He
said you could name her anything you wanted to, and he didn't like
Gladys anyway.

I never liked Gladys either. I was afraid he'd say Maybird was a
silly name, but Whippy Bird said anybody who'd gone through life
with the name of Pink shouldn't be too critical.

After she got Pink, Whippy Bird tracked down May Anna at the
studio, where she told the telephone operator it was a family emergency, which it was, I guess, us being the only family May Anna had
left. Whippy Bird informed May Anna I wanted both of them to be
the godmother and that the baby was named half for her. May Anna
said she never was so honored in her life even though later on they
named airplanes and even an aircraft carrier after her.

While Whippy Bird was telling me about the phone calls, a delivery boy came over from Hennessy's with a present wrapped in white
paper with a pink bow that had a duck on it. Inside there was enough
tissue paper to last us through Christmas and wrapped in it was a bed
jacket. It was a whole lot of lace on a little bit of silk.

"May Anna," I said, then both me and Whippy Bird giggled.

"Do you suppose she remembers what winter's like in Butte?"
Whippy Bird asked.

"Or how cold houses are in Centerville?" But it was nice of her
and I put it on over my flannel nightgown.

Then Whippy Bird gave me her present. It was a Sunbonnet Sue
baby quilt she'd made by hand, not even using the sewing machine.

There were nine little Sues, and they all had embroidered faces. Whippy Bird said she had a feeling it would be a girl. But she made one with boys, too, just in case. What got me was when she did it, with me around all the time. "I'll make her one with Maybirds for her first birthday," Whippy Bird said when she saw how much I liked it.

Of course, there never was a first birthday, but at least we had that happy time to dream about it. Maybird wasn't more than three or four days old when the doctor said there was something wrong. He thought little Maybird's lungs hadn't developed enough, and she couldn't get air.

It wasn't right, I told Whippy Bird. I accepted the will of God when we lost that first baby because we didn't ever have a chance to love it. But I loved Maybird. Whippy Bird told me we should be grateful for whatever time we had with that precious child. She said it was better to have Maybird for just a few days than not to have her at all. Like she always did, Whippy Bird helped ease the pain.

Whippy Bird telegraphed May Anna to let her know Maybird wasn't going to live long. May Anna called the hospital and had me moved into a private room. She told Whippy Bird it wasn't fair to me to be around the other mothers. May Anna knew me and Pink would be too proud to let her pay, just like she was too proud to take money from Ma long ago, so she told Whippy Bird to say the hospital had the extra room available and moved me in for nothing. I didn't know May Anna paid the bill until much, much later.

It was the sorrow of my life that Pink never saw his little baby girl, never held her in his great big hand. He could have, she was that small. At the end, they let me hold the baby for her last minutes. The doctor brought her in to my bed, and Whippy Bird sat there next

to me with the nurse at the window. I'd forgotten about that nurse.
They were shorthanded because of the war, but she stayed with me
while Maybird Varscoe expired. The baby was breathing one minute
and not breathing the next. The nurse let me hold her a little while
longer, then she took her out of my arms like she was still a sweet
living thing and said, "God has taken her, Mrs. Varscoe."

Chick said he thought Pink would go crazy. Pink said he had to
be with me, but the army wouldn't let him come to the funeral. He
threatened to come anyway, but Chick told him he'd be in a jail
instead, and that wouldn't do me any good. Pink blamed himself
because he'd joined the army when he didn't have to. He thought
if he'd been there, he could have taken care of me, but nobody could
have done a better job than Whippy Bird. It wasn't meant to be.

We had a funeral with just family. Little Maybird was in the tiniest
coffin I ever saw, lined with pink silk. May Anna ordered it, and she
told Father Pig Face to light candles for Maybird though Whippy
Bird said it wasn't necessary. A baby as sweet as that would go straight
to heaven. Whippy Bird said the candles were for May Anna herself
since it was the closest she ever came to being a mother.

When I got home, I sat down in the rocking chair in the living
room. Moon crawled up in my lap and said, "I love you, Aunt Effa
Commander," and he went to sleep with me holding him. Whippy
Bird sharing Moon with me like that made it easier. Pink got over
it, too. When he found out I was all right, he said we'd have other
babies, though we never did.

May Anna never forgot. Every year on the day little Maybird died,
there was a notice in the paper under "In Memoriam." It read:
"Beloved Maybird. Sadly missed. MAK."

CHAPTER
12

When the boys left for Europe on the troop carrier, me and Whippy Bird remembered about that fight on the raft at the pond when we were kids. "Funny, isn't it? Buster and Pig Face were the toughest boys in the gang, and they're not going," Whippy Bird said. We didn't blame Buster, of course, but it did seem strange that the United States government thought Pig Face lighting candles was an "essential industry."

Maybe it was the praying that was essential. Me and Whippy Bird didn't need Pig Face for that, though. We did enough of it for Pink and Chick and every other soldier from Butte, Montana. There were other things we did, too, like saving bacon grease for the war effort and planting a victory garden. Moon collected newspapers in his little wagon and took them to the paper drive at school. It wasn't so bad when the boys were in camp. Then all we had to worry about was them getting into trouble from too many drunks. It was them being shipped out that really mattered to us.

They came home before that, though. We celebrated at the Pekin and at the Rocky Mountain where we ordered Shawn O's and bottles of red, but it wasn't the same. We knew the boys were going to war. Me and Pink were still in mourning, too. I took Pink to the cemetery to show him Maybird's grave the day before they left. We sat on the grass for a long time, just holding hands. I knew Pink was crying inside though he wasn't the kind to show it. Afterward we picked out a stone with a little lamb on it for her grave. I waited for him to come home so we could choose it together. Pink had to order the writing by himself, though, because I was too torn up to say Maybird's name out loud to a stranger. I sat on a bench with my arms wrapped around me trying not to cry while Pink finished up. The stone was installed after he left, and I cried when I saw that it read MAYBIRD EFFA VARSCOE. Since I didn't have a middle name, I never thought about giving our baby one. But Pink did, God bless him.

We didn't know where the boys had gone; the army wouldn't let them tell us. But we found out from May Anna. She saw them in North Africa at a USO show.

May Anna was one of the brightest stars in the Hollywood Sky by then, and one of Warner Bros.' biggest money-makers, too. Me and Whippy Bird thought she was getting a little long in the tooth to play gangster molls, but May Anna said Sing Sing didn't want to mess with a winning formula.

You surely could not argue about May Anna drawing them in. Every picture she made was a blockbuster. Millions of people went to see her getting killed or sitting around a cocktail lounge drinking martinis and or pushing gangsters down the elevator shaft.

We always knew what to expect in her movies because they were always the same. They started out with May Anna working in a nightclub, and they always included a scene where she walked down a dark street that was lit by a flashing neon sign. Then she had to run because somebody was after her. The audience would hear her high heels clicking on the street and the sound would get fainter and fainter as she disappeared in the fog. Sometimes she stood on top of a hill in the wind, wearing a white dress that blew up around her, but she would always be looking off to the Pacific Ocean and not notice. Then there were the bedrooms, which were always draped in satin, with a quilted satin headboard and satin sheets and white phones. May Anna never talked on anything but a white phone.

May Anna even had her own fan club with members from every state in the union, and it personally requested me and Whippy Bird to write an article about May Anna as a little girl. You bet we were proud! Lots of people knew May Anna in Butte, but May Anna's fan club turned to us when they needed a true picture. Hunter Harper listed that article in the back of his book, though he said it was folklore and not fact. A damn fool like that wouldn't know a true fact if you served it to him with syrup and butter, Whippy Bird said when she read that. If only we had stayed with our literary career after me and Whippy Bird wrote that piece, we would not have such a hard time writing about May Anna now.

We talked about the article for a long time and decided it wasn't necessary to mention that May Anna's mother never got married. We also decided to leave out Jackfish. Since they wanted us to tell about May Anna as a little girl, we skipped over the part about Venus Alley.

Me and Whippy Bird must have used up two of Moon's Big Chief tablets working on that article. It took us almost a month to finish. Then Whippy Bird took it down to the Anaconda office and typed it on her lunch hour. We thought it was real good. It started out:

The first time we saw May Anna Kovaks, our friend who became
the famous Marion Street, star of radio and motion picture
fame, she was standing at the edge of the Little Annie glory hole
looking like Merle Oberon in *Wuthering Heights,* and we saved
her from falling in.

Maybe the fan club didn't like us taking credit for saving May

Anna's life because it changed the story to say: "We always knew our

friend Marion Street would be a star." Then they took out the rest

of what we sent them and wrote a lot of other stuff they made up.

They left our names, though. We got ten free copies of the newsletter

where the story was printed so we mailed one to Pink and Chick. Pink

wrote back, asking how come we never told him we knew May Anna

would be a famous star. He said he'd put his money on Effa Com-

mander to be the world-famous beauty, but then Pink always did

flatter me.

May Anna was a major supporter of the war, which was why she

volunteered for the USO tours for the soldiers overseas. She said the

tours were organized like vaudeville shows—one singer, one come-

dian, one pretty girl, one famous athlete, and one singer. May Anna

was the pretty girl because she surely was not the singer. The come-

dian was the master of ceremonies, and May Anna wrote us he always

introduced her by announcing, "Why, look who's here! It's that

lovely actress of stage and screen, Miss Marion Street!" just like he

forgot she was part of the show and he'd been putting the make on

her for three weeks.

Whippy Bird said what stage was May Anna ever on, but I think

stage-and-screen is just a saying.

May Anna didn't do much except walk around in a bathing suit or a strapless sundress and look sexy and pout and tell dirty jokes. But she liked doing it. May Anna said she had a lot of respect for those boys in the service. She didn't think so much of the officers, who were always trying to get her to go to bed with them, though. May Anna said she didn't go to Europe to get laid on an army cot.

But May Anna liked being with the soldiers, and they knew it. She was in big demand because she made them laugh and took their minds off the war.

"Are any of you boys from my home town of Butte, Montana?" she always asked. Anybody who said yes got a kiss. She said she was surprised how many soldiers said they were from Butte.

It was when May Anna was strutting around a wobbly stage in Tunisia, sweating in the heat even though she was wearing a strapless dress and high-heeled sandals when she found Pink and Chick. Or they found her. "Hey, May Anna!" she heard somebody yell over the heads of the crowd. She said she almost fainted.

"Is there somebody here from Butte, Montana?"

Whippy Bird said she bet every soldier in the audience yelled, "I am!"

She heard her name called again, and saw, way at the back, a hand waving at her. "You there, come on down here!" she called. When she saw it was Pink, May Anna rushed to the edge of the stage and held out her arms and squealed, "Pink Varscoe! I can't believe it! You get right up here on this stage!"

Pink jumped up on the platform, and May Anna dragged him over to the microphone, where she hugged him and kissed him while the soldiers cheered. "This is Pink Varscoe from Butte, Montana. He married my best friend. Now, I'll bet Chick O'Reilly is out there, too.

Chick, where are you?" About five hundred men raised their hands, but Pink told her Chick was on duty. So May Anna looked down at a colonel sitting in the front row and told him, "You go get Chick O'Reilly! On the double, soldier!" Everybody laughed and clapped while the colonel's aide ran to get Chick.

While they waited for Chick, the comedian made a few cracks about May Anna having a soldier in every port. "Two in this port," she said as Chick ran up on the stage where May Anna hugged and kissed him, too. Then she introduced him, saying he was married to her other best friend. "You boys want to see something pretty, you ought to see the two girls these boys left at home. Real pinups, I'll tell you." Pink and Chick liked that a lot, especially the catcalls. Me and Whippy Bird thought it was nice of May Anna to say even though it wasn't true.

Pink wrote that being with May Anna was the best time they had in the army. He said seeing her was like being back at the Brown Jug. It pleased me to think she had brought a little bit of Butte to our husbands overseas. Later on, of course, me and Whippy Bird were especially glad that if we couldn't be there, they at least had time with May Anna. She stayed with them the whole day, even took them to the lunch the officers held for her. Pink said that some of the big shots wanted to meet her so much they pretended they were personally acquainted with him. Even after May Anna left, Pink and Chick got special treatment.

About a week after Pink's letter arrived, we got an official United States Army envelope. Inside was a picture of May Anna with her arms around Pink and Chick. She'd written across it: "A New Unholy Three Alliance. Love Marion Street (May Anna Kovaks)." We framed that picture and put it over the living room sofa because it was the last picture ever taken of Pink and Chick during their lifetimes.

In the meantime, me and Whippy Bird and Moon figured out a pretty good life for ourselves. I worked weekends at Gamer's in the kitchen where I did baking. It didn't pay as good as waitressing since sometimes I could make twenty-five dollars a day on tips. But I wanted to learn to cook so when Pink got back, he would come home to the best damn cook in Butte, Montana. Along with the baking, I had a job two nights a week at Gamer's as the hostess. Whippy Bird worked days as a professional typist at the Anaconda Company, and that way one of us was always at home if Moon needed us. Sometimes when there was a school vacation day, me and Moon took the Jackpot uptown and met Whippy Bird for lunch at the Creamery Cafe. Whippy Bird didn't have much time to eat, so me and Moon went in early and ordered. That way, only a minute after she came in, her lunch was sitting right there in front of her.

Moon liked that. We talked about what to order Whippy Bird, and we worried that her lunch might come before she did and get cold, but Whippy Bird always told Moon her lunch was just right. If the weather was nice, we walked Whippy Bird back to the Anaconda office, which was above Hennessy's. Then me and Moon would stand on the street until she came to the office window to wave good-bye. As a treat, every now and then, I took Moon to the movies in the afternoon, where he thought every one of the blond actresses he saw was May Anna. It wasn't such a bad way to spend the war, at least, until that morning in November.

I was fixing the peanut butter sandwiches for Moon's lunch when wouldn't you know it, I ran out of bread. "No need for you to go for it since I already put my coat on. I'll just run over to the Nickel for a loaf of Holsum before I go to work," Whippy Bird told me. "There's plenty of time."

So when I heard the doorbell a few minutes later, I smiled, thinking Whippy Bird forgot her key. Then I realized it wouldn't make any difference because we never locked the door. That's when I heard Moon open the door and say, "I can take it." In a minute, he came in with a telegram.

"Aunt May Anna?" Moon asked, handing it to me. There was a big grin on his face because every telegram he'd ever seen came from May Anna, and he knew me and Whippy Bird loved getting them.

"Why I expect so," I said, wiping my hands on my apron. "Me and you are going to read this now, and you can tell your mother what's in it when she comes back."

I ripped open the yellow envelope with my fingernail and read it through. Then I read it again, thinking there was a May Anna joke in there that I'd missed. Sometimes her jokes weren't too funny. Other times the telegraph office mixed up the words, and they didn't make sense, but when I read it the second time there wasn't any joke, and the words were in the right order. Then I looked hard at the envelope. It was addressed to Whippy Bird. Not to me and Whippy Bird. And the telegram said Chick was dead.

I sat there staring across the room with that yellow piece of paper in my hand, letting the message sink in. REGRET . . . STOP . . . DIED . . . STOP . . . KINDLY WIRE . . . STOP . . . DEEPEST SYMPATHY . . . STOP. I wondered if the man who sent it knew Chick personally and if he was hurting when he wrote the telegram. For a minute I felt sorry for him having to send Western Union messages like that. But I didn't think about him for long because it was Whippy Bird I cared about. What was I going to say to Whippy Bird? And Moon? I looked down at little Moon, who had his face turned up to me waiting to hear something funny to tell his mother.

"Oh, honey," I said, putting my arm around him.

"What's wrong, Aunt Effa Commander?"

I just shook my head and pulled him to me, trying to keep the tears from falling, hugging him while I tried to think how to tell Whippy Bird about her sorrow. I thought back to the last time Chick was home and how excited he was to see Whippy Bird. He didn't even wait for the train to stop. When he saw her, he jumped onto the platform and swung her up in the air. Then he picked up Moon and put him on his shoulder even though Moon was almost seven years old. They were the happiest family I ever saw. Tears came to my eyes when I saw them together that wonderful day, just like the tears I was fighting off that awful morning. That's when I decided to send Moon to the school before Whippy Bird came back. She would need her time alone before she explained to Moon.

"What's wrong?" I said, pulling myself together. "What's wrong is you're going to be late for second grade. You run along, and I'll bring your lunch up to school later." Moon looked surprised, but he did as he was told, putting on his little sweater and hurrying up the street. I leaned against the door and watched as he caught up with a friend in the next block, then the two of them squatted down on the sidewalk to look at something. I was glad he could have this day without knowing about Chick. I wished Whippy Bird could, too, and for a second I wondered what would have happened if the telegram had gone to the wrong address. Or if Moon and I hadn't been home to sign for it? But that wouldn't make Chick any less dead.

Not a minute after Moon disappeared around the corner, I saw Whippy Bird coming back in the opposite direction. She waved, holding up the grocery sack so I could see she'd gotten the bread. When I realized Chick would never see that pretty girl walking down the street again, wearing a smile on her face like she always did, I had to go inside to compose myself.

"I wish I'd taken our ration book," Whippy Bird chattered as she came through the door. "The Nickel had more sugar than I've seen since the war started." She handed me the bread. "I surely did take my time down there looking at it. I hope Moon won't be late for school."

"I sent him on already. I can take his lunch later."

"Oh, you don't have to do that, Effa Commander. I'll go by on my way to work and take the bus from there." When I didn't reply or even move to make Moon's sandwiches, Whippy Bird looked at me closely. "What's going on?" Then she saw the telegram in my hand. "Is that from May Anna?" But I could tell from her voice she knew it wasn't. I tried to answer her, but there was a lump in my throat like a chunk of ore so I just shook my head.

"Then it's not from May Anna?" she asked again.

"No," I said. "It's from the army." She looked at that piece of paper in my hand for the longest time.

"Chick or Pink?" she whispered at last.

"Chick. Honey, I'm so sorry. He's dead." I put out my arms, and she fell into them sobbing.

"Pink?" Whippy Bird asked, the tears still streaming down her face. That was just like Whippy Bird to think of me while her own heart was breaking.

"He's all right," I said, though I didn't know any such thing. I kept telling myself if he wasn't, there would have been two telegrams instead of one. I hoped Pink was with Chick in his final hour. I couldn't bear it if Chick died among strangers.

"Moon?" she asked. "Does Moon know?"

"No. We can tell him when he comes home." I remembered how Whippy Bird had helped me with my sorrow when Maybird died, letting me cry and cry until I was numb. Whippy Bird needed her cry now just like I did then. There would be time enough for poor little Moon later.

Whippy Bird held on to me, her head against my shoulder, crying until the tears wouldn't come any more. When she was quiet, I patted her on the back, just the way I had comforted little Maybird when I held her. "Do you want to read the telegram?" I asked at last. It was still wadded up in my hand. Whippy Bird wiped her eyes with her hands then took the paper and read it slowly. When she finished she handed the telegram back to me, and I straightened it and put it in the envelope.

Whippy Bird watched as I set it on the table, then gave a long sigh and took off her coat. It was bright green with a black velvet collar. Chick gave it to her for her thirty-first birthday, just before he went overseas. I got out a hanger but Whippy Bird shook her head. "Remember how surprised I was when Chick bought me this coat?" She blew her nose. "I wore it to the station when the boys left. Chick made me promise to wear it when he came back, even if it was the middle of July."

Whippy Bird folded her coat lengthwise with the sleeves inside, then folded it in half and in half again until it was the size of a pillow. She pressed the thick wool to her cheek then lay down on the sofa with the coat tucked under head and closed her eyes. I sat on the arm of the sofa smoothing her hair with my hand. When I thought she was asleep, I got up for a blanket.

"Don't go, Effa Commander," Whippy Bird said softly without opening her eyes.

"I'm right here." I sat down on the floor next to Whippy Bird.

"Green was Chick's favorite color," she said.

"That's because your eyes are green," I told her.

"Do you think he was in pain?"

I thought it over. "I hope not. The telegram said they'd send a letter. Pink will write, too, of course." That made me feel better because I knew Pink would tell Whippy Bird Chick died easy. Pink would never in this world let Whippy Bird know if Chick suffered.

"I hope he was close by."

"You know Pink was right there. Nothing could keep those two boys apart. Pink would give his life for Chick."

"I know." Whippy Bird said as she reached for my hand. "They've always been close."

"Just as thick as the Unholy Three," I told her.

Chick was buried overseas in a soldiers' cemetery, but we still held a service in Butte. May Anna wanted to come, but she was in the middle of a picture so Whippy Bird told her to stay where she was, that it meant more to her that she had been with Chick in North

Africa. Buster and Toney couldn't come either since Buster was training for a fight, but Toney called Whippy Bird and talked for thirty minutes long-distance, telling her if she needed anything at all, to let him know. He told me that, too, and was disappointed when I couldn't think of anything for him to take care of.

The telegram about Pink came exactly four weeks later, the very same day, a Wednesday. Moon was at school. The first thing I did this time was look at the name on the envelope. It was addressed to Mrs. P. M. Varscoe, and that told me what was inside. Nobody but me and Whippy Bird and the army knew there was a P. M. Varscoe. I closed the door and sat down in the rocker before I opened the envelope.

The words were the same as in the telegram about Chick, only there was Pink's name instead.

I knew we might lose one of the boys, but not both of them. When Chick was killed, I thought in my heart that meant Pink was safe. Now he was gone, too, and it wasn't fair, just like it wasn't fair to lose Maybird. But this time I didn't cry. I just sat there and rocked. I remembered how happy I was that day Pink gave me the rocker. I was pregnant for the first time, and he was always bringing surprises like toys for the baby or orchid corsages for me. Pink bought the rocker while I was at work, and when I came home, he was sitting in it with a big smile on his face. "Hi, Mom," he said when I came through the door. Then he pulled me down on his lap, and we rocked back and forth like that while I thought I surely was the luckiest girl in the world. I grieved for Pink and Maybird. Then I grieved for Chick again, and for me and Whippy Bird and Moon.

I don't know how long after that the phone rang. Somehow I got up out of the chair to answer it.

"Effa Commander. Were you outside? One of the girls here invited me and you and Moon for supper tonight. I thought it might be nice to get Moon out of the house, that is if you haven't started cooking." When I didn't answer, Whippy Bird said, "Effa Commander? Is something wrong?"

"It's Pink."

"Pink?"

"Killed."

"Oh, honey. I'll be right there."

So me and Whippy Bird clung to each other again, and when Moon came home from school, he cried with us.

"No Uncle Pink either?" he whispered to Whippy Bird.

She shook her head.

"No daddies," Moon said after he thought it over. "But you and Aunt Effa Commander can still be my mamas."

"I guess he's the man of the family now," I told Whippy Bird through my tears.

May Anna sent even more roses for Pink's service. When I talked to her on the telephone, she told me she knew Pink was with little Maybird. That was a comfort to hear, and it was exactly what Whippy Bird told me when she got home after my telegram came. Buster couldn't attend the service because he had a fight scheduled in Los Angeles, but Toney came, which surprised me. The two of them lived on the West Coast now, and Toney'd always been with Buster at his fights.

Afterward, when I stood in front of the church, shaking hands with the people who came to remember Pink, Toney gave both me and Whippy Bird a hug and said it wasn't right, two of his best friends being taken like that. He asked if he could do anything for me, but I said just him being there meant a lot.

"There's one thing," Toney said, looking everywhere but at us. "After Chick died . . . well, I bought that house you're renting. I wanted to make sure you had a place to live. I'm going to put it in both of your names just in case something happens to me. I'm only telling you about it now because I'm joining up tomorrow."

Me and Whippy Bird looked at him like he was crazy. "Why would you do a thing like that?" Whippy Bird asked him.

"It's my duty."

"To buy us a house?" I said. Even May Anna didn't buy us houses.

"Oh, that's nothing. Me and Buster have lots of money. It was Buster's idea anyway."

But it wasn't. Later on, when I thanked Buster for that generous thought, he told us he wished he could claim it, but he couldn't. He said Toney always did look out for Whippy Bird even if she never knew it. That made me and Whippy Bird think about Toney in a new way. He'd always been Buster's brother, Toney the hustler. Now we thought about him being a separate person, and a fine person, too.

Toney just laughed at me and Whippy Bird standing there, struck dumb. "It's worth it to see the look on your faces. Maybe I ought to buy a house for Moon, too." That's when he sounded more like the old Toney, who did things just for the hell of it.

Then Whippy Bird remembered Toney said he was joining up.

"You don't have to do that," she told him. "You can get out of it. We already lost Chick and Pink. We don't have to give every damn boy in Butte to the war."

Toney tried to explain, but I could see it wasn't easy for him. He was used to talking big. He wasn't used to saying what was in his heart. "It just isn't right," he said finally. "Chick and Pink gave their lives, and what am I doing? Sitting around throwing down the booze with May Anna's friends and getting on Buster to skip rope. I'm not so proud of myself. So I talked it over with Buster, and he agrees that me joining up is the right thing to do."

"Why, Toney, you've got a conscience!" I told him. He blushed, but he didn't deny it. The next day Toney joined the navy, and we didn't see him again until the end of the war.

We had our grief, me and Whippy Bird. I'd get home from work just after midnight and see Whippy Bird through the window, sitting in the rocker with her head in her hands, crying. She had to hold herself together during the day because of her job and because of Moon. It was hardest for her in the evenings, when I was at Gamer's, and Moon was in bed, and she was alone. When I came home and found her like that, I would fix us a bourbon and seven and put some records on the victrola. Then we'd talk about the days when we used to go to the Brown Jug before the war started and it was turned into a pig farm.

Sometimes, at three in the morning, Whippy Bird would hear me stirring and know I was having a hard time. So she'd bring in hot chocolate and marshmallows, and we'd sit there in our nightgowns, talking just the way we did when we were little girls spending the night together.

Whippy Bird was the only one who understood what I was going through because she was going through the same thing. Ditto for me. We helped each other with our sorrow. She even understood about my having a double loss. She had Moon at least. But I'd lost both Pink and my little girl, and there were times when I didn't care if I lived or died. That was when she told me how much Moon loved me and how she'd never be able to raise him without me.

When I was really blue, Whippy Bird told me I ought to think about a career in the restaurant business. That was hard to imagine because I never in my life wanted to be anything more than Pink's wife. I never thought about having a job after Pink came home. Now I could see that I would have to support myself for the rest of my life. "I should have been smart like May Anna and gone to Venus Alley when I had the chance," I said.

"What chance was that?" Whippy Bird asked, and I had to laugh because I surely was not cut out to be a hooker. Whippy Bird told me I had a talent for cooking just the way May Anna had a talent for other things, and I ought not to waste it. I told her May Anna was at the head of the line when they passed out talent, and I was at the tail end, stuck with the leftovers.

May Anna let us have our grief. She let us go through that awful winter. She'd lived through enough Butte winters to know how cold and depressing they were even if you didn't have sorrows. Maybe that was the reason she sent that silly little lace jacket when Maybird was born. There were weeks when the sun didn't come out at all, and the coal smoke hung over the town like a black cloud. It got so cold you thought you'd never get warm again. You couldn't walk more than a block without ducking into a store to get warmed up. We'd do a fine business selling pasties at Gamer's to people who came in just for a minute to get out of the cold. That fresh, crusty smell alone warmed them and they bought the hot pasties to put in their pockets to keep their hands from freezing.

One time it was so cold, I stopped in a florist shop and pretended I was going to buy flowers. It was steamy inside, and the windows were striped from drops of water that rolled down the panes. The smell of flowers was so sweet it made me think of the gardenias Mrs. Kovaks wore, but when I told Lottie Palagi, who ran the shop, I wanted a gardenia to take with me, she said it would freeze in the cold. She knew I wasn't there to buy flowers anyway and let me stay as long as I wanted. Lottie said she always stopped in Gamer's for the same reason.

After a cold spell like that, there were warm days with the sky so blue, it hurt your eyes. Those were the days we bundled Moon up and took him out on his sled. When we got home, his face was sunburned. Then just when we thought spring was surely coming, the weather turned again, and it was always worse than before.

After we went through that first winter without the boys, May Anna called us up long-distance and said she was sending us tickets on the North Coast Limited to come and visit her. Whippy Bird refused at first. "You can't do that, May Anna. You spent too much money on us already."

"God almighty, Whippy Bird, if you don't get out of Butte, you'll turn gray and old, just like the snow," she said.

"And most likely melt out in the spring," I added since Whippy Bird held the receiver so we could both hear.

"You, Effa Commander. Just wait until you see the flowers. You never saw anything in your life like the flowers in California."

We thanked her for the kindness but said no. Whippy Bird told her she wouldn't leave Moon, and I said I couldn't get off work. "You have to. You just have to," May Anna pleaded. "Won't you do it for me? I need you."

"What do you need us for, May Anna?" I asked.

She paused a minute then answered. "I need my friends. People out here, well, they don't really care about you. You can't trust them. With Toney gone and Buster away so much, I need somebody to talk to. Sometimes I get so lonely, I can't stand it."

Me and Whippy Bird knew about being lonely, so we talked it over and agreed it wasn't right to let May Anna down. We sent her a telegram saying UNHOLY THREE BACK IN BUSINESS SOON.

Two weeks later on the train to California, I asked Whippy Bird, "Do you think May Anna was acting when she said she needed us?"

"Sometimes you're a damn fool, Effa Commander," Whippy Bird replied.

CHAPTER
13

It didn't cost us one dime to go to California except for our meals in the diner, which I thought were overpriced. Working at a restaurant, I knew what food cost. The train had linen napkins and tablecloths and heavy silverware, though, so maybe their expenses were high. I ordered chicken loaf, which came with a nice ball of mashed potatoes that was dished up with an ice cream scoop, just like we did at Gamer's.

Sitting there in the diner over our coffee and lemon pie, we felt like queens looking out the windows at people sitting in their cars at the crossings. They always waved, and we waved right back. We liked to listen to the crossing signals as they got louder and louder, then faded away.

The club car was the best part—watching the world go by from an overstuffed chair and reading the magazines that we brought with us. We knew the magazines they sold on the train and even in the depot cost more than at regular newsstands, so we bought ours ahead of time. We also knew you didn't buy cigarettes from the porter because he expected a tip, so we brought along our own carton of Luckies. We sat there just as elegant as May Anna, smoking ciga-

rettes and ordering Manhattans and reading *The Saturday Evening
Post* and *Look*.

After our supper the second night, we went into the club car again,
where a man in a matching suit, the kind that comes with a coat, two
pairs of pants, and a reversible vest, bought us a nightcap and asked
where we were going.

"To the coast," Whippy Bird said, just like we went to California
every day. She could surely put on the dog when she wanted to.

"Live there?" he asked. He used a cigarette holder, and later me
and Whippy Bird bought one. President Roosevelt used one, too.

"No. We're visiting friends."

"LA?" he asked.

"Hollywood," she said, blowing smoke past him. That wasn't true.
May Anna lived in Beverly Hills, but it didn't sound as fine as
Hollywood. "Movie people."

He looked at her like he didn't believe her. "Joan Crawford or
Hedy Lamarr?" he asked. He thought he was a real card.

"Joan Crawford's not from Butte," I told him. "Hedy Lamarr isn't
even an American."

"Nobody's from Butte," he said. I surely didn't like him.

"Marion Street's from Butte," Whippy Bird said, but he only
laughed. She looked at me to say something, but I shook my head.
We never bragged about knowing May Anna, and I wouldn't start
now with a jerk like that.

"You're friends of Marion Street's then," he said. I could see Mr.
Matching Suit couldn't believe it.

"That's for us to know, and for you to find out," I told him, and me and Whippy Bird got up and went back to our compartment. May Anna, being the first-class movie star she was, didn't just send us ordinary train tickets. She sent us tickets for a private compartment that had its own bathroom, so we didn't have to wait in line in the ladies' with your ordinary train people.

We forgot we were put out at that man the minute we opened the door because there was a silver bucket with a big bottle of champagne in it waiting for us. "May Anna thinks of everything," Whippy Bird said. She took out the champagne while I opened the envelope.

"It's not from May Anna," I said. Whippy Bird stopped opening the bottle.

"Not that dumb man in the club car," she asked, putting the champagne back in the bucket. "I'm not drinking his champagne."

"Buster," I told her. "It says right here: 'Bottoms up to the Unholy Three. Love Buster.'"

So we drank a toast to Buster. Then we drank a toast to May Anna, and by the time we finished we drank a toast to the man in the club car. We drank ourselves to sleep, and when we woke up the next morning, we had arrived in the Land of Sunshine.

May Anna wrote us to get off the train at the Los Angeles depot and stand right by the car so her chauffeur could meet us. I never saw so many people in my life except when we stood outside the newspaper office during the Buster Midnight championship fight. I didn't know how anybody could spot us until, just like magic, a man in a gray uniform with a little hat and leather boots came right up and asked, "Mrs. O'Reilly and Mrs. Varscoe?" We knew right away he was a chauffeur because we'd seen them in the movies.

Me and Whippy Bird looked at him with our mouths open. We

knew May Anna made a lot of money, but it hit us when we saw that chauffeur that she wasn't just rich; she was loaded. "Mrs. O'Reilly?" he asked me.

"I'm Effa Commander. She's Whippy Bird."

"I'm Thomas. I'll take care of your luggage. Would you follow me, please? Miss Street's car is just outside." Just as he said that, the man with the two-pair-of-pants suit walked by, and his mouth fell open. Whippy Bird sent him a snooty glance that would have done May Anna proud in any of her movies. The chauffeur snapped his fingers, and before you knew it a porter had picked up our suitcases. He put them on a rack, and we followed the chauffeur down the track to the biggest limousine you ever saw.

It was white. A white Cadillac. White outside and white inside. In fact, everything May Anna owned was white. "May I fix you a drink before we start?" the chauffeur asked.

"At nine o'clock in the morning?" Whippy Bird asked. We could belt them down, all right, but not thirty minutes after breakfast.

"Very good," he said, and me and Whippy Bird had to be careful not to laugh and hurt his feelings.

"We'll be going directly to Miss Street's home. Beverly Hills," he said when we got going. "She's between films just now, so she'll be there. She doesn't like to meet people at the station." Thomas sounded English, but we learned everybody in Hollywood sounded English.

Me and Whippy Bird didn't know if you were supposed to talk to the chauffeur, but we did anyway. We asked him if it was true Alan Ladd was only five feet two, and did he know where Grauman's Chinese Theatre was, and could we visit the tar pits, and would he

take us by Hollywood and Vine. We said please call us Whippy Bird
and Effa Commander because we forgot he meant us when he said
Mrs. O'Reilly and Mrs. Varscoe. Whippy Bird said if he didn't, we'd
call him Tommy. He told us he was at our disposal the whole time
we were there, and he would give us a grand tour, but right now "Miss
Street would be most distressed if I didn't take you directly to her."

"You mean May Anna said she'd have your ass," Whippy Bird
said, and Thomas laughed. By the time we got to May Anna's house,
he didn't talk English anymore.

I guess you'd call it a house, though it looked more like a hospital.
No porches. No towers. Just long white brick walls, and bathroom
windows. There were lots of bushes trimmed in different shapes like
circles and upside-down ice cream cones, and we could see in the back
where there was a swimming pool and a lot of white lawn furniture.

"May Anna sure has it made with a dump like this," Whippy Bird
said, and Thomas laughed.

A lady with a white apron over a black dress and a little bit of
ribbon tied around her head came to the door. "Miss Street's expecting you," she announced.

Whippy Bird said, "I surely hope so."

There was a big white marble floor with a white iron staircase that
made half a circle to the second floor. It was covered with white
carpet. Everything in that room was white, and so was May Anna.
White slacks and blouse and platinum hair. The only thing that
wasn't white was her nail polish and her lipstick, which were bright
red. She looked like a cherry sundae. And she smelled even better
than Evening in Paris.

She was just coming down the stairs when we walked in, and later on Whippy Bird asked me did I suppose May Anna was waiting there for us so she could make her grand entrance. I said why would May Anna do that for us, so we decided it was just a coincidence. She came down those stairs just as smooth as rainwater sliding out of a barrel.

Maybe she did want to make a grand entrance, but by the time she got to the bottom, she was the old May Anna. "You darlings," she said, hugging us. "I'm so glad you're here. I didn't sleep a wink last night I was so excited!" You couldn't tell it by us because May Anna didn't have a line on her face or any black smudges under her eyes. She didn't look any older than when she worked Venus Alley.

"You don't weigh any more than Moon," I told her when we got through saying how good everybody looked even though me and Whippy Bird looked about like we'd been riding herd for a week in the Beartooth Mountains. I took out a Kleenex and rubbed May Anna's lipstick off Whippy Bird's face, then she did the same for me.

"I should of had you bring him," May Anna said.

"No, you shouldn't. In about five minutes your house wouldn't be white anymore," said Whippy Bird, though that wasn't true. Moon always minded just fine, though he did spill sometimes.

"How do you like it?" May Anna asked.

"Well, it looks like every window goes to a bathroom," I told her.

"That's glass block. People here use it everywhere. It lets in the light but not the view. You ought to use it in Butte."

If anybody else said that about Butte, we wouldn't have liked it, but May Anna was us, and we knew just what she meant.

"Come and see my bedroom," she said, and we went up the circle stairs and down a hall to a room that had a round satin bed.

"Where do you buy round sheets?" Whippy Bird asked.

"How do I know? I don't go shopping for sheets. That's the maid's job. I help out sometimes though. I make the bed myself every morning."

"That'll take a load off somebody," I told her.

There were mirrors everywhere. "Nell Nolan would love it," May Anna said. Well, who wouldn't except a fat lady or Eleanor Roosevelt. She had mirrors on all the walls, the doors, inside the closet, and even the ceiling. They were all over the bathroom, too, but I wouldn't care to see that much of myself in there.

Still, the bathroom was swell. It looked like the pictures of the Romans throwing an orgy that you see in the *National Geographic*. There was a marble tub and a separate shower where the water came out of a duck's mouth. A fish spit out the water in the sink.

"I wish my mama could have seen this," May Anna said.

"She'd be proud, all right," I said.

"And clean," Whippy Bird added. When we first met May Anna, the Kovakses didn't even have indoor plumbing.

Off the bathroom May Anna had what she called a wardrobe, which was a room the size of our house. It had closets for dresses and for shoes and for furs. There was an entire bureau for her stockings, too. Real nylon. The war could last ten years, and May Anna wouldn't have to show a bare leg.

She took us for a tour of the whole house. The rest of it was just like the bedroom, with lots of white and some stainless steel. Snazzy, like the front of the Jim Hill. She was like a little kid showing us her Christmas stocking, I told Whippy Bird later. Whippy Bird asked me when did May Anna ever have a Christmas stocking? There was a wall between the living room and dining room that was a fish tank with goldfish the size of dinner plates swimming around in it. "Hey, May Anna, I forgot you were a fish eater. There's enough here for a fish fry for you and Pig Face, and everybody else at Blessed Sacrament," Whippy Bird said, and we all laughed. May Anna's maid put her hand over her mouth in horror. Well, hell, me and Whippy Bird knew you didn't catch goldfish in your house and eat them for dinner. It was just a joke.

The room I liked best was the sun room, which was shaped like half a circle with windows all around and a white leather couch that ran along the wall. It looked like the world's biggest restaurant booth. I told Whippy Bird if May Anna ever got hard up she could put up a sign that said WORLD'S BIGGEST RESTAURANT BOOTH and charge admission. You could sit there and look out the windows—real windows, not glass blocks—and see the swimming pool with black designs May Anna called Greek fretwork painted in the bottom.

"May Anna," Whippy Bird said after she saw the house, "when you left Butte, I thought you were a damn fool. But now I think you have done all right for yourself. I think you may have gotten even richer than me and Effa Commander." May Anna laughed and snapped her fingers for the maid, who brought in a silver tray with three glasses and a bottle of champagne and cold toast, caviar, and chopped egg for a snack. That was when May Anna told us that caviar was just fish eggs.

A week later, we were sitting around May Anna's pool looking at the statues and playing down-the-hatch with fish eggs and Ditches (whiskey and water was what we were drinking in Butte in those days) when me and Whippy Bird decided this wasn't such a bad way to live after all. We'd never seen so many naked statues at one time—especially ones of men with all their parts.

"Hell, May Anna, if you've got so much money, why don't you buy these folks some clothes?" Whippy Bird asked. "Or if you get me the material, I'll make dresses for them myself."

"Even the men?" May Anna asked.

"They can't wear pants with their legs glued together like that. That's for sure. Maybe towels."

"No," May Anna said. "Not for all of them anyway. I kind of like that second one in. His business is the size of a sweet potato. It makes my men friends jealous."

May Anna was lying on a lounge chair in a white Catalina swimming suit that looked as if it would dissolve like Jell-O in water if she went in the pool. She didn't have to worry about that because nobody in Hollywood used swimming pools for swimming. They just stretched out next to them. Or when they got drunk, they jumped into the swimming pool with all their clothes on, May Anna said. She was rubbing suntan lotion on her legs. This was the first time we ever heard of suntan lotion. But why would we know about it? Nobody in Butte ever sat in the backyard in a bathing suit.

"Were you thinking of strapless dresses?" I asked Whippy Bird.

"Whatever May Anna wants. They're her statues."

"Maybe a variety. Like a fashion show," May Anna said. "That one in the middle. She ought to have a gabardine suit. Don't you think she looks like the world history teacher we had in Butte, Effa Commander?"

"Don't ask me. She doesn't have a head," I told her.

"Well, she stands like her then."

I studied the statue for a minute, but I couldn't see it. "She doesn't have any arms, either," I told her.

"May Anna, you ought to buy whole people," Whippy Bird told her.

"White dresses," I said. "To match everything else around here. May Anna, how come everything's white?"

"A decorator from Sing Sing did it. Besides, it's not all white since you got here." That was surely true.

Me and Whippy Bird gave a lot of thought to a present to bring May Anna. She already had about a hundred pictures of Moon, and we sent her candy from Gamer's on her birthday every year. May Anna said bring her some snow, so Moon filled up a jar with snow, but it melted into brown water. Just before we left, Whippy Bird came up with the right answer, as she always does.

We gave May Anna her present right after she showed us the house. It was wrapped in a big grocery sack and tied with a bunch of string. May Anna untied every single knot, even though she didn't save the string, then she slid the present out of the sack and laughed and laughed. It was the wood cutout of the jug from the Brown Jug. "I got married to Buster under that sign. This is a wedding present," she said. "How did you get it?"

"Stole it. What else?" Whippy Bird replied.

May Anna was so pleased, she took down a mirror in her living room and hung the sign in its place. It was dirty, because me and Whippy Bird never thought about dusting it off before we wrapped it, and May Anna got cobwebs on her slacks when she was hanging it up. She didn't mind. We all admired how fine that brown jug looked in May Anna's white house. It hung there for the rest of her life.

May Anna handed me the suntan lotion, but I shook my head because the sun never hurt me. "May Anna, isn't there anything to do around here?" I asked her, and we all laughed.

The truth was this was the first time we'd sat down in the week we'd been there. May Anna took us to the Brown Derby for lunch. It was a restaurant in a big brown hat where they charged too much. May Anna said people from Nebraska went there and mistook each other for movie stars. She was surely right because somebody asked me for my autograph, probably because I was wearing one of May Anna's hats, one with a veil that covered my face and made it hard to eat.

Mostly, though, May Anna sent us off in the Caddie by ourselves. She said if she was along, we'd never get to see anything because of the people asking for autographs, and that was surely true. Every time she was with us and we stopped, people gathered around May Anna and asked would she sign something personal in their autograph books. Or would she pose for a picture. They asked whether she was going to marry Clark Gable even though she'd never met him. Me and Whippy Bird had to stand there for about twenty minutes waiting for her to finish.

Me and Whippy Bird liked riding around in the Cadillac because people stared and tried to figure out who we were. Sometimes Whippy Bird waved her arm as she got out of the car and said, "No autographs. Please, no autographs."

The best thing we did in Hollywood was go to Warner Bros. with

May Anna and visit her trailer and even sit in the chair that said MARION STREET on the back. It wasn't so comfortable. I'd rather have overstuffed. Then we went into the cafeteria, which everyone calls the commissary, at Warner Bros., which everyone calls Sing Sing, which you already know. We saw all the famous people who were working there that day. We even saw Bette Davis's back. She was dressed in lace and jewels, only the jewels were glass. You could have fooled me. Whippy Bird says fooling you is no big trick, Effa Commander.

Everybody called everybody else darling, and so did May Anna. Anna Bates, who was once May Anna's roommate though she never became a star like May Anna, came by and said, "Darling, I'm so sorry . . ." but she didn't say what she was sorry about, and we didn't ask. May Anna introduced us as her best friends. "How quaint," she said. She must have liked us.

After she left, Whippy Bird said she didn't think Anna Bates was sincere. May Anna said sincerity in Hollywood was as hard to find as virginity in Venus Alley.

When John Garfield stopped by, May Anna introduced us and said we were friends of hers from Butte. Now we'd never cared much about John Garfield until he said, "Nice place, Butte. Nice mountains." So you can believe he was one of our favorites after that.

May Anna didn't pay much attention to him. She was watching a fat man in red pants make his way past the tables. When he reached ours, May Anna grabbed for his hand. "David!"

"Oh, hiya, honey."

May Anna was all keyed up, and me and Whippy Bird looked at each other wondering what was going on. "When I read the script for *Debutantes at War* I thought, oh, my God, the part of Esther was written just for me. I know it was," May Anna said, not letting go of his hand.

He wasn't what you'd call friendly. He looked down his nose and said, "Sorry, honey. It's an ingénue role." Then he pulled his hand away, leaving May Anna looking crushed. Then he noticed Whippy Bird's curls. "Are they real?" he asked.

"Are yours?" Whippy Bird asked, looking at his bald head.

"Son of a bitch," May Anna said when he left.

"Damn fool," Whippy Bird said. After she explained to me what *ingénue* meant, I asked why May Anna didn't play women her own age.

"How many movies have you seen with thirty-one-year-old heroines?" Whippy Bird replied.

I thought about that later while I sat next to May Anna's swimming pool, watching her slap on suntan lotion. Maybe it wasn't so easy being a famous movie star.

We heard the phone ring. Then the maid came out and announced it was May Anna's agent. She went inside, and we couldn't help but hear her. "The son of a bitch told me I was too old. Twenty-six is not too old!" Me and Whippy Bird looked at each other. "You tell him I can sing like a bird."

Me and Whippy Bird were still looking at each other when Whippy Bird said, "Is a chicken a bird?"

Then we heard May Anna say, "It's a good thing Sing Sing didn't produce *Snow White.* They'd of cast me as the old witch. Listen, I need that job. I need the smack. They're talking about not renewing my contract. You get the part for me or I'll find somebody who can."

"May Anna has troubles," Whippy Bird said.

"She doesn't live a life of ease like we thought," I replied.

We heard May Anna slam down the phone. A minute later she came out with a cigarette in her hand, flicking little bits of ash off her bathing suit.

"Why don't you retire, May Anna?" I asked her. "You've got plenty of money. You could sell this house and live any place in the world and never have to work again. You wouldn't have to go back to Butte. You must make more money than Franklin Delano Roosevelt."

"Franklin Delano Roosevelt doesn't pay rent. And he gets free limo service. I don't own this place, I rent it," she said. "And I owe for three months."

"Then why don't you move someplace you can afford?" Whippy Bird asked her.

"Ha!" May Anna said and stubbed out her cigarette on the table then threw the butt behind a statue. She lit another with a silver table lighter then took a long draw. "Nobody lives any place they can afford in this town. It's all appearance. You have to look successful. It's a rotten place, where everybody's always watching for signs you're on the skids." She picked bits of tobacco out of her porcelain teeth with the red nail of her little finger then sat down with her feet in the pool.

"The funny thing is, I didn't care about being an actress when I came here. I wanted to make money and be famous, be a movie star is what I mean. Now I want to be good. I've been taking acting lessons, and I think I'm getting better." She looked embarrassed when she said it, but she didn't need to. It's OK to brag to your best friends.

Whippy Bird sat down next to her by the pool and splashed her
feet in the water. "May Anna, we know you're better. People used
to go to see you because you're beautiful. Now they go to see you
because you're an actress." You might think that Whippy Bird said
that because she was May Anna's friend, but that's not so. Whippy
Bird is a good judge of acting. In the fifties, while we were watching
Medic, a doctor show on television, Whippy Bird saw an actor she
liked. She wrote him a letter of encouragement, maybe it was the first
fan letter of his career. He even wrote back to say thanks for your
support. That actor today is Dennis Hopper.

"Why don't you quit the movies and marry Buster?" I asked her.
For a minute, I was afraid I'd gone too far. Buster and May Anna
weren't any of my business. I didn't know what was going on between
them. We hadn't seen Buster in a long time. We hoped to see him
in California, but May Anna told us he had gone to New York for
a fight.

"Sometimes I wonder myself why I don't marry Buster. I guess it's
always in the back of my mind. I know that someday I will. But in
this town, marriages don't last very long. Everybody tries to get you
married. If you're married, they try to get you divorced. Besides, I've
been dating one or two other men."

The maid came back out and said May Anna's agent wanted her
again. While she was on the phone, Whippy Bird said, "Effa Commander, we have to stop spending May Anna's money."

"You mean the money she hasn't got," I said.

"We can stop taking the limo for one thing and find a street car,
and swear off these fish eggs."

"I should have brought along our gas ration coupons," I said.

May Anna was smiling when she came back. "I'm going to have a party on Saturday night. A farewell party for my two best friends from Butte, since they're going home on Sunday. My agent will bring David Veder. He's the producer of *Debutantes at War*. The one you met. I'll sing."

Me and Whippy Bird stared at May Anna. "Oh, I know. I sound like a dump truck. But I'll hire a loud band. David's hard of hearing anyway. Everyone will tell him I'm wonderful. Besides, I think having a party is a fine idea. You can meet everybody—and they can meet you."

Having a party is an easy thing to do in Hollywood. A secretary from the studio invited all the people, and May Anna's cook did all the work. I don't know why May Anna even had a cook because all she ate was dry toast and tuna fish out of a can. In fact, on the cook's day off, when I fixed pasties and apple pie, May Anna said it was the only decent meal she'd had since she left Butte, even though she didn't eat much of it. She said she had to be careful since the movie screen made you look fat.

Since me and Whippy Bird decided to help May Anna save money, Whippy Bird told the maid she would help clean the house, but the maid got mad and said the house was already clean. I told Cook—May Anna just called her Cook—I'd help her in the kitchen. She said she didn't need me, but after May Anna talked to her, she said she did.

I thought ham sandwiches with plenty of mustard would be nice or maybe egg and onion sandwiches, which was a favorite of Buster's.

But Cook said people liked little cream cheese sandwiches with the
crusts cut off. They didn't sound very good to me, but I guess people
who like fish eggs eat other damn fool things, too.

Whippy Bird said I ought to make something special for the party,
so I decided on Ginger Ale Salad, which is one of Whippy Bird's
favorites. Cook said I didn't have to go to all that trouble, but it's not
as much trouble as you might think. Besides, it was for May Anna,
wasn't it? Whippy Bird said it was the best thing at the party, but
she's always handing out the compliments. I will admit, though, that
when the party was over, the Ginger Ale Salad was gone but there
were plenty of cream cheese sandwiches left. The Ginger Ale Salad
only serves eight, though, and May Anna invited about a hundred
and fifty people. I was surely a dummy for not making more.

Now I'm going to tell you who ate my Ginger Ale Salad. Mr. Errol
Flynn, that's who. Me and Whippy Bird saw him standing there by
himself, and we dared each other to go up and say hello. We knew
the best way to break the ice would be to say could we have your
autograph. But after seeing how people were always after May Anna,
we thought if we asked for an autograph we would look like a pair
of amateurs instead of childhood friends of the famous star Marion
Street. We had to find another way to meet him, which Whippy Bird
did, as you might expect.

She marched right up to Mr. Flynn and said, "Hi, I'm Whippy
Bird, and this is Effa Commander."

"You mean there really is a Whippy Bird and an Effa Commander?" he asked, giving us his famous smile that you have seen
light up the screen. You can bet that made us feel fine to think May

Anna told people in Hollywood about us. Then he lifted his finger, and in about three seconds, there was a waiter with a tray of champagne glasses. He gave one to each of us.

When the waiter left, Mr. Flynn offered us a cigarette from a silver case. We said we didn't mind if we did. It hit me and Whippy Bird at the same time that we were in Hollywood, California, drinking champagne and having Errol Flynn light our cigarettes.

He asked if we were having a good time and even complimented us on our dresses, which was nice because May Anna bought them for us as a treat that morning. She said she wanted to show us off and didn't expect we'd packed our cocktail dresses.

So she sent us in the limo to a dress shop. We didn't want her to pay, but May Anna told us she got dresses for a discount because she was a movie star, and shops wanted her to wear their clothes as an advertisement. Me and Whippy Bird never figured out why that shop would want to sell dresses to May Anna's friends at a discount. Maybe they thought people in Butte would send them mail orders.

The clerk was waiting for us when we got there. I wanted the red dress that had sparkles all over it, but the clerk said the black one looked better, and Whippy Bird whispered that maybe May Anna had already ordered the black one for me. We thought since it didn't have sparkles, it might be cheaper, though we couldn't tell for sure because there weren't any price tags. We each got a strapless black dress. The clerk wrapped them up and put them in the limo for us. We didn't even have to carry the shopping bags.

That night, after we admired ourselves in the mirror, Whippy Bird said, "Maybe we are destined to be rich and famous."

"I'd rather have Pink," I said, starting to cry.

"The boys would be so proud of us dressed up like this," Whippy Bird said, and she began to cry, too.

We sat on the bed and cried until May Anna's maid knocked on the door to tell us the guests were ringing the door bell. I wiped my eyes and smiled at Whippy Bird and said, "The boys surely would not like those fish eggs."

"Chick would tell May Anna to let them hatch."

After Mr. Flynn told us how nice we looked, a waiter came by with a plate of cream cheese sandwiches, which we all turned down, and that's when Whippy Bird said to be sure and try the Ginger Ale Salad because I'd made it. Mr. Flynn said he surely would. I told him I would send him the recipe, which I did, and got a nice note back from his secretary saying Mr. Flynn asked her to write and thank me.

After he left, I told Whippy Bird to come with me to the powder room, which is what they call a bathroom that doesn't have a bathtub. That was so she could pull up my bra. Since I'm flat chested, my strapless bra kept slipping down, and every now and then Whippy Bird had to hike it up in the back. With all those skinny women at the party, the powder room surely was busy.

When we came out, we stood for a few minutes looking at all the movie stars. There was Ann Sheridan and Ida Lupino and Dennis Morgan and John Reide, who was English and had a little mustache. May Anna told us he was one of the other men she was dating, so we looked him over. He wasn't as handsome as Buster, and he was throwing down May Anna's booze, which we did not appreciate, knowing she was strapped. Me and Whippy Bird thought we'd say hello, but he turned away and snapped his fingers for a waiter. We forgot about him, though, when we saw David Veder. "There's the damn fool son of a bitch," I told Whippy Bird. He was off by himself in a corner looking like a pig with pink pig skin and a flat pig nose and no hair.

"Come on," Whippy Bird said. "We're going to help May Anna get that part." We marched right up to him, and Whippy Bird used the same line that had been so successful with Mr. Flynn. She said, "Hi, I'm Whippy Bird, and this is Effa Commander."

The son of a bitch looked at her like she was crazy. "Yeah?" he said. "What kind of bird is a Whippy Bird?"

Whippy Bird laughed and laughed just like she hadn't heard that line hundreds of times in her life already. "Why that's what Marion Street asked me the first time I met her in Butte, Montana," she said.

"Butte?" he said. "Butte, Montana?"

"That's our hometown," I said. "Marion Street's, too." We practiced saying Marion Street instead of May Anna. If she wanted people to think that was her name, we wouldn't give her away.

"My grandfather was from Butte. Moses Veder. He had a pushcart."

"That's a hell of a way to make a living. Especially in the winter," I told him.

"Yeah. That's what he said. Froze his feet once. Nice old guy. My father left because of the winters. Not my grandfather. He's buried there."

"We'll look for his grave," I said.

"What?"

"We'll put flowers on his grave."

"Why would you do that?"

"We take the Jackpot—that's our car—down to the cemetery every month. Me and Whippy Bird have three generations of family to visit there. Sometimes we have too many flowers, so we put them on the graves that don't have any. It's sad. People move away, and there isn't anybody to take care of their plots. Sometimes me and Moon—he's Whippy Bird's little boy—we walk around and look at the stones. Now he'll have a name to look for. Moon reads good." I didn't see any reason to tell him there were five cemeteries in Butte.

"So you're friends of Marion's from Butte?" he said, which was dumb because he already knew that. "She show you the studio?"

"We ate in the commissary," Whippy Bird said, but he didn't remember us. "You stopped by our table. Marion asked you about *Debutantes at War.*"

"Yeah, she sure wants that part. Must be pushing thirty- thirty-one."

"Twenty-six," we said together.

"Yeah? Ain't that something? So am I. I been twenty-six since 1910."

"She was always the prettiest girl at school," I said. "There wasn't anything she couldn't do. Act. Dance. And she sings like a bird."

"Yeah, I heard her sing." He looked at us so long that both me and Whippy Bird burst out laughing. We were mortified until he started laughing, too. "You girls are all right."

"If you ever come to Butte, we'll take you to the Rocky Mountain Cafe," Whippy Bird told him.

"Our treat," I added.

When a waiter came by, Mr. Veder put his glass on the tray and said he was leaving.

"But you can't leave before she sings. She's been taking lessons," Whippy Bird said.

"You ever heard of dubbing?" he asked us. "You tell Marion Street not everybody is lucky enough to have real friends."

He turned to walk away, then he stopped. "I doubt there's a stone," he said. "Any grave will do."

Me and Whippy Bird were glad he hadn't stayed to hear May Anna sing because Whippy Bird lied when she said May Anna was taking lessons. Even with the band playing as loud as it could, May Anna didn't sound like much. Still, everybody clapped and said, "That was so moving, darling," and "You've got yourself a real voice there." Whippy Bird said, "People sure tell a lot of lies around here."

"Like you," I said.

Of course, we never told May Anna about our conversation with Mr. Veder, and it was just as well. *Debutantes at War* was the worst movie she ever made. We didn't do a favor for either May Anna or Mr. Veder, though it did keep May Anna working for the next year.

After everybody left, May Anna said we were her good luck charms because Mr. Veder told her agent to call him in the morning.

"I guess he's not a son of a bitch anymore," I told Whippy Bird and May Anna.

"But he's still a damn fool," Whippy Bird said.

The next day, we took the train back to Butte. All across the miles me and Whippy Bird nudged each other, saying, "I saw Errol Flynn look down the front of your dress," and "Did I tell you Ann Sheridan ate your Ginger Ale Salad?" We had so many good things to remember being together as the Unholy Three again. Still, as much fun as we had, we knew May Anna wasn't a happy person, any more than she'd been happy in Butte.

"It looks like there's one thing that matters more to May Anna than anything else in this world, and that is being a movie star," Whippy Bird said. "She cares more about that than she cares even about Buster."

"That's a terrible thing to say."

Whippy Bird thought that over. "You're right, Effa Commander. I take it back. I was wrong."

But she wasn't.

CHAPTER
14

I was fixing Moon's Cheerios and Ovaltine when the telephone rang. I set the bowl down in front of him and patted the top of his head.

"Phone," Moon said, picking up his Charlie McCarthy spoon and digging in.

Whippy Bird didn't even let me get through the hello. "Effa Commander, have you seen the paper?" It was a silly question because we only read the paper of an evening so how would I have seen it? "No," I said. "I was just giving Moon—"

"Oh, of course, you haven't. That was a stupid thing to ask," Whippy Bird said. "Besides, you would have called me if you had. I was just hoping not to have to tell you."

"Tell me what?" The first thing that came into my mind was that Toney had been killed.

"It's Buster."

Buster wasn't in the war. That didn't make sense. I thought, Pull yourself together, Effa Commander, and let your mind catch up.

"Buster's in jail," she said.

"Jail?"

"For murder."

"Murder?" I asked. Moon stopped drinking his Ovaltine. "Who?"

"May Anna—" Then somebody interrupted Whippy Bird before she could finish what she was saying. As long as I live, I'll never forget the pain that went through me when she said Buster killed May Anna. It was like a hot poker sizzling through ice. I started to shake.

Moon jumped up from the table and grabbed my hand. "Telegram?" That poor boy. Once he thought a telegram meant happy times. But after he saw the telegrams about Pink and Chick, he knew they meant death, too. Looking at my face, he thought we had gotten another one. And looking at his, I could tell he was afraid. I wiped off his Ovaltine mustache with the hem of my apron then put my arm around him.

"Whippy Bird, what happened?" I yelled into the phone trying to get her back. Buster loved May Anna. He had been protecting her since she was five years old. He wouldn't hurt her. Never in his life. I wouldn't believe that Buster would murder May Anna. Not on purpose and not by accident, either. "Whippy Bird!" I yelled.

"Sorry, Effa Commander," she said. "It's right here in the *Standard.* I bought it on the street and had to call you as soon as I got to the office. I still have my coat on. The headline says: 'Butte Boxer Charged with Murder.' "

"Why would he kill May Anna?"

"Kill May Anna? He didn't kill May Anna! Buster wouldn't kill May Anna! It was at May Anna's house. He killed that John Reide. Remember him? May Anna had him on her string."

I heaved such a big sigh of relief I had to sit down on the kitchen chair we kept by the phone. "It's all right," I whispered to Moon. "Go finish your breakfast." He didn't move.

"Did Buster beat him up?" I asked Whippy Bird.

"He shot him."

"With a gun?"

"It's the best way to shoot people, Effa Commander."

"Buster never used a gun. Why would he do that? With fists like he's got he doesn't need a gun."

"It was May Anna's gun. It says right here that Buster and John Reide got into a fight at May Anna's house. They were struggling over the gun, and it went off," Whippy Bird said.

"That's not murder," I told her.

"Well, hell, Effa Commander, all I know is what's right here. It says: 'Murder charges were filed against the boxer.' That's Buster."

"What did May Anna say?"

"Nothing. The paper says she's in seclusion."

"Seclusion? What the hell is seclusion? Why isn't she there helping Buster?"

"How would I know. Maybe she's in jail. Maybe she and Buster had a fight. It doesn't say. Now what are we going to do?"

I knew what we were going to do. "Whippy Bird, I'll call May Anna. We have to get to the bottom of this."

When I hung up the phone, little Moon looked up at me with his head cocked to one side and said, "Troubles?"

He was such a smart little boy—already in third grade—and me and Whippy Bird always treated him like a man. "Like nobody's business," I told him.

"Did Uncle Buster shoot Aunt May Anna?" It hurt me just to look at Moon's sorry little face.

"No such a thing. Your Uncle Buster's fine, and Aunt May Anna's fine. Now you pick up Charlie McCarthy and eat those Cheerios before they get soggy."

Moon sat down at the table again, stirring his cereal around and listening while I placed a long-distance call to May Anna. Calling her was strange because we always wrote to her. She was the one who did the telephoning except for the time Whippy Bird called her about Maybird. We sent her telegrams when Pink and Chick died. I'd never called her long-distance before so it took me ten minutes to find where we'd written down her phone number.

Once the operator came on the line, I told her it was an emergency. Still, it took twenty minutes before I got a connection. Even at that, it wasn't May Anna. It was her maid.

"Hazel, where's May Anna?" I asked. I didn't want to pay for a long-distance phone call to talk to any maid.

"She's not taking calls," Hazel said.

"This is Effa Commander. You remember, me and Whippy Bird visited last year. Tell May Anna I'm on the phone."

"I'm sorry. She's asleep. We've had some trouble here."

"I know that. Why else would I be calling? How come she's in bed when Buster's in trouble?"

"The doctor gave her a sedative. She's exhausted. She can't talk now."

"Then you tell me what happened," I told the maid.

"I'm not allowed."

"That's crap." I looked to see if Moon heard, but his attention was all on Charlie McCarthy, pushing the cereal to the side of the bowl and mashing it up. "May Anna would want you to tell me."

There was a long pause while Hazel thought that over. Then she said, "I don't know anything. I wasn't here when it happened. None of us was. It was our day off. When we came in, they were taking away Mr. Reide's body, and the police had handcuffs on Mr. Midnight, and Miss Street was hysterical. She was hurt."

"Shot?" I was so mad at May Anna for not calling, I hadn't thought about her not being all right.

"No. It looked like she was beat up. You won't tell anybody I said that, will you? We don't want the fan magazines to know. Louella Parsons called here three times already. And that other one with the ugly hats, she yelled at me. You won't talk to them, will you?"

No I wouldn't, I told her. I was glad May Anna had Hazel to protect her, but she didn't have to protect her from me and Whippy Bird. "I'm May Anna's friend, remember? Is she all right?"

"I think so. Mostly, she just acted crazy. I like Buster Midnight. I hope nothing happens to him." She sniffed. I told her not to worry, that it most likely was an accident. Buster wouldn't hurt anybody outside of a boxing ring, I told her, though I knew that wasn't true. He would have killed Pig Face if he'd had the chance. Then I wondered what if he felt that way about Mr. Reide? After all, May Anna went out with him on dates. Maybe Buster was jealous. I tried to think was Buster jealous. He never seemed to be jealous of May Anna's johns when she worked in Venus Alley. "You tell May Anna to call Effa Commander in Butte, Montana, when she wakes up," I told the maid and hung up.

I sat by the phone all day so I could answer it on the first ring. It was always Whippy Bird on the other end, though, asking if May Anna had telephoned. May Anna didn't call until late in the afternoon. Her voice was so quiet and sad, you wouldn't have known it was May Anna. "Oh, Effa Commander. I wish you were here."

"Are you all right, May Anna?"

"He beat me up. That's not right. Even when I was a hooker, I never got beat up."

"Buster beat you up?" I asked. "Buster wouldn't beat you up," I added, answering my own question.

"No, of course not. It was John. He was drunk. He slapped me. He tried to take advantage of me," May Anna said, which was some statement because May Anna once earned her living letting men take advantage of her. Still, just because she used to work in a cathouse didn't mean she had to sleep with anybody who wanted her, no matter how famous he was. "Then Buster . . . showed up," May Anna continued. "I didn't even know he was there. I forgot he has a key. He came in and heard all the noise, and"—May Anna had to stop for a minute to blow her nose—"he shot John." Then she covered up the telephone receiver with her hand and said something to someone I couldn't hear. I knew she wasn't alone.

"May Anna!" I yelled into the phone. "The paper said it was your gun. Why did Buster get your gun? Why didn't he just pop that man?"

"Oh, I didn't tell you. When John hit me, I got out my revolver and told him I'd shoot him if he didn't leave. He laughed and said I wouldn't do it. He was right. I wouldn't have shot him. I'd never shoot anybody. You know that, don't you, Effa Commander? Then when Buster came in, John took the gun away from me and pointed it at Buster." Her voice faded away, then came back. "Buster grabbed his arm, and they fought, and the gun went off. Buster didn't mean to do anything. It was an accident." May Anna sounded far away, but maybe that was the connection. You didn't get good phone connections back then like you do now.

"Are you all right now, May Anna?"

"I think so. The doctor gave me something. My face is bruised, but I think I can cover it with makeup."

"Maybe you shouldn't," I told her. "If people see you looking beat up, they'll know Buster was defending you."

"Oh, but I couldn't let anybody see me like this. I look so awful."

"May Anna, you listen to me. You're still hysterical. Buster's in jail, and you have to get him out. Who the hell cares what you look like," I told her. There was a long silence, and I thought we'd been cut off. "Hello? Hello?" I yelled.

"Effa Commander, it's going to be all right, isn't it?" May Anna said at last.

Maybe I'd been too hard on her. "I think so, honey. It sounds like self-defense to me," I said. "I wish Toney was here. He'd know what to do." He wasn't though. He was fighting overseas. So I had to step in. "Does Buster have a lawyer?"

"The studio got him one. I didn't know who else to call. They're used to dealing with scandals. They'll know how to hush this up."

"Hush it up?" I asked. "Hush it up? What's there to hush up?"

"Oh, you know what it could do to my career."

That didn't make any sense to me. This wasn't about May Anna's career. It was about getting Buster out of jail, but what did I know?

"Do you think there'll be a trial?" May Anna asked.

"Don't ask me," I said.

"I'll be the best witness there ever was. I'll wear black and cry, and they'll never find Buster guilty. Never."

May Anna was only partly right. There was a trial, and she cried, and she wore black. But they found Buster guilty anyway. The whole thing went on for a long time, and the papers were filled with it every day. Walter Winchell wrote about it, and Louella Parsons had it in her column. She always called May Anna "Poor Marion Street" like "poor" was her first name. It seemed for six months you couldn't open the paper without reading about the Buster Midnight–John Reide–Marion Street Hollywood Love Triangle Murder, which is what they called it. Or the Tinsel Town Crime of Passion.

As it turned out there was more to it than May Anna told me over the phone that day. She'd been going out with John Reide for a long time, even before me and Whippy Bird went to Hollywood. He even wanted to marry her, though, of course, May Anna never said yes. In fact, she was tired of him because he made a drunken nuisance of himself. Sometimes he yelled at her, calling her whore and bitch so loud that the neighbors threatened to call the police, and May Anna had to let him in the house until he shut up.

Of course, none of that was ever in the newspapers. If you're a Hollywood celebrity, you can do all kinds of things and get away with it. You can have loud parties and drive drunk and sleep with anybody you want to and still play the Virgin Mary in the movies, May Anna told us. And if you die, the reporters out there turn you into a saint. But if they make up their minds they don't like you, they print everything you ever did in your whole life. Or make it up.

That's what happened to Buster. The newspapers wrote that Buster was jealous of John Reide. They said Mr. Reide and May Anna were having a quiet dinner at her house, a nice romantic candlelight dinner that May Anna cooked herself, which we knew was a lie unless Mr. Reide thought pork and beans or tuna from a can was a romantic dinner. Then they wrote that Buster broke into the house. May Anna ran to get her gun, they said, then Buster grabbed it and shot Mr. Reide.

Of course, if that was all true, why would they troop up to May Anna's bedroom so Buster could shoot Mr. Reide there?

May Anna said the papers had it all wrong. She held a press conference to say that Buster was only protecting her since Mr. Reide had beat her up. Nobody except me and Whippy Bird believed her, though. That's because the papers printed that Buster was a slacker.

Now, we knew Buster was not a war slacker, and so do you. Nobody else did though since even after the murder, he never told anyone he'd been turned down by the armed services for physical reasons. So the papers never printed the truth about why he wasn't in the war. If Toney had been around, he would have made Buster speak up or maybe leaked the story to the press, as the fellow says. But the navy wouldn't let Toney out to help Buster. May Anna tried hard, but she couldn't convince Buster to tell people why he wasn't in the war. So people just naturally assumed that story about Buster was true.

What made it worse was the papers printed that John Reide was said to be an English war hero and a friend of Princess Elizabeth. They said he was a British pilot who got shot down and injured and couldn't fight anymore even though he tried and tried to join the army in England. That was why he came to America, the papers said.

He didn't come here to get in the movies. He wanted to join the United States Army, and they wouldn't take him because of his war wounds.

May Anna told us that was hogwash. Mr. Reide was a crummy English actor who got hurt in a bombing raid when he fell off a bar stool. He came to America so he wouldn't have to fight in the war because he was chicken. Not only that, she said he was also a queer, so he wouldn't dare join the United States Army either.

Whippy Bird said how come he wanted to marry May Anna and how come he tried to take advantage of her if he was a fruit. May Anna told us sometimes they were like that. Besides, he had to keep up appearances since there were rumors going around about him. If his fans found out he was a homo, he'd be dead in that town, May Anna said. She told us that some of your most famous leading men were homosexuals, and they were even married and had kids. When Whippy Bird said that was a rotten thing to do to your wife, May Anna explained that some of the wives were homosexuals, too, so it didn't matter. Whippy Bird told her two wrongs don't make a right.

Mr. Reide beat up May Anna because she told him she wouldn't go out with him anymore. She threatened to tell people about him if he didn't leave her alone. May Anna couldn't tell all that to the reporters, because how would it look if she was dating a homosexual? Besides, people might not believe her, and feel sorry for John Reide instead of Buster.

By the time the trial date was set, May Anna wasn't talking to the reporters any longer, so they interviewed other people about her, like the preacher who marched back and forth in front of the courthouse with a sign saying THE WAGES OF SIN IS DEATH. When I told Whippy

Bird about him, she said she thought the wages of sin in Hollywood was a big white house with naked statues.

The odd thing was with all that snooping around, those reporters never found out May Anna had been a hooker. One newspaper man called me and Whippy Bird, though, and asked wasn't it true that May Anna and Buster had a baby named Moon that we were raising. He'd found out May Anna had pictures of a little boy all over her house.

Whippy Bird wasn't mad. She just laughed and laughed and invited the man to come to Butte and she'd show him Moon's birth certificate. Besides, she said, May Anna was already in Hollywood when Moon was born.

Just before the trial started, May Anna called and begged us to come and stay with her. She was hysterical because studio people were telling her different things she should do and she didn't know which way to turn. Unless we were with her, she said, she couldn't get through the trial.

Whippy Bird asked, but the Anaconda Company wouldn't let her take any vacation, so I had to go by myself. May Anna said she'd send me a ticket, but I told her no. I owed Buster plenty, and I would spend my own money.

I took a Pullman instead of getting a private room, and I couldn't help thinking that I surely had a much better time when me and Whippy Bird went to see May Anna than I had by myself. I didn't even enjoy the food, though I ordered meat loaf, which I usually like, and a baked potato, which came in a separate dish with a little flag on it. I couldn't eat it, which is a switch for me. Even when Pink died, I kept my good appetite.

Thomas, the chauffeur, met me again, but we didn't talk about any Grauman's Chinese Theatre or tar pits. I wanted to sit up front with him so he could tell me what was going on, but he said that wasn't proper, that May Anna wouldn't like it. So I sat in the back and leaned forward, but he still didn't say much that me and Whippy Bird didn't know already. He told me May Anna was still upset, which I knew, and that they were all surprised that the newspapers were against Buster, which we knew, too. Thomas called Mr. Reide a faggot worm because whenever he borrowed the limo, he never tipped.

That was the first time I knew you were supposed to tip the limo driver, and I surely was embarrassed. I said me and Whippy Bird were a pair of nincompoops from Butte, Montana, and I owed him money. He told me it was a pure pleasure to drive us around, and he didn't want any tip from us because he had such a nice time. He must have meant it because when he drove me back to the depot after the trial, I tried to give him some money, but he told me to save it to buy a drink in the club car.

He warned me not to talk to any of the reporters, who were always hanging around May Anna's house, but I knew about dealing with them from the days of Buster's training camp. Two of them were standing in May Anna's driveway. "No comment," I said when I got out of the car before they could even ask me a question. Thomas said I didn't have to worry about them since they were guards the studio sent over.

"I'm glad you're here, Effa Commander," he said when he carried my suitcases up to the front door. "So many people are telling Miss

Street what to do, it's good she's got somebody around who loves her."

"And Buster, too," I said. Like Whippy Bird said, I wasn't out there just to help out May Anna.

When I walked into the living room, I saw right off May Anna surely did not look like the Queen of the Silver Screen. Her eyes were red. There were lines on her face that I hadn't seen when we were there the year before, and she'd lost weight. She must have weighed less than ninety pounds. She was nervous, too, pacing back and forth, putting her cigarette down then forgetting it was there and lighting another. But I didn't say you look like hell, May Anna. Instead, I hugged her and said that since Whippy Bird was right with us in spirit, we were the Unholy Three together again.

I recognized May Anna's agent, whose name was Eddie Baum. She introduced me to another man named Jim McDonald, who was a press agent from Sing Sing. They were discussing her testimony, and when I asked where's the lawyer, the agent said he didn't want to take up my time when he was sure I was tired and wanted to rest up after my trip. May Anna said she felt better with me in the room, though, and since I didn't come all the way from Butte to rest up, I stayed. So they ignored me.

"Now that we've settled the makeup, wardrobe is making up a black suit. Fitted waist but not cut too low," Jim, the press agent said.

"Don't you think a dress would be better, maybe a little Peter Pan collar? You know, innocence?" Eddie asked. He patted May Anna's hand until she put it in her lap.

"Nope. Confusing. She'll never play Joan of Arc after this. But if

Marion pulls it off, she's got a shot at *The Sin of Rachel Babcock*.
She needs it after that *Debutantes at War* bomb. We don't want her
to look like she's in training for the Virgin Mary."

"Do you really think I have a chance?" May Anna asked.

"A good one, baby, if you handle yourself right," Eddie told her.
He moved to sit on the arm of her chair then leaned against her
shoulder.

May Anna nodded. "What about a hat? Maybe a little black one
with a veil." May Anna stood up, walked back and forth for a minute,
then sat down in another chair.

"No veil. We don't want to cover the face. The cameras'll zero in
on it. A picture hat's too flashy. I'll talk to wardrobe. A bow, maybe.
You could start a fashion trend," Jim told her.

They talked about her shoes and her purse and even whether her
hanky ought to have lace or not—they decided lace.

"You know, you're dead in the water if you say Reide was queer,
don't you?" Jim told her. "You hear me? The man's a fallen idol. You
say he's queer, and they'll tear you apart. Remember, fallen idol."

May Anna nodded.

"But watch the tough act. You want to generate a little sympathy
for yourself, too," Eddie added. "It means scratch, kiddo. The Lux
endorsement is riding on this. You tie yourself in too close to Buster,
and you'll lose it."

"Buster saved her life," I said. I knew they didn't want me to
interrupt, but I had to. They were talking about the wrong things.

"What the hell does that have to do with anything?" Eddie said.
"We are talking about saving a major screen talent here."

"And you're not talking about saving Buster," I said.

"Your friend is already dead. Nothing'll save his career. You want Marion here to go down right along with him? You're nuts."

I looked at May Anna, but she was lighting another cigarette. Nobody said anything. Finally May Anna looked up and met my eyes and shrugged. "I'm so tired, Effa Commander," she said. "That's why I wanted you to come. I need a friend."

"It looks like Buster needs a friend, too."

"I'm trying to be one, but I don't know what else I can do."

I tried, but just then I didn't feel as sorry for her as I did for Buster. After all, Buster saved May Anna's life. It didn't look like May Anna was going to return the favor. "What you have to do," I said while the two men glared at me, "what you have to do is tell the truth."

"Oh, truth," said Jim after he gave a silly little laugh. "What's truth? There's truth and there's truth. The truth is your friend Buster did the world a favor by rubbing out that scum John Reide, who was a queer and a drunk and a cocaine head. I'm sorry Buster's in the soup for croaking him. Nice guy, too. But the truth is, Marion Street will never star in another picture if she squawks because she'll be tarred with the same brush. Ever heard of Fatty Arbuckle? You want to put the kibosh on your chum's career?"

"The way I see it, I got two chums. I'm trying to keep one of them out of jail. What you're saying is a God-damned bunch of hooey."

"Says who? Are you a big lawyer who knows all about defending a murderer?" Jim sneered. I wished in the worst way that Whippy Bird was there. She'd know what to say.

"Now why don't you write some picture postcards or go bowling?" Jim said. "You want to go on a tour of the studio? We can arrange it."

"I don't want to do anything but stay with May Anna," I told him.

I looked at May Anna. Her face was so sad. Then I noticed the bottle of gin and the empty glass beside it on the table. May Anna filled it and swallowed the gin in two gulps then filled up the glass again. I remembered once Whippy Bird said Hollywood was a lush place and so were the people, and I wondered if May Anna was one of them now. "Please, Effa Commander," May Anna said.

I didn't know what she was saying please about, but it seemed to me they weren't listening to anything I said, and I was making May Anna more upset. Besides, Buster had a lawyer. He surely knew what to do without my help, so I backed off. "I think I'll walk down to the drugstore and get a soda."

"Take the limo. You can't walk," May Anna said. So Thomas took me all the way over to the drugstore where Lana Turner was discovered. I treated him to a Barney Google, which you make with marshmallow syrup poured over a coke. I had a black-and-white, which is a chocolate soda with vanilla ice cream. I figured since he'd been driving me around, I could pay, and he said thanks to you, Effa Commander.

I didn't say anything more to May Anna about her testimony. What good would it do anyway? Instead, I tried to calm her down by acting like we were kids again. At night we pretended it was a regular slumber party like me and Whippy Bird and May Anna had in Butte, only this time we didn't sleep three in a bed. I put on my nightgown and May Anna got into her silk pajamas. Then I brushed her hair, and she set mine in pincurls. After that, we put on nail polish, only it wasn't Cutex but some expensive kind that was made

up in a special color just for May Anna. And all the time we drank
bourbon and ate chocolate popcorn that I made.

I didn't spend all my time with May Anna. Half my reason for
being there was to help Buster, so I took the limo down to the jail
once to see him. The guard said he couldn't have any more visitors.
I said Buster was family, but the policeman said that's what they all
say. So I didn't see Buster until the trial. I sat right in front of him.
He didn't know I was staying at May Anna's, and when he spotted
me, he broke into the biggest grin you ever saw. I was glad I was there
because it looked to me like I was Buster's only friend.

The trial just went on and on and was the most boring thing I ever
went to even though I tried hard to follow it so I could write it up
every night for Whippy Bird. The highlight was May Anna's testimony. The day she took the stand was the only time she came to
court because the studio made her stay away. Besides, there were
crowds that gathered around her when she went out in public, and
she couldn't stand that. I was with her in the limo on the trip to the
courthouse that day. May Anna was as nervous as she was when she
went to the charity tea party on West Broadway. The minute we got
out of the car, flashbulbs popped in our faces just like at a movie
premiere. Whippy Bird saved me a picture from the *Montana Standard* that showed May Anna with me behind her, only it didn't give
my name or say I was from Butte.

May Anna did just what she said she would. She cried little dainty
tears and dabbed at her eyes with the lace hanky. She told the jury
John Reide beat her up so she ran to her bedroom to get her gun.
Then Buster came in and fought with Mr. Reide, and the gun went

off. But she didn't say Mr. Reide was a queer and a drug user. Of course, it wasn't May Anna's fault because the studio ordered her not to.

The prosecutor called May Anna a liar who was trying to protect Buster because she was afraid of him. Then he called Buster a jealous maniac and a drunk who gunned down a true English war hero on purpose.

The jury was out for a day. When they came back, they said Buster was guilty of involuntary manslaughter. Later one of the reporters interviewed a juror who said Buster hurt his case by not testifying. He said if May Anna was telling the truth, why wasn't she there every day, backing up her man?

Of course, Buster took it like the champ he always was. He didn't complain. Buster never in his life said he'd been robbed in a fight, and he didn't say he'd been robbed in a court of law. Before they took him away, he hugged me and said not to worry. I told him May Anna should have been there, but he said it didn't matter. "I did the right thing. I know I did the right thing." He hugged me again even though the policeman was pulling at him. "You and Whippy Bird are the best friends May Anna ever had. She needs you now that I can't be here. She's got to have somebody watch out over her. Don't blame her. She did the best she could." I told Whippy Bird he worried more about May Anna than he did about going off to prison. Whippy Bird said it wasn't the first time in his life Buster was a sap about May Anna.

After they hauled Buster off I got in the limo and went right to May Anna's to tell her Buster was found guilty, but she already knew.

In fact, she was in the middle of a press conference in her living room. She was wearing white again, and I heard her say that Buster was her dear friend who was only defending her virtue, whatever that was. She also said John Reide was a poor misguided man, and she would miss him. I didn't want to hear any more of that, so I went upstairs to May Anna's bedroom and called Whippy Bird. Not collect. I figured May Anna could pay for it now.

"How do you feel about May Anna?" Whippy Bird asked after I told her the whole story.

"I don't know. She testified in Buster's favor, but she could have done more. A lot more. But Buster says she needs us."

Whippy Bird thought that over and said, "Buster's right. You know, Effa Commander, we're May Anna's best friends. That means we have to stick by her even when she does something that stinks. She's not as strong as us. She could crack. If Buster doesn't blame her, then it's not our business to blame her either."

I felt like somebody was on either side of me, pulling, like I was going to be split down the middle. It hurt to think that May Anna had not been a true friend to Buster like he always was to her. Then I thought maybe she did the best she could. I decided Whippy Bird was right, like she always is. This was between Buster and May Anna. Our job was to be May Anna's friend. Being a friend meant helping the other person even when she was wrong. That's why I told May Anna her testimony kept Buster from being found guilty of a worse charge, like voluntary manslaughter. Or first degree.

I could see that May Anna thought over what I said but I don't know if she believed it.

Buster got two years. The newspapers printed headlines about him for a few days. I remember one in particular that said: MIDNIGHT FOR BUTTE BOXER BUSTER. Then everybody forgot about him.

I wrote Buster every week when he was in prison, and though he never wrote back, I knew he got the letters. Toney, who'd been writing Whippy Bird since the day he joined the navy, said my letters cheered up Buster more than anything. May Anna wrote him, too. She said she'd wait for him. She wanted to pay for the lawyer, but Buster said no. He also told her not to write him anymore. He explained that when he got out, he wouldn't be seeing her again. They ought to forget each other. Being together wouldn't be any good for either of their careers. Whippy Bird said what career did Buster have left anymore, anyway.

The trial was the beginning of what they called May Anna's mature career and of the series of movies that made her rank as one of the Ten Best Motion Picture Actresses of All Time. The reviewers said May Anna had an air of tragedy about her. "Baptism by fire," one of them wrote. Of course, you know May Anna won the Academy Award for *The Sin of Rachel Babcock*. She was nominated twice after that. She never had to play a gangster moll again or anything else she didn't want to. From then until the end of her life, May Anna wrote her own ticket in that town.

Life changed after the trial for me and Whippy Bird, too. When the war ended, Toney came home minus one leg and with a purple heart. Three days later he and Whippy Bird got married.

CHAPTER

15

Buster served his two years and was released not long after Whippy Bird and Toney got married. Then he hit the road. He wasn't Buster Midnight anymore. He was too old and out of shape to defend his championship title even if he still retained it, which he didn't. I don't think he had the will to fight either. Every now and then we'd hear about him. He sent Toney a picture postcard from Australia saying he was fighting there under another name. Then there was a story in the paper about a television wrestler in New York called the Butte Bomber that the reporter claimed was really Buster Midnight. There weren't any pictures, and we didn't get TV in Butte then so we never saw those wrestling matches. We knew it was the real Butte Bomber, though, because about that time Toney got a postcard from Buster saying he was in charge of a crew of Mexicans picking oranges in Florida. Later on, I got a crate of oranges in the mail. There wasn't any card with it, but I knew they were from Buster. I shared them with Whippy Bird and Toney and with Moon, who sometimes stopped by my house after school even though he was in the fifth grade and had his own friends.

A couple of months later, I got a sterling silver teaspoon with oranges on the handle from Florida, and I knew that came from Buster, too.

Of course, I moved out when Whippy Bird and Toney got married. Toney insisted he'd given the house to both of us and that he wanted to buy my share. I told him what he'd done was given me a place to live free throughout the war. I surely was grateful for that, but I always thought of it as Whippy Bird's house, not mine. Besides, I was sure Toney had gone through his money, and what was he going to use to buy my half? So I gave Whippy Bird and Toney my part of the house as a wedding gift. They lived there until Toney bought a house off South Main by where the Pay and Takit Market used to be.

It was a happy wedding, but it was different from when Whippy Bird and Chick were married. They were older, and Toney was a disabled war veteran, so we celebrated with champagne and a cake I made, instead of getting drunk on Shawn O's like we did the first time she got married. I knew from the day Whippy Bird got the first letter from Toney, which was addressed exclusively to her and not to me and her, that if Toney survived the war, he would come home to Whippy Bird. Toney always was sweet on her though she didn't care about him when she was young because she was crazy about Chick. But in his letters, Whippy Bird saw a new Toney. "Chick will always be in my heart, just like Pink for you," she told me. "You don't live on memories, though, and it's time Moon had a father." She was surely right.

Me and Whippy Bird always acted like Moon was the man of the house, and she worried that he wouldn't like Toney taking over. That's because sometimes Toney treated Moon like a little kid.

Whippy Bird loved Toney, but Moon was her son. But they both loved Whippy Bird, so they made it work. Right after the wedding, Toney held out his hand to Moon and said, "Hi, soldier."

Moon took that hand and said, "Hi, Dad." And that's the way it always was with those two. They shared Whippy Bird.

When he was grown up, I asked Moon what he thought about Toney taking Chick's place. "I never minded because Toney and Buster were my heroes. Remember how Toney treated me like a mascot at Buster's training camp?" Moon replied. "Besides, Toney didn't take my dad's place. He took yours. That's what I resented. But it turned out you were always around our place anyway so I didn't mind after a while. What really happened was I ended up with three parents."

Whippy Bird worried about me, also. "You know, Effa Commander, I'm never going to have as much fun with a husband as I did with you. I'm going to have to learn to cook, too, because Toney's used to eating in fancy places. And you're going to be a lady of leisure with nobody to look after but yourself." That meant she was afraid I'd be lonely.

"Don't you worry about me, Whippy Bird. I'm going to sleep till noon and eat chocolates without worrying about Moon seeing me and not even make my bed if I don't want to."

"You're always welcome at our house. Always," she said.

"I know that," I told her. "I also know things are different now. Me and you've been running in neutral for a long time, but it's time to shift and get in gear. You've already done it. Now I've got to get myself up the pass." That was surely true. When I said that, I realized I'd been using Whippy Bird and Moon as a reason not to get on with my life. I knew with Whippy Bird and Toney married, they didn't want me hanging around all the time. Whippy Bird had her work cut out for her because Toney was used to the big time, and there wasn't going to be the big time for him anymore. What's more, except for the navy, he'd never held a real job.

When I moved, I didn't just move out of the house. I left Centerville and rented a place over on West Quartz. Me and Whippy Bird still got together for lunch, and Moon developed the habit of stopping by after school when I wasn't working. I went to Centerville for dinner every week, and sometimes me and Whippy Bird and Toney went out on the town. For the first time in my life, though, I was on my own.

You know what? I liked it. I was just kidding when I told Whippy Bird I'd sleep till noon because I never did that in my life. Sometimes, though, I lay in bed and read *Reader's Digest.* Or I spread the Sunday paper all over the living room and let it stay there for three or four days until I was good and ready to throw it out.

My little house had just enough backyard for a clothesline and a garden. I had the best lettuce and spinach you ever ate. I grew peas and beets and onions, too. I planted climbing roses that grew up over the fence, and all summer, my house had the sweetest smells. Moon said one of the reasons he liked to visit me was my house always smelled good, from the flowers—or else from something in the oven. "Go on!" I said. "What you mean is have I made any cookies today?"

Two months after I moved into that house, I started on a new career. It was as though somebody, maybe Pink up there, was directing a whole new Effa Commander. Joe Bonnet offered me a job as the manager of the West Park Cafe. Now, I'd been a waitress and a cook and a hostess, but I'd never been a manager. I told Whippy Bird I was scared.

Whippy Bird looked me straight in the eye and said, "Effa Commander, there is nothing in this world you cannot do." Well, that's not true, but I did do a good job of managing the restaurant after all, with Whippy Bird right there to give me advice.

It was good advice, like it always is. "You have to be cheap," she said, and we were that. Coffee for a nickel, a burger for fifteen cents, a fried ham sand for a quarter, and pie à la mode for twenty cents.

You have to be fast, too, Whippy Bird also advised me, because "when you've got only thirty minutes for lunch like we secretaries at the Anaconda Company, you don't want to spend it waiting." That's when I came up with Jiffy Lunch Specials. We guaranteed to have them on the table in five minutes or you ate free. They were a smash hit right off the bat. People liked quick, but they liked free even better. They were happy if their lunch came right away without having to wait, but they were even happier when it didn't, and they got a free meal.

Once a week or so, Whippy Bird took a late lunch, coming in after the rush so we could eat together. She worked because she never was much for sitting around, even now, which is why she helps out at the Jim Hill today. But the main reason she kept on working at the Anaconda Company after she got married was to take the pressure off Toney, give him time to look for a job. Finding a job wasn't easy for Toney because he didn't know what he wanted. Except for the navy, the only work he'd ever done was bootlegging and managing Buster. Those were out, and with his leg gone, he couldn't work in the mines.

Whippy Bird arranged for Toney to talk to the Anaconda Company about working in the publicity department, where he was offered a job. Toney turned it down, telling Whippy Bird he could not be the voice of the Anaconda Company if it meant talking against the union during negotiations. Besides, he said, the only reason the Anaconda Company wanted to hire him was because he was Buster Midnight's brother.

Finally, Toney leased a filling station, the Toney McKnight Texaco down on the Flats. They tore it down a few years ago for a Kentucky Fried Chicken. Toney worked hard at being a filling station man, and he did a good job. Once gasoline rationing was off, people hit the road in Chrysler Town and Country Woodies and those funny-looking Studebakers that looked the same in the front and back so you couldn't tell if they were coming or going. They burned a lot of gasoline driving all over the state of Montana to see the mountains and read the Burma Shave signs. You'd see cars with license plates from as far away as Louisiana and West Virginia, big water bags hanging down the front and California coolers sticking out the window. People were throwing up tourist cabins for them to stay in as quick as you could say sucker.

Every day Toney wore a fresh white shirt and pants with that Texaco star on them. He said appearances were important. Whippy Bird said that was because he didn't do the washing. Even with one leg, Toney could get out to the car and say, "Fill 'er up?" before the driver turned off the motor. He said people liked a go-getter. When drivers saw him humping like that just to sell gas, it put them in a better mind for buying new batteries or fan belts or having the oil changed.

"Once a hustler," Whippy Bird told him, and she was right.

Both me and Whippy Bird knew Toney's heart wasn't in filling your tank, though. Sometimes when we had lunch in the Park Cafe, Whippy Bird wished there was something else for Toney to do, but she didn't know what.

Even though he was moody, which Whippy Bird blamed on him missing the limelight, Whippy Bird was as happy with Toney as she was with Chick. He was a good father to Moon and helpful to her in ways Chick never was. He advised Whippy Bird how to ask for a promotion to the accounting department at the Anaconda Company, which she received. He cooked and helped with the dishes and even put in a garden. Whippy Bird told me she hoped I'd find somebody as good as Toney.

"I had Pink," I told her. "I don't ever need anybody else."

"That is surely true, Effa Commander," she said. "Now that you're a career gal, you can manage just fine on your own. But I wish you'd meet a good man just the same." Every now and then Whippy Bird and Toney would set me up with a good man, too, and the four of us would paint the town, but I wasn't interested in getting serious, so I never saw any of them more than once or twice. I had my job and my house. In the summer, I worked in the yard of an evening, and in the winter I read or listened to the radio. I still had the nice Emerson that Buster bought to listen to May Anna in her early years as a starlet and which he gave to Pink later on. I left Pink's RCA with Whippy Bird because it seemed to go with that house.

And I had Butte. In those years after the war, that town was always going. It was as crowded on West Park at four in the morning after a shift change as it was at twelve o'clock noon. There were people to watch and places to go. We closed the West Park Cafe at midnight, but there were other restaurants where you could go for a bite. You'd think working in a cafe all day, I would want to go home, but I liked to go out and eat. Sometimes Joe Bonnet came in at closing time, and we went off to Meaderville for Italian. Then we fooled around with the slot machines until almost sunrise. Whippy Bird said I could do worse than Joe Bonnet. Toney said I could do better.

When I started at the West Park Cafe, I worked an early shift, getting in before we opened in the morning then staying till dinnertime. I liked working late, too. So I'd do a week early then switch off. Sometimes I left at midnight and wasn't even tired, so I went for a walk. Of course, you can't do that today, but back then you were as safe as if it was broad daylight.

One night I walked all the way down to the Milwaukee depot on Montana. To this day I don't know why. My feet just took me there. I set out, and that's where I ended up. I usually didn't go that far, but it was a nice fall night, and it felt good to be outside in the breeze.

It was about one in the morning, and a train had just pulled in, westbound. Passengers rushed out of the depot grabbing taxis or looking for a streetcar. I liked trains, though the only time I ever went anywhere far away on a train was to visit May Anna. Trains always made me wish I was going someplace. But where would I go?

I stood there across the street from the depot watching the people inside as they went from window to window, pushing open the doors and walking out into the bright spots under the streetlights. Some of them stopped for a minute, looking up at the lights on the Hill or shifting their suitcases. Then they moved on into the shadows and disappeared. It was quiet, but I kept on watching, looking up at that big tower the Milwaukee depot had. It's a television station now, but it was a fine depot then. It seemed like I was planted there.

He was the last one out of the station, and when I saw him I felt gladness in my heart. He came out slow and stood there like a buck sniffing the air. I never did ask him why he came in on the Milwaukee or where he came from. He just stood holding a suitcase and looking at the Hill like he was trying to convince himself he was finally home. He didn't see me until I came right up next to him.

"Hi, Buster."

At first Buster looked at me like he didn't recognize me. Then he shook his head and his eyes focused and he stared at me a long time. Then he put down the suitcase and grinned. "Hi, babe." He put his arms around me so tight I could hardly breathe, and when he let loose and I saw his face, there were tears in his eyes. "Effa Commander, you sure look good."

"I'm glad you're home, Buster," I said. "It's about time." He nodded, then he took my hand, and we began to walk uptown. "Don't you want to take the streetcar?" I asked.

"I used to race delivery wagons up and down Montana Street, remember?"

It seemed like old times walking up Montana with Buster. We talked easy, not about jail or May Anna, but about things you'd say if you'd seen the other person just the day before—like what a fine night it was and the price of copper and would he like to stop and have a nice cup of coffee.

"I run the West Park Cafe now," I said. "It's closed, but I have a key, and I'll fix you a pot of coffee." I had the feeling he didn't want to see anybody.

Buster never talked much, but that night I couldn't stop him. We must have made five pots of coffee and eaten about a dozen sinkers that had been delivered for morning. He told me he'd been knocking around all over the country for two years, doing odd jobs, running that orange picker crew, loading trucks, bartending. Then he wound up in New York and thought he'd get a job as a sparring partner, maybe hit up some of the gyms that would like the idea of using a one-time champion as a has-been punching bag for the fighters coming up. He was sitting on a bench in a park in New York City thinking about this when somebody said aren't you Buster Midnight and asked for his autograph. That made Buster ask himself what was he doing asking for a job to get punched out. "Effa Commander, I said to myself, I was the champ. I'm going out with some dignity, even if everybody in America hates me for killing a creep they called a war hero. That's when I decided to come home."

"I don't know about the rest of the world, but in Butte, Montana, you're still Buster Midnight, the champ," I said. "Around here, people don't talk about the murder. They just remember you were the champion. And that you're a Butte boy."

I talked, too, telling Buster how happy Whippy Bird and Toney were. Buster said Toney with one leg was more of a man than anybody else with two. When I said I still missed Pink, Buster put his arms around me and let me have a cry. We talked until the crew came in to open up. Jimmy Soo, the short-order cook, came up to Buster shyly and held out his hand. "Remember me, Mr. Midnight?" Buster said he surely did. Then Jimmy turned to Toady Madden, the dishwasher, and whispered, "Looky there. The champ's home."

"It's what I've been telling you all night, Buster. You belong in Butte, Montana."

We walked outside. It was still dark though we saw the miners hustle up and down the street, getting ready to go on shift. A few of the hookers from Venus Alley, which was still wide open, headed home while a drunk or two looked for a doorway to sleep in for a couple of hours. There were sounds of men working on the Hill, of trucks heaving and whistles blowing. You could set your Bulova by the whistles blowing shift changes on the Hill. "There's no place like Butte," I told Buster, and he said I surely was right.

"Toney didn't know I was planning to come. I'll walk you home, then I'll check into a hotel uptown."

"You can stay at my place. There's no need for you to get a hotel room this late at night," I told him.

"Effa Commander . . ."

"On the couch. It isn't the best place in the world to sleep, but it's free. We're old friends, Buster, but I'm not giving up my bed for you."

Whippy Bird says right here that me giving up my bed was not what Buster was thinking about. Well, I know that, but Buster was still May Anna's man as far as I was concerned. I wasn't going to make any mistake there. So Buster slept on the couch, and I slept in the bed. Being on the night shift, I slept late. It was almost noon when I got up, and Buster had breakfast on the table.

Toney wanted Buster to stay with them. "You can sleep with Moon," he said.

"Yippee!" Moon yelled.

"Sure. I'll roll over and flatten him out, and Whippy Bird will kill me with a fry pan." So Buster got a room over a bank on Park, and he took his meals at the cafe. I think the real reason he turned down Toney was he wanted to be alone. He had to find out if he really could come back to Butte.

It was even harder for Buster to get a job than Toney, not that he didn't have offers. He called most of them freak-show jobs. Car dealers, for instance, wanted to hire Buster to sell Kaiser-Frazers or step-down Hudsons, because they thought people would come in just to meet him. Buster said too many people already took him for a ride in his life, so he turned them down. Whippy Bird told me Buster was broke. What he hadn't spent on having a good time when he was a champ went to the fancy lawyer May Anna's studio got for him, which was a waste of money since he didn't keep Buster out of jail. So he worked a day or two a week down at the Texaco with Toney to earn enough to pay his hotel and board.

Sometimes Toney took a day off to go fishing with Buster. Whippy Bird said they both needed time to adjust. I told her it wasn't as easy for a man as old as Toney, who was more than forty, to get married for the first time and settle down with a ready-made family. But we both knew that wasn't the problem. The two of them were restless. After spending most of their lives in the big time, they weren't happy pumping gas. She said we had to give them time to work it out.

Meanwhile, people got used to seeing Buster in Butte. They would call, "Hey, champ!" and pretend to take a poke at him when they ran into him around town. After a while when he realized they weren't being smart alecks, Buster liked it. He knew he was accepted back in Butte at last. "Do you notice Buster doesn't stoop anymore?" Whippy Bird asked one day, and she was right. He stood up tall and looked people straight in the eye, just the way he did when he was a fighter.

We were at Whippy Bird's one night, full of pot roast and vinegar pie, when we made our big decision about the future. Me and Whippy Bird figured something was going on in Toney's head since he was so keyed up. All night he smiled to himself, and once he even whistled a little tune. We knew it wouldn't do any good to push him, though. He'd take his own sweet time to tell us.

"I got it," he said at last, after me and Whippy Bird had finished the dishes and taken off our aprons.

"Got what?" Whippy Bird asked.

"We are going to get rich," Toney said, sitting back, proud of himself.

"So, we're going to break the bank, are we?" Whippy Bird asked.

"I'm not kidding." Toney leaned forward, looking at each one of us. "We're going to open a restaurant. We'll call it Buster Midnight's Restaurant. Buster'll be the greeter, Effa Commander can be the manager, you'll be the bookkeeper, and I'll be bartender." I never saw Toney look that proud of himself since the day he told Buster he could be a famous boxer.

Whippy Bird turned around and looked at Toney with her mouth open. Then she shut it and kept quiet. We were all quiet, sitting around the table thinking it over.

"Yeah? What'll we do for money?" Buster finally asked.

"I ain't Toney the hustler for nothing. You let me worry about that. I know plenty of people who'll invest in a sure thing."

"What if it doesn't work? We'll all be out of a job." I said.

"Jobs. Jobs. We can always get jobs. This is a career opportunity. Once in a lifetime. You have to take a chance in this life, Effa Commander." Toney lit a cigarette. "We open a steakhouse uptown. Real deluxe. Get a big picture of Buster in neon lights out front and load the place down wall-to-wall with pictures of Buster as the champ. People'll roll in off the street just to meet him. You ever see people around here look at Buster like he's a reincarnated Butte Copper King? They'll pay money just to shake his hand. Then they'll come back because Effa Commander is the best cook in the world."

"I don't know how to run a restaurant," Buster said.

"You don't have to. Effa Commander does," Toney told him. "All you have to do is say hello to the folks and sign autographs."

"Right, Tone. Effa Commander would like that," Buster said sarcastically. "She'll be cooking up a storm in the kitchen while I'm shaking hands."

"It won't be that easy, Buster," I told him. "There's all kinds of things you'll have to do like talking people into having a drink when we don't have a table ready for them and calming them down when their dinners don't arrive on time."

"Somebody'll have to deal with drunks, too," Whippy Bird added.

We talked about that restaurant all night, and the thing of it was, none of us could find anything really wrong with the idea except for the money. Toney said that was his department, and the money was as good as in the bank. By the time me and Buster climbed in the Jackpot to leave, we'd designed the kitchen and the bar and a nice area to wait for your table. I'd worked out a menu, which was heavy on steaks and big shrimp cocktails with hot sauce. Toney said to make sure we gave them plenty to eat since our customers would be miners, and they wouldn't come back if we skimped.

Buster, who had been in some of the great restaurants of America, had ideas, too. First he said call it Buster Midnight's Cafe, not Buster Midnight's Restaurant. He said *cafe* was a Hollywood word that people thought was spiffy. Toney liked that because it'd be cheaper to spell out *cafe* in neon than *restaurant*. And have plenty of booths, Buster said. People in Hollywood and New York like little tables with chairs, but in Montana, we eat in booths.

Also, Buster knew just the right building on Galena Street for us, not too far from where the Jim Hill is today. If we made our sign big enough, the miners could see it from the Hill. Then Buster told us he'd be the bartender instead of the greeter. That way people would have to buy a drink to introduce themselves. People in Butte never ordered anything other than a Shawn O or a Ditch or a Sage, which is a Ditch with 7Up, and he knew how to fix those with his eyes closed. That way Toney could handle the buying and work with the suppliers; he was used to wheeling and dealing.

Whippy Bird said she'd take a class in accounting at night just so she wouldn't miss any tricks keeping the books.

Even so, we weren't as smart as we thought about the restaurant business. Deciding to open the restaurant was like the time we all sat around at the Rocky Mountain Cafe and turned Buster into a champion. If we'd known more, we wouldn't have done it, so it's a good thing we were such dummies.

Toney was wrong about getting rich, too. None of us got rich, at least not rich like May Anna or even Toney and Buster during the championship days. Still, we made a comfortable living, and we had fun, too. Running Buster Midnight's Cafe surely was a good life for all of us for a lot of years.

It was just before our grand opening—almost a year after Buster came back to Butte—that he stopped to see me one afternoon. I was in the backyard. It was fall, after the first hard frost, because I was picking rose hips to make jelly.

"You look nervous," I told him. "Are you having second thoughts?" I leaned against the fence and ran my fingers through the rose hips. "It's OK. I've been having second thoughts since the night we decided to do this, but I think it's going to work out fine. Toney knows how to pick a winner."

"It's not that," Buster said. "The restaurant's fine. I've just been wondering if I ought to let my wife work."

"What?" I said. My rose hips sounded like marbles hitting a sidewalk as they slid back into the bowl.

"That's a proposal of marriage, Effa Commander. I want you to marry me."

Whippy Bird said I shouldn't have been surprised. I saw Buster almost every day after he came back, and we had as good a time together as any two people ever did. Still, I'd spent so many years thinking Buster would marry May Anna that it didn't seem right to think about him and me. Of course, Whippy Bird and Toney said they knew from the first that sooner or later we'd tie the knot. But I didn't, and I surely didn't know what to say.

"I think we ought to get the cafe open first then we can talk about it," I told Buster, trying to buy time. My mind surely wasn't working.

"I think we ought to talk about it now, babe," he said.

So I went to sit next to him on the porch steps and put down my bowl of rose hips. It was the old yelloware bowl, the one with the brown stripe that I got for a quarter at the secondhand store on North Main. I held my hands together in my lap while I thought how to explain it. "The truth is, Buster . . ." I stopped for a minute wondering if it was my business to say what I needed to. Then I decided it was my business, since Buster had asked me to marry him. "The truth is, Buster, you will always love May Anna Kovaks."

"And the truth is, Effa Commander, you will always love Pink Varscoe. But both of them are dead. There isn't any May Anna anymore. I knew that when I went to prison. She's Marion Street now. That's why I told her I didn't want to see her again. I didn't love who she'd turned into. She wasn't a little girl falling into glory holes and getting hit with tomatoes anymore. Me and May Anna had some good times, and so did you and Pink. But we have to go on, just like I had to stop being a fighter and go into the restaurant business.

"I don't want you to think you're second choice to May Anna because you're not. I'm not asking you to marry me because May Anna turned me down. The old Buster wanted to marry May Anna. This here's a new Buster, and he loves you. You're the strongest and finest person I know. You always stuck by me, and you never expected anything from me. I think me and you can have a fine life together, Effa Commander."

That was the most I ever heard Buster say in one breath. I thought about Whippy Bird and Toney making a good marriage. I thought about Pink, and how he surely would want me to be happy, then about Buster, who was fine and loyal. Last, I looked in my heart and knew I loved Buster back. So I said yes, which, as Whippy Bird said later, is the shortest answer I've ever given anyone in my life.

We got married right after the restaurant opened. Then we had a big celebration at Buster Midnight's Cafe with champagne and free drinks and steak dinners. People poured in to wish us luck, just like we were Princess Elizabeth and Prince Philip.

There were flowers all over "like a funeral," Toney said.

Whippy Bird poked him in the ribs with her elbow and said, "There surely will be a funeral if you keep talking like that—yours."

Folks we didn't even know sent us little bouquets and big flower arrangements that we lined up on the bar. Of course, I had my bridal bouquet, which was a white orchid that went nicely with my pink suit, which the bridal department at Hennessy's recommended, this being a second wedding. The biggest bouquet of all was a giant horseshoe of white roses with GOOD LUCK in gold letters. It came with a little white card that said: "Love always, May Anna."

Ours was the best marriage that anybody ever had. Buster was the kindest man in the world. He never raised a hand to me or spoke a harsh word. Even working together all day, Buster and I never had a fight. Our marriage lasted a long time, almost thirty years, and you couldn't have found two happier people. I surely was a lucky woman. To think I spent all those years looking for a man as good as Pink, and when I found him, he turned out to be old Buster.

CHAPTER

16

May Anna still wrote and sent presents at Christmas. She called Moon on his birthday and sent us telegrams every time she was nominated for the Academy Award. Sometimes when she drank too much, she even called us at the restaurant. But we never saw her. You don't have a lot of days off when you work as a movie star, and I guess that's why she never made it back to Butte. Whippy Bird says would you be so kind as to stop talking like a damn fool, Effa Commander. You know as well as I do that May Anna always thought we blamed her for letting Buster down. Even though we all tried hard, things never were the same after the trial—or after I married Buster either.

Then we got the phone call one Friday night.

Friday was our hardest night at the cafe, and sometimes I wasn't sure I'd make it to Sunday morning. On Friday we had all that spaghetti and ravioli to fix as side dishes for the weekend as well as the steaks people ordered that night. Sometimes they changed their mind and wanted them rare instead of medium even after they'd eaten half. We never argued with the customers even though the moochers cost us plenty. After working all week, folks wanted to relax over their dinners even though they could see there were people waiting for their table. We had to keep those folks from throwing up their hands and walking out.

Whippy Bird always came down on Friday night to help me and Jimmy Soo in the kitchen. She said since me and Buster and Toney were there, she'd be lonely taking her time off at home. The truth was, you could always count on Whippy Bird. Even Moon came in on Friday night and worked as a busboy.

I already told you me and Buster never had a fight. But we never even had a fight with Toney and Whippy Bird either. We all owned that cafe together, and we all worked hard to make it a success. If there was a job to do, why we just did it, whether it was waiting tables or carrying out the trash. That restaurant was as important to me and Whippy Bird and Toney as it was to Buster even though our names weren't on it. People knew that. Lots of them called the cafe Buster and Toney's. And some even called it the McKnights', which meant the four of us plus Moon, even though he kept the name O'Reilly. Sometimes Moon winked at me and called it Aunt Effa Commander's Cafe.

After two years, the restaurant was a real success, but that Friday night was even more of a madhouse than usual. One of the ovens wouldn't go over 300 degrees, and I was having a hell of a time getting the orders out. Whippy Bird knocked over a bottle of bourbon, and people tracked it across the carpet before she had a chance to clean it up. Buster was chipping ice off the sidewalk in front because two customers had slipped and fallen down.

"You got a phone call," one of the waitresses told me.

"Tell them we don't take reservations," I said. Sometimes people thought if they called me or Buster, they'd get special service.

"It's not a reservation. It's long distance."

"I don't have time. It's some damn supplier who wants an order. They always think you'll drop everything for a long-distance telephone call." I was more concerned about the restaurant than any phone call. "You better get a new hanky. That one's got spaghetti sauce on it." The waitresses wore big flowered handkerchiefs spread out across their chests. "Don't chew gum."

"His name's Eddie Baum."

"Who? I don't know any Eddie Baum."

The waitress went to the phone again and came back. "He's Marion Street's agent. He says it's urgent. I wish she'd call herself. Think of what my kids would say if I told them I talked to a movie star."

I was too worried about the oven to give it much thought. I just wiped my hands on my apron and went to the phone, the one in the closet we called an office. "Yeah?" I said.

"You don't remember me, Effa Commander—" he said, but I cut him off.

"I remember you. You were the one who designed May Anna's dress for Buster's trial."

There was a long pause. "Sorry. I didn't know then you had the hots for Buster."

"You don't know much about anything as far as I'm concerned. What the hell do you want? I got a restaurant to run."

"Marion is sick. Real sick," he said.

I forgot about the fifty people in the dining room ready to die of hunger. His words cut through me. He wouldn't have called unless something was wrong. All I could think of was Mrs. Kovaks all curled up on her living room floor.

"What's wrong? What is it?" I bit the inside of my mouth to keep from crying.

"Cancer."

"Cancer? Cancer of what?"

"Cancer all over."

I leaned my head against the wall. "Her mother died of cancer. Is she . . . you know . . ." I couldn't bring myself to ask.

"Yes."

"Oh, my God." I slid down the wall so I was sitting on the floor. "God damn."

"She wants you to come. She's got things to say. I checked the train schedules. You can get out first thing tomorrow morning. The ticket will be waiting for you. With the weather, we can't depend on a plane. The train's the best way. You leave in the morning."

"I'm not sure me and Whippy Bird can get away that fast. Saturday night's as bad as Friday. We have to find somebody to take over."

"Your friend doesn't have to come. Marion just asked for you."

"Then you didn't hear her right. Me and Whippy Bird are both May Anna's best friend."

"Of course," he said. "I'll have two tickets waiting. You'll come tomorrow, won't you? I don't know how much time . . ." He had to stop for a minute to collect himself. "We weren't sure she'd make it through last night."

"Then why didn't you call us before?"

"Marion didn't want anyone to know. Then today, she asked to see you. She said she wanted to die in peace."

"We'll be there. Only don't leave any tickets. Me and Whippy Bird will pay for ourselves."

When I hung up, I sat like that for a long time until Whippy Bird came to find me. "What's going on?" she asked.

"It's May Anna. She's going to die of cancer. Maybe tonight." Whippy Bird started to cry. I thought about May Anna dying all alone in her white house, without even her best friends near her, and I cried, too. We cried until Whippy Bird said there were now one hundred hungry people in the other room ready to hang us from a light post if they didn't get their dinners.

"They can wait one more minute. I have to tell Buster."

"You can't tell him in the bar," Whippy Bird said. "I'll go get him."

I explained to Buster as gently as I could. "Poor May Anna," he said when I was finished. "She was afraid of that. I wish I could . . ." He shrugged. He didn't have to finish. I knew what he meant. He was still Little Buster McKnight looking out for May Anna.

"She wants to see me and Whippy Bird. That Eddie fellow who called. He wants us to leave in the morning."

"Then do it. She's your best friend, after all. Toney and I, we'll take care of things." The next morning when I got on the train, Buster didn't tell me to say hello to May Anna for him. He just gave me a big hug as strong as a Buster Midnight punch that made me feel my bones would snap. Then he kissed me and told me he loved me. "Come back soon, babe."

Toney got the tickets, and when we climbed on board the train, we found he'd bought us a private compartment. "It doesn't seem right about May Anna getting sick," Whippy Bird said when we were settled in our roomette.

"You mean May Anna dying," I corrected her. "It's not fair either. Pink and Chick, they were in the war. You can accept men getting killed in a war. But it's hard to accept other people you know dying, especially this young. May Anna isn't even forty."

"Not hardly more than thirty if you read what the studio puts out," Whippy Bird said.

"How old was her mother when she died?"

Whippy Bird thought it over. "Maybe not much older. You think of our mothers being older than God, but they weren't. May Anna's mother was even younger than they were."

"Now I know how Ma must have felt when Mrs. Kovaks died."

"Do you think May Anna was happy?" Now Whippy Bird was talking about her like she was already dead.

"Not like us. We had two good men apiece. May Anna never had anybody."

"She could have had Buster." Now you might think Whippy Bird should keep her mouth shut, but we always said what we thought to each other. Besides, I'd been thinking that, too.

"She could have. Maybe she should have. But I'm not sure she would have been happy."

"I know Buster wouldn't have been, not as happy as he is now anyway," said Whippy Bird. That was nice of her, but I always thought that, too.

"May Anna wouldn't have been happy with the pope," I said.

"The only man May Anna ever truly wanted was Jackfish Cook."

. . .

We were sorry Eddie came with Thomas to meet us at the train because we wanted to talk to Thomas alone. "I was afraid he wouldn't recognize you," Eddie explained. He had on one of those argyle sweaters and white slip-on shoes that made him look too flashy for somebody taking us to see a dying woman.

"He always did before," I told him.

"Look, I know you don't like me much, but I appreciate you girls coming out."

"We didn't come to see you," Whippy Bird told him.

"He's probably busy figuring out what dress to bury May Anna in," I whispered loud enough for Eddie to hear.

"How is she?" Whippy Bird asked Thomas.

He looked over his shoulder. "I don't know. She hangs on, but it's not good. She'll feel better with you here though. I said before somebody ought to call you. She looks bad."

"That's off the record," Eddie said. "There are some reporters around who'll want to talk to you. You can say she was dressed all in white, and she was beautiful to the end."

"You shut up. She's not dead yet," Whippy Bird told him.

I was right behind her: "We came out here to see our best friend, not to protect any Hollywood legend."

"I'm just saying Marion worked hard to become a star. She wants her fans to remember her that way."

"Do you think we don't know that?" I asked him, but he just shrugged.

We rode the rest of the way to May Anna's house without talking.

As Thomas opened the door he whispered, "She's been asking for you all day, Effa Commander. She wants to talk to you about Mr. Midnight."

"Looks like she's not running away from him this time," said Whippy Bird, thinking about how May Anna left Butte without saying good-bye to Buster.

"I think she wants to know Buster forgives her, but hell, what's to forgive?" I asked. "He knew May Anna did the best she could. Buster doesn't have any hard feelings about the trial. Buster understands her better than anybody. Maybe better than us."

"I always hoped Miss Street would marry him," the chauffeur said. Then he remembered Buster was married to me. "But he couldn't have done any better than you."

"Why, thank you for the compliment," I told him. "And if we have the time, I'll take you out for another Barney Google."

As it turned out, we never left the house, hardly even left May Anna's bedroom. I couldn't help thinking when we hurried up those fancy stairs to see her that things were a lot different from the first time we were there. I thought back to when me and Whippy Bird came down the stairs that time in the black dresses to May Anna's party where we got her the role in that awful *Debutantes at War*. I also remembered the other time I was there, for Buster's trial. Now I knew we were in that house for the last time.

May Anna was skinny like she was when she was a girl. With no makeup, her face was blotchy, making me think of that day on the raft when it was smeared with old tomatoes. Instead of the blond halo the fan magazines always wrote about, her hair was back to the color of mine runoff. May Anna looked like a little kid in Butte again, not the famous Marion Street. Seeing her that way broke my heart.

The room didn't look much like a movie queen's bedroom either. The satin quilt was put away, and the fancy perfume bottles on her dressing table were shoved to one side to make room for enamel pans and syringes. The smell in the room that day was the smell of sickness and Lysol instead of the lily scent May Anna loved. Me and Whippy Bird tiptoed in and stood there for a minute, not sure if she was asleep. Then she opened her eyes and smiled. Not the smile with her hand in front of her mouth—there were tubes in her arm—but the funny crooked smile she gave us the first day we saw her at the Little Annie.

"Your eyes still look like glory holes," I told her after I kissed her. "Big enough for a kid to fall into. How come I always think about you and glory holes?"

"If it hadn't been for you, I'd be at the bottom of one right now," May Anna whispered.

"Or China," Whippy Bird said.

May Anna smiled again. The nurse shushed us, but the doctor shook his head. "It can't do her any harm to talk to them for a few minutes," he said.

"I never went to China, did I? I always wanted to. The closest I came was *Shanghai Operative.*"

That was one of May Anna's gun moll movies.

"There were lots of places you never made it to, like back to Butte," Whippy Bird said. "When you get well and come back to Butte, Moon O'Reilly will be the most popular boy in the entire school. He'll make enough selling your autograph to put himself through college."

May Anna just smiled again like she knew Whippy Bird was trying to make her feel better. Later on, we remembered that smile when we found out she left Moon twenty-five thousand dollars in her will for his education. I don't know what college she was thinking of because that was enough to send Moon's entire graduating class to the university.

"You've been good friends to me, the best a girl ever had." She sounded so final. Me and Whippy Bird looked at each other, both of us wondering if May Anna knew she was dying. I turned to the doctor, hoping he would let us know, but he was bent over a chart.

"We always will be," I said at last.

"No, Effa Commander." She stopped because it was hard for her to talk. "You know I'm dying. I know it, too. I've had the cancer a long time. I'm luckier than my mother, though. I don't have to worry about the pain. They give me anything I want. But I told them to hold off so I'd be awake when you came. I want to play it straight. Last night, they didn't think I'd make it, but I knew I would because I have to tell you . . ."

It took her a big effort to say all that, and I could see she was hurting.

The nurse came over to give her more medicine, but May Anna shook her head. "Not yet," she said. I could see her trying to move her hand to push the nurse away, but she didn't have the strength. She opened and closed her fingers on the sheet, which was cotton, not the satin sheets May Anna liked, so I took hold of her hand and noticed it was probably the first time since she was twelve she wasn't wearing nail polish. "Come close," she whispered to me and Whippy Bird. The nurse brought folding chairs, and we sat down on either side of the bed. We still had our coats on.

"Did Buster tell you?" she asked me.

"Tell me what?"

"What happened that night with John Reide."

"We never talked about it. It's none of my business." I didn't want May Anna to talk about it either. Not now.

"Buster's loyal, all right. I should have married him when I had the chance. I wish I had. You're a lucky girl, Effa Commander." She gave me a tiny squeeze with her hand. "Buster's lucky, too."

I heard somebody move behind me and turned to see Eddie standing there. There were tears in his eyes. I wanted him to go away. Then I thought, no, he had a right to be there, too. He cared about May Anna just like me and Whippy Bird did, even though he wasn't as close to her as we were. I didn't like him because he hadn't done anything for Buster during the trial. Still, he helped save May Anna's career, and we owed him for that.

"You mustn't talk anymore," the doctor said. He was standing next to May Anna with a needle in his hand.

"No," May Anna said. "Why do you think I stayed alive so long? I have to say this."

"Honey, there's nothing you have to say," I told her. I could see there was pain all over May Anna, and I wanted her to have that shot. The picture of Mrs. Kovaks dying in the fourplex came back to my mind, and for a second I thought about my own mother and how she

made Mrs. Kovaks custard and beef tea. I wondered if anybody had
fixed that for May Anna.

She took a deep breath like she was gathering strength to go on.
"Buster didn't kill John Reide. I did. Buster covered up for me." She
sank back in the pillow and closed her eyes.

Her words rolled over me. I was stunned. Whippy Bird's face froze
in shock. After what seemed like forever, Whippy Bird turned to me,
and I saw tears streaming down her face—for Buster and May Anna
and maybe for me, too. "What happened, May Anna?" she asked for
both of us.

May Anna didn't answer right away. She'd spent so much of her
strength saying what she had to that all she could do for a minute
was open and close her eyes. Behind me, I heard the doctor whisper
something, but I couldn't make out the words. The nurse went into
May Anna's bathroom and turned on the faucet then came back and
handed me a glass of water. I shook my head but didn't look at her.
I kept staring at May Anna, waiting for her to speak.

At last May Anna said, "John and I had a fight. I shot him. Then
I called Buster, and when he came, I gave the performance of my life.
I should have won an Oscar for it." Her lips turned up just a little.
"You know how I can cry when I want to. So Buster confessed. I
knew he would. I didn't have to ask him. He always looked out for
me."

I was so weak I grabbed the edge of the bed with both hands to
keep from falling off the chair. May Anna had ruined Buster in the
prime of his career. On purpose. That good man gave up his life's
work for her, sacrificed his reputation, and went to prison for something he didn't do. She had done a terrible thing. Terrible.

Whippy Bird was waiting for me to speak, but the words didn't come. We were all silent for a long time. Only the nurse moved. She straightened May Anna's pillows and brushed a strand of hair off her forehead.

Whippy Bird whispered at last, "Effa Commander . . . say something." I knew how upset Whippy Bird was when she turned to me for words.

Still, I didn't know what to say. All I could do was think that the person Buster had loved most in the world almost destroyed him—and for no better reason than to keep on being a movie star. Then I told myself, Effa Commander, you can't let a dying woman know what an awful thing she did. Besides, it wasn't my place to say it to her. What happened was between Buster and May Anna. If Buster didn't hold it against her, how could I?

When I was in control of myself again, I took her hand. "It was Buster's decision, May Anna. It's over."

"No, it's not," May Anna said. "There's an envelope for you. I wrote it all out last week. The attorney signed it, so it's legal. I want you to tell the newspapers. It's time I made it up to Buster. Please, Effa Commander, let me do right by Buster." There were tears in her eyes, maybe the first real tears of her life. I could feel just the slightest pressure from her hand, so I squeezed back. While I did, I thought that May Anna Kovaks had made a bad mistake, but she surely had some kind of courage. She waited for us in pain, and she was willing to ruin the legend of Marion Street to make things up to Buster.

"You're a good person, May Anna," I said. "I'll do the right thing."

May Anna closed her eyes then shivered as the pain shot through her. I could see she needed the medicine fast and motioned for the doctor to give her a shot. In a minute she was asleep. Peaceful.

Eddie walked over to the bed and kissed May Anna on the cheek. Then he left. Me and Whippy Bird got up and took off our coats. "Does she still know we're here?" Whippy Bird asked the doctor.

"I don't know. She might. You can sit with her if you like. Sometimes we think voices penetrate."

So me and Whippy Bird sat by May Anna's bed all that day and through the night, one of us on each side, holding her hands. We talked to her about Jackfish and laughed when we remembered the April Fools' Day joke. "I never heard you crack up the way you did that day, May Anna." Whippy Bird shook her head. "Me and Effa Commander were sure a pair of damn fools, all right."

We remembered the raft, too, telling May Anna if she hadn't gotten a tomato in the face, Buster never would have become a famous boxer.

Once Whippy Bird asked the nurse, "Would you be so kind as to bring us some coffee?" Then we both burst out laughing. After that we cried for a long, long time.

We talked about the movie stars we saw at May Anna's party, though we didn't mention John Reide. I said, "May Anna, do you know because of you, me and Whippy Bird got to meet some of the most famous people in the world? Why if it wasn't for you, we'd be just two Butte nobodies."

"We still are," Whippy Bird said.

The doctor laughed. "That sounds like something Marion would say. You girls must have had a good time together. You're three of a kind."

"We surely are," I said. "We were the Unholy Three."

"She was going to be a nun once—before she decided to become a movie star," Whippy Bird told him. Then she looked at May Anna. "I wonder what would have happened if you'd gone ahead and become a nun."

"Buster McKnight would have slit his throat. You surely saved his soul when you turned out," I said.

"And yours, too, Effa Commander," Whippy Bird added.

"She'll see Pink and Chick before we do," I told Whippy Bird at about three in the morning.

"She'll meet Maybird, too," said Whippy Bird. It made me smile to think she would get to meet my little girl.

In the morning, May Anna died.

We didn't stay for the service. It was Marion Street's funeral, not May Anna's. We didn't want to see flashbulbs go off and crazy people cry and grab flowers for keepsakes. It was bad enough with the people who came to the house or called. Reporters mostly. Louella Parsons wrote that "the heavens burn brighter tonight because one of Hollywood's shining stars has joined them."

"That's a bunch of crap," Whippy Bird said, and she surely was right.

We wanted May Anna to be buried in Butte, next to her mother, but Eddie said she told him to cremate her and spread the ashes over a field of white lilies not far from her house.

May Anna's lawyer wanted us to stay and listen to the will since she left us something, but we said we weren't gold diggers. We came to be with May Anna in her final hour. So the lawyer sent us the things May Anna left us, which included the stuff I already told you about and some of her better jewelry, and fifty thousand dollars each, which was enough to live on for the rest of our lives. She also canceled the loan on the cafe. Even though she was the bookkeeper, Whippy Bird never knew Toney got the money from May Anna. He told us he had friends from Buster's boxing days who wanted to invest in the place. If we'd thought about it, though, we'd have figured out he went straight to May Anna.

Before we left, Eddie asked me what I planned to do about the letter May Anna wrote. I said I would talk it over with Buster before I sent it to the newspapers. Eddie told us he didn't know anything about May Anna doing the shooting until she wrote the letter. Still, he hoped we would not throw mud on a legend now that May Anna was dead. I told Whippy Bird he was in love with May Anna, and she said so what else is new.

Father Pig Face gave a service for May Anna only an hour after we got back to Butte. Toney was running the restaurant, so Buster met us at the train and told us about it. He refused to go. He said he still wanted to bust Pig Face after all those years. May Anna didn't have many friends left in Butte, so me and Whippy Bird decided we ought to be there. She had a lot of fans in Butte, though, because the church was jammed.

It wasn't a funeral. It was just a memory service with Pig Face talking about May Anna and how much joy she gave the world. I thought he laid it on a little thick about him growing up with her and being good friends, which we knew they weren't. Whippy Bird said that was all right because priests had an in with God, and it might do May Anna some good. He looked truly sad when he talked about her, which Whippy Bird said he had reason to be since May Anna wouldn't be sending him any more money for candles. There were plenty of candles lit for May Anna that day. I thought Pig Face was responsible. Whippy Bird said that might be so since he could light them for free.

Buster being the loyal person he was waited for me on the steps until the service ended. He and Pig Face nodded at each other, but they didn't shake hands. It looked to me like Pig Face was still afraid of him.

"I didn't bring the Jackpot. I thought maybe you'd like to walk home," Buster said. It was winter, but the sun was out, shining so bright it made your eyes sting. We said good-bye to Whippy Bird, and Buster waved to Nell Nolan. Then we walked down North Main. It was the first time I'd been alone with Buster since I got back.

"How did Pig Face get his name?" I asked.

"You ever look at him?" Buster said, and we laughed. It surely was easy being married to Buster, I thought as we walked along. We both liked to walk, and our strides matched.

"May Anna was awake when we got there," I said.

Buster nodded.

"We had a chance to say good-bye."

"That's good."

"She talked, too." I stopped by a cribbing that held back the hill on Woolman Street and looked up at Buster. "May Anna told me. She told me she killed John Reide, not you. It was her deathbed confession."

Buster looked at the headframes on the Hill. After a minute, he rubbed his hand across his forehead, and I saw his eyes were red, so I looked away.

"She wrote it all down," I continued. "It's in a letter in my purse. She told me to tell the newspapers." He didn't reply. Then he took my arm, and we walked on. "It's what she wanted. Now's the time to tell the truth. That's what May Anna said."

Whatever went through Buster's mind just then, he didn't tell me. He put his arm around me and squeezed so hard I thought he'd bust me in half. It was cold, and we walked the last few blocks as fast as we could. When we got home, Buster put three logs in the fireplace and lit them then he sat down in the easy chair. I hung up our coats and perched on the footstool next to him. For the first time since I left Butte, I felt warm, and it wasn't just because of the fire.

I opened my pocketbook and took out the letter. It was addressed to me. "Me and Whippy Bird read it about a dozen times," I said, handing it to Buster. "The lawyer wrote it all down, just the way May Anna told us."

Buster let the envelope sit in his lap while he stared into the fire. "You want a drink?" I asked, but he shook his head. "May Anna's a good person. She loved you. She proved it when she wrote that letter." Maybe I should have been jealous, but I wasn't. May Anna was dead, and I could surely share Buster with her memory.

We sat by that fire a long time, maybe an hour. The flames died down, so I wadded up some newspaper and lit it with a match. After it caught, I added more logs. Outside, it turned dark and a thick snow started blowing against the house. After a while, I went to the window to watch the lights come on all over the Hill. Then I turned on the lamp and sat down on the arm of Buster's easy chair. "Read it, Buster," I said, picking up the envelope from his lap and handing it to him.

Buster sighed then took the letter out of the envelope and looked at it for a few minutes until he could focus on the words. First, he read it slowly, then he read it again. The fire flared up as pitch seeped from a log, and out of the corner of my eye I saw the flame light up Buster's face. He was still the handsomest man I ever knew. At last he folded the letter and put it back in the envelope.

"Babe," Buster said at last, "May Anna lied." He tore the letter in half and threw both pieces into the fire.

CHAPTER
17

I finished this book without the inspiration of Whippy Bird. She passed on in the spring, just before the roses bloomed at the house on West Broadway I bought with some of my inherited money from May Anna. The day I signed the papers, I told Whippy Bird I surely wished May Anna knew she'd bought me a house on West Broadway.

"She knows," Whippy Bird said. That was thirty-five years ago.

One of the last things Whippy Bird told me before she crossed over was: "You have a mission, Effa Commander, and it is to polish a golden Hollywood legend that Hunter Harper tarnished. Even if I'm not here to push you. You have a responsibility to finish the book." Once more, she was right.

After his book came out I never looked at Hunter Harper without wanting to lob an ore chunk at his pea brain for writing down that he had investigated and discovered Marion Street committed the murder of John Reide, and Buster covered it up. Besides being wrong, that was not a major scoop on his part anyway because the story was Hollywood gossip for years after May Anna died—courtesy of the nurse at her deathbed or maybe the attorney. Still, after Hunter Harper's book came out, *People* magazine and *Parade* and all the others picked up the story and printed it. That was why me and

Whippy Bird thought it was important to write the true facts and why I finished the book even without the help of my lifetime friend, Whippy Bird O'Reilly McKnight.

"It was May Anna's goodness that made her tell us she killed that man," Whippy Bird said once.

"And Buster's goodness that he didn't let us believe it," I said.

"She was willing to sacrifice her world reputation for our friendship. And for love of Buster, too."

"I guess in the end, there's nothing that matters more than friends. But you and me always knew that, Whippy Bird," I told her.

It was the cancer. Whippy Bird was brave as she always was. She never complained even when her hair fell out from the chemo and she couldn't eat. Moon's oldest boy, Bumbo, brought her marijuana cigarettes to make her feel better, and me and Whippy Bird sat in her bedroom and smoked them until we both felt fine. I said since I gave up tobacco cigarettes with Whippy Bird, it made sense to start smoking dope with her.

"Funny, isn't it, you losing your two best friends from cancer, even though I've lived twice as long as May Anna," Whippy Bird said. "We're both going out on cotton sheets, too. I never did understand why they wouldn't let May Anna die on satin. I always wondered, were May Anna's cotton sheets round like her bed?"

"Square like your head. I haven't lost you yet. I could still go first," I told her.

"No you won't, Effa Commander, and you'll have to plan the funeral. No cremation either. That's because no matter where you scatter my ashes, they'll blow into the mine pit, and I'll end up as a copper pipe in somebody's bathroom."

"You want a Pig Face service?" I asked. Pig Face gave a nice funeral for Toney when he died, even though he wasn't Catholic. But I wouldn't let him touch Buster.

"No, but I think it would be real nice if you lobbed a tomato at him. You can put in the paper that instead of flowers, people should throw tomatoes at BS. You know, Buster beat up Pig Face because May Anna got a tomato in the face, but I must have got a dozen, and he didn't do anything."

"I'll see what I can do," I told her.

I was with her at the end, me on one side and Moon on the other, holding her hands, just like me and Whippy Bird were with May Anna. The last thing she said to me was: "It's not dying I mind, Effa Commander. It's leaving Butte."

"What she means is leaving you," Moon said.

I knew that. Because we were one person. Losing Whippy Bird was like the ore vein in me had pinched out. I can't remember when she wasn't my best friend. We were closer to each other than we were even to our husbands. Part of me died with Whippy Bird that day.

Not long after we buried Whippy Bird, I was having a sandwich in Pork Chop John's Uptown, when Pig Face sat down on the stool next to me and ordered one loaded. "We're the only ones left, Effa Commander," he said. "We're the last of a great era." I nodded. We were the same era, all right, but Pig Face wasn't privileged to be part of the gang of me and Whippy Bird, Pink and Chick, Buster and Toney, and May Anna Kovaks.

Those memories kept me going during the terrible days after I lost Whippy Bird. I tried to go on as I always had, watching television at my little house on West Broadway or listening to Oakie O'Connor and other Butte people I knew on Buster's old Emerson radio. There was the Senior Center for when I wanted to go out. And every week Moon invited me for dinner with his wife and the boys.

A few months later, after I'd begun feeling better, Moon came by with a big cardboard box for me from Whippy Bird. Inside were the things May Anna left her along with Whippy Bird's snapshot album of when we were kids and Toney's collection of Buster Midnight stuff. There was the scrapbook Toney kept on Buster throughout his career, and some posters of Buster as the champ. They're worth about a hundred dollars each now, but you'd never get me to sell them. "I will surely enjoy these, but you made an extra trip for yourself," I said. "You'll have to come back and pick them up when I cross over." After Buster died, I drew up a will leaving everything to Moon.

"That won't be for a long time," Moon said. Then he invited me down to the Jim Hill for a cup of coffee. "You have to get on with your life, Aunt Effa Commander," he said.

"You are just like your mother, telling me that," I said wiping away a tear. "She told me that every time something of serious importance happened to me." Like when Buster and Toney died, ten years ago, only a few months apart. Once more, we were widows together. We grieved for a time, just as we had before, with me refusing to step foot inside the restaurant after we sold it. Then one day Whippy Bird said "Effa Commander, we have to get on with our lives. It's time me and you had lunch," and she marched us right into Buster Midnight's Cafe, only they'd changed the name to the Kopper Kamp Kafe by then. We ordered a BLT and an iced tea. From then on, I didn't have any trouble walking inside.

The new owners asked to buy all Buster's photographs and trophies and ribbons and even Toney's old purple silk trunks that Buster wore when he fought at Columbia Gardens. Me and Whippy Bird said no. They should go to the history museum as a memorial, which is where they are now, in the Buster Midnight Room. We wouldn't let them use Buster's name on the restaurant either. We thought the people might not buy the cafe when we told them that. Then they decided the location was good, and if they kept the old menu, people would keep on coming in.

There's a room at the museum for May Anna, too, which also has things we donated, like the fur scarf she gave Ma and the dresses she sent us during the war. Also the Brown Jug sign, though I am the only one left who knows it's true historical significance for Buster Midnight and Marion Street. She's a big tourist attraction in Butte these days. The city council wanted to name a street for her until they found out there already is a Marion Street.

Some people think the sculptor used May Anna's face on the "Madonna of the Mountains," the statue they put up outside Butte, but me and Whippy Bird knew it didn't look anything like May Anna. We like the "Madonna" anyway. "Work of art," Whippy Bird said when she saw it gleaming in the sun. "Work of art."

Moon was right. It was time to go on with my life and visit the Jim Hill once more, though it was hard knowing I'd never see Whippy Bird behind the counter again. So one morning I woke up and said today's the day, Effa Commander. I waited until 11 A.M., too late for breakfast and too early for lunch. Just the regulars were there along with a few tourists. I waved to Joe Mapes who was sitting in his office, then I sat down at the end of the counter.

"Hi, honey, you want a cheese sand?" Alta asked me. That's what she says to everybody, and sometimes it works. You go in there to get a cup of coffee, and you end up having a sandwich, too. I tell her just the regular. I don't have to tell her no decaf because she knows. "Here you go, kid," she said putting down the cup on the counter. Since I was there the last time, Joe Mapes bought new cups with two green rings on them, a wide ring at the top, and a narrow one below it. I missed the old china mugs where you could feel the scratches with your tongue.

Everybody was watching Hunter Harper talking to a pair of tourists. Not much has changed, I thought, except that everybody got a little older in the six months since I'd been there. That, and the fact it was Hunter Harper entertaining the tourists instead of Whippy Bird. Alta doesn't like to talk to people she doesn't know. Once me and Whippy Bird heard a reporter try to get her to say something he could put in his newspaper, so he asked, "How's tips?"

Alta leaned against the counter, took a puff on her Kent, which she put back in the ash tray in front of the reporter so the smoke went in his face, and said, "They're worse than the shits, honey."

So now Hunter Harper was the geyser of information. I didn't pay any attention to him, just sat there and tried to think about Whippy Bird standing behind the counter, making pancakes, wondering if I ought to order some for old times' sake even though I already had my breakfast. I nodded down the counter at Jimmy Soo, who was a cook at the West Park when I ran it and at Buster Midnight's Cafe, too. Jimmy's mind wanders these days, and sometimes when things get dull, he dumps his food on the counter and eats his ham and eggs right off the Formica. Whippy Bird claimed there was nothing wrong with him when he did that since the counter was as clean as the plate. It was when he put a tea bag in his coffee that you knew his mind had gone.

I heard a tourist ask about Marion Street and smiled at my coffee while I waited for Hunter Harper to say that Marion Street sounds like an *ay*-dress. That's what Whippy Bird would have said. I heard her say that hundreds of times and laughed at every one. He didn't, though. Hunter was not a wit like Whippy Bird.

Little bits of Hunter Harper's story came down the bar to me for a few minutes, but I was too wrapped up in my memories to pay much attention. I started to listen, though, when I heard him say my name.

"There were three of them. Two of them were good friends of mine. Marion Street, whose real name was May Anna Kovak," which wasn't true. As you know, it was Kovaks with an *s*. Then he said, "The other two were Whippy Bird and Effa Commander. God knows what their real names were." He stopped so the tourists could laugh. "They called themselves the Holy Three."

"Unholy Three," I muttered. The man on the next stool glared at me like I was older than God and moved his coffee away.

"You know, Whippy worked behind this counter until she died a few months ago." I curled my lip when I heard that, since only people who didn't know Whippy Bird called her Whippy.

"Effa Commander's in a rest home, God bless her soul," he continued. I glanced at Alta, who blew smoke at Hunter for that. I wasn't any more in a rest home than he was. I was only seventy-five, though like May Anna, I liked to shave the years a little.

"Three peas in a pod, they were," he continued. "All worked in Venus Alley, which is what we called the red-light district here in

Butte. That's how come they knew Buster Midnight. He was a real ladies' man." He stopped, and one of the tourists asked him a question I couldn't hear.

"No, Marion Street was just a working girl. I think Whippy was the madam. I'm revising my book, and I'm going to include that."

I was used to people making up lies about May Anna and even Buster. They were legend, and there wasn't anything I could do about it. But not Whippy Bird. And not by a jackass like Hunter Harper.

I put down my coffee, real slow, so I wouldn't spill it because I was so mad I was shaking. Then I got down off the stool. Joe Mapes heard what Hunter Harper said, and he came out of his little office to shut him up. Jimmy Soo stood up, too, being the gentleman your Orientals always were in Butte, but I shook my head at them. Nobody had to fight battles for me and Whippy Bird. And nobody was going to talk about Whippy Bird like that when Effa Commander was around.

I walked down the counter to Hunter Harper and tapped him on the shoulder. He turned around and blinked at me like he didn't know who I was.

"I'm your old friend, Effa Commander, escaped from the rest home," I told him. Then I saw everybody watching me, and I remembered May Anna losing her nerve at the end of the charity tea with the food basket ladies, when she'd started to tell them she'd moved to Venus Alley but said Hollywood instead. May Anna chickened out, but I wasn't going to back down. I was the defender of Whippy Bird. "Put this in your damn fool book," I told him. Then I smiled a little, looked away, wound up, and decked him with a Buster Midnight.